Prairie Flower

James B. Hendryx

Alpha Editions

This edition published in 2024

ISBN 9789361473890

Design and Setting By

Alpha Editions

www.alphaedis.com

Email - info@alphaedis.com

As per information held with us this book is in Public Domain.
This book is a reproduction of an important historical work.
Alpha Editions uses the best technology to reproduce historical work
in the same manner it was first published to preserve its original nature.
Any marks or number seen are left intentionally to preserve.

Contents

A PROLOGUE	- 1 -
CHAPTER I	- 6 -
AN ANNIVERSARY	- 6 -
CHAPTER II	- 11 -
KANGAROO COURT	- 11 -
CHAPTER III	- 17 -
THE STAGE ARRIVES	- 17 -
CHAPTER IV	- 22 -
Y BAR COLSTON TALKS	- 22 -
CHAPTER V	- 28 -
ALICE TAKES A RIDE	- 28 -
CHAPTER VI	- 34 -
AT THE RED FRONT	- 34 -
CHAPTER VII	- 39 -
THE TEXAN "COMES A-SHOOTIN'"	- 39 -
CHAPTER VIII	- 47 -
THE ESCAPE	- 47 -
CHAPTER IX	- 54 -
ON THE RIVER	- 54 -
CHAPTER X	- 62 -
JANET MCWHORTER	- 62 -
CHAPTER XI	- 69 -
AT THE MOUTH OF THE COULEE	- 69 -
CHAPTER XII	- 75 -
IN TIMBER CITY	- 75 -

CHAPTER XIII	- 82 -
A MAN ALL BAD	- 82 -
CHAPTER XIV	- 89 -
THE INSURGENT	- 89 -
CHAPTER XV	- 93 -
PURDY MAKES A RIDE	- 93 -
CHAPTER XVI	- 98 -
BIRDS OF A FEATHER	- 98 -
CHAPTER XVII	- 104 -
IN THE SCRUB	- 104 -
CHAPTER XVIII	- 108 -
THE TEXAN TAKES THE TRAIL	- 108 -
CHAPTER XIX	- 113 -
AT MCWHORTER'S RANCH	- 113 -
CHAPTER XX	- 120 -
AT CINNABAR JOE'S	- 120 -
CHAPTER XXI	- 126 -
THE PASSING OF LONG BILL KEARNEY	- 126 -
CHAPTER XXII	- 132 -
CASS GRIMSHAW—HORSE-THIEF	- 132 -
CHAPTER XXIII	- 138 -
CINNABAR JOE TELLS A STORY	- 138 -
CHAPTER XXIV	- 146 -
"ALL FRIENDS TOGETHER"	- 146 -
CHAPTER XXV	- 154 -
JANET PAYS A CALL	- 154 -
CHAPTER XXVI	- 159 -

THE OTHER WOMAN	- 159 -
CHAPTER XXVII	- 166 -
SOME SHOOTING	- 166 -
CHAPTER XXVIII	- 175 -
BACK ON RED SAND	- 175 -
AN EPILOGUE	- 181 -

A PROLOGUE

The grey roadster purred up the driveway, and Alice Endicott thrust the "home edition" aside and hurried out onto the porch to greet her husband as he stepped around from the garage.

"Did the deal go through?" she asked, as her eyes eagerly sought the eyes of the man who ascended the steps.

"Yes, dear," laughed Endicott, "the deal went through. You see before you a gentleman of elegant leisure—foot-loose, and unfettered—free to roam where the gods will."

"Or will not," laughed his wife, giving him a playful hug. "But, oh, Win, aren't you glad! Isn't it just grand to feel that you don't have to go to the horrible, smoky old city every morning? And don't the soft air, and the young leaves, and the green grass, and the nesting birds make you *crazy* to get out into the big open places? To get into a saddle and just ride, and ride, and ride? Remember how the sun looked as it rose like a great ball of fire beyond the miles and miles of open bench?"

Endicott grinned: "And how it beat down on us along about noon until we could fairly feel ourselves shrivel———"

"And how it sank to rest behind the mountains. And the long twilight glow. And how the stars came out one by one. And the night came deliciously cool—and how good the blankets felt."

The man's glance rested upon the close-cropped lawn where the grackles and robins were industriously picking up their evening meal. "You love the country out there—you must love it, to remember only the sunrises, and the sunsets, and the stars; and forget the torture of long hours in the saddle and that terrific downpour of rain that burst the reservoir and so nearly cost us our lives, and the dust storm in the bad lands, and that night of horrible thirst. Why those few days we spent in Montana, between the time of the wreck at Wolf River and our wedding at Timber City, were the most tumultuously adventurous days of our lives!"

His wife's eyes were shining: "Wasn't it awful—the suspense and the excitement! And, yet, wasn't it just grand? We'll never forget it as long as we live———"

Endicott smiled grimly: "We never will," he agreed, with emphasis. "A man isn't likely to forget—things like that."

Alice seated herself upon the porch lounge where her husband joined her, and for several minutes they watched a robin divide a fat worm between the scrawny necked fledglings that thrust their ugly mouths above the edge of the nest in the honeysuckle vine close beside them.

"It was nearly a year ago, Win," the girl breathed, softly; "our anniversary is just thirteen days away."

"And you still want to spend it in Timber City?"

"Indeed I do! Why it would just break my heart not to be right there in that ugly little wooden town on that day."

"And you really—seriously—want to live out there?"

"Of course I do! Why wouldn't anyone want to live there? That's real living—with the wonderful air, and the mountains, and the boundless unfenced range! Not right in Timber City, or any of the other towns, but on a ranch, somewhere. We could stay there till we got tired of it, and then go to California, or New York, or Florida for a change. But we could call the ranch home, and live there most of the time. Now that you have closed out your business, there is no earthly reason why we should live in this place—it's neither east nor west, nor north, nor south—it's just half way between everything. I wish we would hear from that Mr. Carlson, or whatever his name is so we could go and look over his ranch the day after our anniversary."

"His name is Colston, and we have heard," smiled Endicott. "I got word this morning."

"Oh, what did he say?"

"He said to come and look the property over. That he was willing to sell, and that he thought there was no doubt about our being able to arrange satisfactory terms."

"Oh, Win, aren't you glad! You must sit right down after dinner and write him. Tell him we'll——"

"I wired him this afternoon to meet us in Timber City."

"Let's see," Alice chattered, excitedly, "it will take—one night to Chicago, and a day to St. Paul, and another day and night, and part of the next day—how many days is that? One, two nights, and two days and a half—that will give us ten days to sell the house and pack the furniture and ship it——"

"Ship it!" exclaimed the man. "We better not do any shipping till we buy the ranch. The deal may not go through——"

"Well, Mr. What's-his-name don't own the only ranch in Montana. If we don't buy his, we'll buy another one. You better see that Mr. Schwabheimer tomorrow—he's wanted this place ever since we bought it, and he's offered more than we paid."

"Oh, it won't be any trouble to sell the house. But, about shipping the furniture until we're sure———"

Alice interrupted impetuously: "We'll ship it right straight away—because when we get it out there we'll just have to buy a ranch to put it in!"

Endicott surrendered with a gesture of mock despair: "If that's the way you feel about it, I guess we'll have to buy. But, I'll give you fair warning—it will be up to you to help run the outfit. I don't know anything about the cattle business———"

"We'll find Tex! And we'll make him foreman—and then, when we get all settled I'll invite Margery Demming out for a long visit—I've picked out Margery for Tex—and we can put them up a nice house right near ours, and Margery and I can———"

"Holy Mackerel!" laughed Endicott. "Just like that! Little things don't matter at all—like the fact that we haven't any ranch yet to invite her to, and that she might not come if you did invite her, and if she did come she might not like the country or Tex, or he might not like her. And last of all, we may never find Tex. We've both written him a half a dozen times—and all the letters have been returned. If we had some ham, we'd have some ham and eggs, if we had some eggs!"

"There you go, with your old practicability! Anyhow, that's what we'll do—and if Tex don't like her I'll invite someone else, and keep on inviting until I find someone he does like—and as for her—no one could help loving the country, and no one could help loving Tex—so there!"

"I hope the course of their true love will run less tempestuously than ours did for those few days we were under the chaperonage of the Texan," grinned the man.

"Of course it will! It's probably very prosaic out there, the same as it is anywhere, most of the time. It was a peculiar combination of circumstances that plunged us into such a maelstrom of adventure. And yet—I don't see why you should hope for such a placid courtship for them. It took just that ordeal to bring out your really fine points. They were there all the time, dear, but I might never have known they were there. Why, I've lived over those few days, step by step, a hundred times! The wreck, the celebration at Wolf River—" she paused and shuddered, and her husband took up the sequence, mercilessly:

"And your ride with Purdy, and Old Bat thrusting the gun into my hand and urging me to follow—and when I looked up and saw you both on the rim of the bench and saw him drag you from your horse—then the mad dash up the steep trail, and the quick shot as he raised above the sage brush—and then, the fake lynching bee—only it was very real to me as I stood there in the moonlight under that cottonwood limb with a noose about my neck. And then the long ride through the night, and the meeting with you at the ford where you were waiting with Old Bat———"

"And the terrible thunder storm, and the bursting reservoir, and the dust storm in the bad lands," continued the girl. "Oh, it was all so—so horrible, and yet—as long as I live I will be glad to have lived those few short days. I learned to know men—big, strong men in action—what they will do—and what they will not do. The Texan with his devil-may-care ways that masked the real character of him. And you, darling—the real you—who had always remained hidden beneath the veneer of your culture and refinement. Then suddenly the veneer was knocked off and for the first time in your life the fine fibre of you—the real *stuff* you are made of, got the chance to assert itself. You stood the test, dear—stood it as not one man in a hundred who had lived your prosaic well-ordered life would have stood it———"

"Nonsense!" laughed the man. "You're grossly prejudiced. You were in love with me anyway—you know you were. You would have married me in time."

"I was not! I wasn't a bit in love with you—and I wouldn't have married you ever, if it hadn't been for the test." She paused suddenly, and her eyes became serious, "But Win, Tex stood the test too—and he really did love me. Do you know that my heart just aches for that boy, out there all alone in the country he loves—for he *is* of different stuff than the rest of them. He likes the men—he is one of them—but he would never choose a wife from among their women, and his big heart is just yearning for a woman's love. I shall never forget the last time I saw him—in that little open glade in the timber. He had lost, and he knew it—and he stood there with his arm thrown over the neck of his horse, staring out over the broad bench toward the mountains that showed hazy-blue in the distance. He was game to the last fibre of him. He tried to conceal his hurt, but he could not conceal it. He spoke highly of you—said you were a *man*—and that I had made no mistake in my choice—and then he spoke the words that filled my cup of happiness to the brim—he told me that you had not killed Purdy—that there was no blood on your hands—and that you were not a fugitive from the law.

"Win, dear—we must find him—we've got to find him!"

"We'll find him—little girl," answered her husband as his arm stole about her shoulders; "I'm just as anxious to find him as you are—*and in ten days we will start!*"

CHAPTER I

AN ANNIVERSARY

The Texan drew up in the centre of a tiny glade that formed an opening in the bull pine woods. Haze purpled the distant mountains of cow-land, and the cowpuncher's gaze strayed slowly from the serried peaks of the Bear Paws to rest upon the broad expanse of the barren, mica-studded bad lands with their dazzling white alkali beds, and their brilliant red and black mosaic of lava rock that trembled and danced and shimmered in the crinkly waves of heat. For a long time he stared at the Missouri whose yellow-brown waters rolled wide and deep from recent rains. From the silver and gold of the flashing waters his eyes strayed to the smoke-grey sage flats that intervened, and then to the cool dark green of the pines.

Very deliberately he slipped from the saddle, letting the reins fall to the ground. He took off his Stetson and removed its thin powdering of white alkali dust by slapping it noisily against his leather chaps. A light breeze fanned his face and involuntarily his eyes sought the base of a huge rock fragment that jutted boldly into the glade, and as he looked, he was conscious that the air was heavy with the scent of the little blue and white prairie flowers that carpeted the ground at his feet. His thin lips twisted into a cynical smile—a smile that added an unpleasant touch to the clean-cut weather-tanned features. In the space of a second he seemed to have aged ten years—not physically, but—he had aged.

He spoke half aloud, with his grey eyes upon the rock: "It—hurts—like hell. I knew it would hurt, an' I came—rode sixty miles to get to this spot at this hour of this day. It was here she said 'good-bye,' an' then she walked slowly around the rock with her flowers held tight, an' the wind ripplin' that lock of hair, just above her right temple, it was—an' then—she was gone." The man's eyes dropped to the ground. A brilliantly striped beetle climbed laboriously to the top of a weed stem, spread his wings in a clumsy effort, and fell to the ground. The cowboy laughed: "A hell of a lot of us that would like to fly has to crawl," he said, and stooping picked a tiny flower, stared at it for a moment, breathed deeply of its fragrance, and thrust it into the band of his hat. Reaching for his reins, he swung into the saddle and once more his eyes sought the painted bad lands with their background of purple mountains. "Prettiest place in the world, I reckon—to look at. Mica flashin' like diamonds, red rocks an' pink ones, white alkali patches, an' black cool-lookin' mud-cracks—an' when you get there—poison water, rattlesnakes, chokin' hot dust, horse-thieves, an' the white bones of dead things! Everything's like that. Come on, old top horse, you an' I'll shove on to Timber City. 'Tain't over a mile, an' when we get there—! Say boy, little old unsuspectin' Timber City is goin' to stage an orgy. We don't aim to pull off no common sordid drunk—not us. What we'll precipitate is goin' to be a classic—a jamboree of sorts, a bacchanalian cataclysm, aided an' abetted by what local talent an' trimmin's the scenery affords. Shake a leg, there! An' we'll forget the bones, an' the poison, an' the dust, an' with the discriminatin' perception of a beltful of rollickin' ferments, we'll enjoy the pink, an' the purple, an' the red. Tomorrow, it'll be different but as Old Bat says 'Wat de hell?'"

Thus adjured, the horse picked his way down the little creek and a few minutes later swung into the trail that stretched dusty white toward the ugly little town whose wooden buildings huddled together a mile to the southward.

Before the door of Red Front saloon the Texan drew up in a swirl of dust, slid from the saddle, and entered. The bartender flashed an appraising glance, and greeted him with professional cordiality, the ritual of which, included the setting out of a bottle and two glasses upon the bar. "Dry?" he invited as he slid the bottle toward the newcomer.

"Middlin'," assented the Texan, as he poured a liberal potion. The other helped himself sparingly and raised his glass.

"Here's how."

"How," responded the Texan, and returning the empty glass to the bar produced papers and tobacco and rolled a cigarette. Then very deliberately, he produced a roll of bills, peeled a yellow one from the outside, and returned the roll to his pocket. Without so much as the flicker of an eyelash, the bartender noted that the next one also was yellow. The cowpuncher laid the bill on the bar, and with a jerk of the thumb, indicated the four engrossed in a game of solo at a table in the rear of the room.

"Don't yer friends imbibe nothin'?" he asked, casually.

The bartender grinned as he glanced toward the table. "Might try 'em, now. I didn't see no call to bust into a solo-tout with no trivial politics like a couple of drinks.

"Gents, what's yourn?"

From across the room came a scraping of chairs, and the four men lined up beside the Texan and measured their drinks.

"Stranger in these parts?" inquired a tall man with a huge sunburned moustache.

"Sort of," replied the Texan, "but let's licker before this sinful decoction evaporates."

"Seems like I've saw you before, somewheres," opined a thick man with round china blue eyes.

"Maybe you have, because astoundin' as it may seem, this ain't my first appearance in public—but you might be nature fakin', at that. Where was it this here episode took place?"

The man shook his head: "I dunno, only it seems like you look sort of nat'chel, somehow."

"I always did—it's got so's it's almost what you might call a fixed habit—like swallowin' when I drink. But, speakin' of towns, Timber City's sure had a boom since I was here last. You've got a new horse trough in front of the livery barn." The tall man ordered another round of drinks, and the Texan paused to fill his glass. They drank, and with an audible suck at his overhanging moustache, the tall man leaned an elbow on the bar: "It ain't noways safe or advisable," he said slowly, looking straight at the Texan, "fer no lone cow-hand to ride in here an' make light of Timber City to our face."

A man with a green vest and white, sleek hands insinuated himself between the two and smiled affably: "Come on, now, boys, they ain't nawthin' in quarrelin'. The gent, here, was only kiddin' us a little an' we ain't got no call to raise the hair on our back for that. What do you say we start a little game of stud? Solo ain't no summer game, nohow—too much thinkin'. How about it stranger, d'you play?"

"Only now an' then, by way of recreation. I don't want your money, I got plenty of my own, an' I never let cards interfere with business. Down in Texas we——"

"But, you ain't workin' today," interrupted the other.

"Well, not what you might call work, maybe. I aimed to get drunk, an' I don't want to get switched off into a card game. Come on, now, an' we'll have another drink, an' then Jo-Jo an' I'll renew our conversation. An' while we're at it, Percy, if I was you I'd stand a little to one side so's I wouldn't get my clothes mussed. Now, Jo-Jo, what was the gist of that there remark of yours?"

"My name's Stork—Ike Stork, an'——"

"You're a bird all right."

"Yes, I'm a bird—an' Timber City's a bird, too. They can't no other town in Montany touch us."

"Wolf River's got a bank———"

"Yes," interrupted the bartender, "an' we could of had a bank, too, but we don't want none. If you want a town to go plumb to hell just you start up a bank. Then everyone runs an' sticks their money in an' don't spend none, an' business stops an' the town's gone plumb to hell!"

"I'd hev you to know," Stork cut in importantly, "that Timber City's a cowtown, an' a sheep town, an' a minin' town, an' a timber town—both of which Wolf River ain't neither, except cattle. We don't depend on no one thing like them railroad towns, an' what's more, it tuck a act of Congress fer to name Timber City———"

"Yes an' it takes an act of God to keep her goin', but He does it offhand an' casual, same as He makes three-year-old steers out of two-year-olds."

The bartender grinned affably, his thoughts on the roll of yellow bills that reposed in the pocket of the Texan. "Don't regard Ike none serious, pardner, he's settin' a little oneasy on account he got his claim all surveyed off into buildin' lots, an' they ain't goin' like, what you might say, hot cakes."

"Oh, I don't know," Stork interrupted, but the bartender ignored him.

"Now, about this here proclamation of yourn to git drunk," continued the bartender. "Not that it ain't any man's privilege to git drunk whenever he feels like, an' not that it's any of my business, 'cause it ain't, an' not that I give a damn one way or the other, 'cause I don't, but just by way of conversation, as you might say; what's the big idea? It ain't neither the Thirteenth of June, nor the Fourth of July, nor Thanksgivin' nor Christmas, nor New Year's, on which dates a man's supposed to git drunk, the revels that comes in between bein' mostly accidental, as you might say. But here comes you, without neither rhyme nor reason, as the feller says in the Bible, just a-honin' to git drunk out of a clear sky as the sayin' goes. Of course they's one other occasion which it's every man's duty to git drunk, an' that's his birthday, so if this is yourn, have another on the house, an' here's hopin' you live till the last sheep dies."

They drank, and the Texan rolled another cigarette: "As long as we've decided to git drunk together, it's no more'n right you-all should know the reason. It ain't my birthday, it's my—my anniversary."

"Married?" asked the man with the china blue eyes.

"Nope."

"Well, no wonder you're celebratin'!"

"Shorty, there, he's married a-plenty," explained the man with the green vest, during the general guffaw that greeted the sally.

Again Shorty asked a question, and the Texan noted a hopeful look in the china blue eyes: "Be'n married an'—quit?"

"Nope."

The hopeful look faded, and removing his hat, the man scratched his head: "Well, if you ain't married, an' ain't be'n married, what's this here anniversary business? An' how in hell do you figger the date?"

The Texan laughed: "A-many a good man's gone bugs foolin' with higher mathmatics, Shorty. Just you slip another jolt of this tornado juice in under your belt, an' by the time you get a couple dozen more with it, you won't care a damn about anniversaries. What'll be botherin' you'll be what kind of meat they feed the sun dogs———"

"Yes, an' I'll catch hell when I git home," whimpered Shorty.

"Every man's got his own brand of troubles," philosophized the Texan, "an' yours sure set light on my shoulders. Come on, barkeep, an' slip us another round of this here inebriatin' fluid. One whole year on crick water an' alkali dust has added, roughly speakin', 365 days an' 5 hours, an' 48 minutes, an' 45-1/2 seconds to my life, an' has whetted my appetite to razor edge—an' that reminds me—" he paused abruptly and picking up the yellow-backed bill that still lay before him upon the bar, crammed it into his pocket.

CHAPTER II

KANGAROO COURT

Bottle in hand, the bartender eyed the cowboy quizzically. "What's the big idee—pinchin' back the *dinero*?" he questioned.

The Texan smiled: "Just happened to think, that this is the identical spot, a year ago, where I imbibed the last shot of red licker that's entered my system till I intruded this peaceful scene today."

"What's all that got to do with you grabbin' that there money which I want two dollars an' a half out of it fer them two rounds of drinks that's on you?"

"Don't go worryin' about that. You'll get all that's comin' to you. But a little reference to back history might fresh up your memory that I've got four dollars change comin' from a year ago———"

"Wha'd ye mean—a year ago? I wasn't here a year ago! My brother run this joint then. I only be'n here a couple of months."

The Texan regarded the man with puckered brow: "Well now, since you mentioned it, there *is* somethin' disparagin' about that face of yours that kind of interfered with me recognizin' it off hand. The Red Front, changin' hands that way, complicates the case to an extent that we'll have to try it out all legal an' regular *pro bono publico*, kangaroo court. I studied law once way back in Texas with a view to abusin' an' evadin' the same, an' enough of it's stuck to me so we can conduct this case *ex post facto*.

"Barkeep, you're the defendant, an' for the purposes of the forthcomin' action your name's John Doe. You four other characters are the jury, an' that don't leave nothin' for me to be except plaintiff, prosecutin' attorney, judge, an' court bailiff." Jerking his gun from its holster the cowboy grasped it by the barrel and rapped loudly upon the bar: "O yes! O yes! You bet! Court is now open! The first case on the docket is Horatio Benton, alias Tex, *vs*. John Doe, John Doe's brother, an' the Red Front saloon *et al*."

"Hey, what's all this here damn nonsense about?" asked the bartender.

For answer the Texan rapped the bar with the butt of his gun: "Silence in the court!" he roared. "An' what's more, you're fined one round of drinks for contempt of court." Taking a match from his pocket he laid it carefully upon the bar, and continued: "The plaintiff will take the stand in his own behalf. Gentlemen of the jury, the facts are these: One year ago today, along about 3:30 P.M., I walked up to this bar an' had five drinks, one of which was on the house an' four on me at two bits a throw. I was packin' a couple of black eyes, the particulars of which is extramundane to this case, an' the barkeep, defendant here's alleged brother, asked certain pertinent an' unmitigated questions concernin' the aforesaid black eyes. In explainin' to him how they were come by, I had occasion to take a shot at a mouse—the bullet hole, an' doubtless his dried-up remains can be seen yonder against the base-board an' constitutes Exhibit A———"

"Well, I'll be damned!" exclaimed Shorty, his china blue eyes round with excitement, "I know'd I'd saw you before!"

"Me, too, we was settin' there playin'———"

Again the six-gun rapped on the bar: "You, Green Vest, you're fined a round of drinks for contempt of court. An' Shorty, you're fined two rounds. Not that there's any doubt about your first statement, but this here *profanus vulgus* business has got to be cut out." Depositing three more matches beside the first upon the bar, the Texan proceeded: "Shortly thereafter, an' right in the middle of my remarks the said barkeep disembarked in tumultuous haste, like he'd be'n sent for an' had to go. I waited around a spell an' not favorin' this spot for a permanent abode, I laid a five dollar gold piece on the bar, an' rode off. Therefore, gentlemen of the jury, it's plain to see that I've got four dollars comin', as an offset to which the present specimen, here, has got a just an' valid claim fer two rounds of drinks to the total value of two dollars an' four bits, leavin' a dollar an' four bits still owin' to me. The case is now closed, owin' to any testimony the defendant, here, might introduce, would be mere hearsay an' therefore irrelevant an' immaterial, he havin' admitted he wasn't here at the time. Now, gentlemen of the jury, what's your verdict?"

Thus appealed to the four gathered at the end of the bar and held whispered conversation, Shorty glancing furtively the while at the gun in the Texan's hand.

Presently, mouthing a corner of his moustache, Ike Stork spoke: "It's the ondivided opinion of the jury, except Shorty disagreein' fer fear he'll git shot, that this here party behind the bar's name ain't John Doe, which it's Pete Barras same as before, an' likewise he's got two dollars an' four bits comin' from you fer the drinks. Them four dollars of yourn is comin' from Sam Barras, which he's runnin' a saloon over to Zortman."

The Texan produced another match and laid it beside the others upon the bar: "You're fined a round of drinks for misnomer of the defendant," he announced, gravely. "An' seein' the jury is hung—why it ain't be'n hung long ago is surprisin' to me—you're discharged—bob-tailed discharge, as they'd say in the army which carries with it a recommendation that you're a bunch of inebriated idiots that's permitted to stand on your hind legs an walk upright so's to make more room for regular folks to move around in. The case is taken out of your hands an' adjoodicated upon its merits which accordin' to the statutes in such cases made an' provided, judgment is rendered for the plaintiff, on account of the above transaction bein' with the saloon, as such, an' not a personal matter with the bartender. Plaintiff is also ordered to take over an' run said saloon to the best of his ability until such time as the said dollar an' four bits is paid."

"Look a-here, pardner," began the bartender, edging along opposite the Texan, "fun's fun, an' kangaroo courts is all right as fer as they go an' as long as they don't mix up no regular money in their carryin's on. Me an' my brother Sam ain't on what you might say, fambly terms, which he'd of skun me to a frazzle on this here deal if the claim I traded him fer the saloon had of be'n worth a damn. But in spite of me an' Sam bein' what you might say, onfriendly relations, I've got to say fer him that he never pays a debt, an' if you've got four dollars comin' from him you might as well set around like a buzzard till he dies, which he's that ornery it prob'ly won't be long, an' then file yer claim ag'in his executioner."

The Texan grinned: "I hope fer your sake that advice is sound, for I'm handin' it back in the original package———"

"You mean you ain't a-goin to pay fer them drinks?" The bartender's voice held a truculent note, and his eyes narrowed. "'Cause, believe me, stranger, if you think you ain't, you're plumb misguided. Things has be'n quiet an' peaceable around here fer quite a spell, but you'll pay fer two rounds of drinks or Timber City's a-goin' to see some excitement."

The Texan noted that the man's hand was reaching along the under side of the bar, and his own dropped unobserved to the butt of the six-gun that he had returned to its holster. "Speakin' of excitement you're sure some prophet," he observed, drily, "an' therefore, prob'ly without honour. But as far as I'm concerned, your brother Sam's nothin' but a pleasant memory while as we say in the law, this saloon here is a corporeal hereditament———"

"You're a damn liar!" flared the aproned one, indignantly: "They ain't no wimin' allowed in here—" With the words the man's hand leaped from behind the bar, there was a crashing report, a heavy six-shooter thudded upon the wooden floor, and with a cry of pain the bartender spun half around clutching at his right arm.

"Backin' up hard words with gun play is dangerous business onless you're a top hand at it," observed the Texan, drily, as he stepped around to the man's side. A movement in front of the bar caused the six-gun once more to leap from its holster and at the action four pairs of hands flew ceilingward. "Just you hombres belly right close up to the rail an' all yer hands open an' above board on top of the bar, an' you, Stork, you come on around here an' tie up this arm or there'll be some more casualties reported. If you're all as plumb languid on the draw as yer fellow citizen here your ranks is sure due to thin out some." The Texan stooped to recover the bartender's gun from the floor and as he did so Ike Stork stepped around the corner of the bar, and taking instant advantage of his position, administered a kick that sent the cowboy sprawling at the feet of the bartender. Pandemonium broke loose in the smashing of glass and the thud of blows. Forgetting his injured arm the bartender joined Stork who had followed up his advantage by leaping upon the struggling Texan. Reaching over the bar, Green Vest sent the heavy whisky bottle crashing into the *mêlée* while his two companions contributed the array of empty glasses and then valiantly bolted for the door. The narrowness of the alley behind the bar undoubtedly saved the struggling Texan from serious mishap. As it was his two assailants hindered and impeded each other and at the same time formed a buffer against the shower of glassware that descended from above. Freeing one hand the Texan began to shoot along the floor. With the first explosion the bartender scrambled to his feet and leaped onto the bar at the precise moment that Green Vest, pausing in his flight toward the door, seized a heavy brass cuspidor and hurled it with both hands. The whirling missile caught the bartender full in the face and without a sound he crashed backward carrying Ike Stork with him to the floor. The next instant the Texan was upon his feet and a gun in each hand, grinned down into the face of the terrified man who lay helplessly pinned by the inert form of the bartender. "Any friends or relations you want notified, Isaac, or any special disposal of the remains?" he questioned, as the guns waved back and forth above the prostrate man's face.

"G'wan, shoot if yer goin' to. I ain't packin' no gun. I done my damnedest when I booted you down, an' we'd of had you at that if them damned eediots hadn't begun bouncin' bottles an' glasses an' spittoons offen our head. Shoot—an' for Christ's sake, make a job of it!"

The Texan's grin broadened, and reaching down he rolled the bartender over, "Get up Ike," he said. "You're a he-one, all right, an' it would be a pity to waste you."

The other struggled to his feet and as he faced him the Texan saw an answering grin widen the mouth beneath the heavy moustache. "Pour us a couple of drinks out of that private stock, an' in the meantime I'll just fog her up a bit as a warnin' to the curious not to intrude on our solitude. An', say, watch this, so you can tell 'em out there I can shoot." Four stacks of chips remained on the table where the players of solo had abandoned their game, and shooting alternately with either hand, and so rapidly that the explosions sounded like shots from an automatic, the Texan cleaned the table and filled the air with a blue-grey haze and a shower of broken chips. Suddenly he glanced at the clock. Its hands pointed to half-past four, and with an oath he sent two bullets crashing into its face. "Four-thirty!" he cried. "A year ago this minute—" He stopped abruptly.

Ike nodded approval and raised his glass: "Now," he pronounced, solemnly, "I've got to own that they ain't none of us in Timber City that's as handy with guns as what you be—but, at that, most of us kin hit a man reasonable often—an' some of us has."

"I'll give you a chance to do it again, then. But, first, you slip down cellar there an' h'ist me up a bunch of beer kegs. I'm goin' to build me a barricade so you birds can't rake the back bar through the window." As Ike passed up the kegs, the Texan arranged them in such a manner that from neither windows nor door could anyone upon the outside cover the space behind the bar, and when Ike came up into the room he shook his head, gloomily: "What's the big idee," he asked, "of startin' a war over a dollar an' four bits? It ain't too late yet fer to leave yer guns in here an' plead guilty to disturbin' the peace. That won't cost you much—but this way, how in hell do you expect to play a lone hand agin a whole town an' git away with it? You're either plumb crazy or drunk or there's somethin' settin' heavy on yer mind——"

"I want my change," insisted the Texan stubbornly, "an' I'm goin' to take it out in trade, an' also them fines—there's twenty or thirty drinks comin', accordin' to the matches. Pour me out a couple of more an' then you've got to take our little friend here an' beat it before the fireworks start. I ain't drunk now, but I'm goin' to be! An' when I am—there's a little song we used to sing way down on the Rio Grande, it runs somethin' like this." Raising his voice the cowboy roared forth the words of his song:

"I'm a howler from the prairie of the West.If you want to die with terror, look at me.I'm chain-lightning—if I ain't, may I be blessed.I'm the snorter of the boundless prairie.

"He's a killer and a hater!He's the great annihilator!He's the terror of the boundless prairie!

"I'm the snoozer from the upper trail!I'm the reveller in murder and in gore!I can bust more Pullman coaches on the railThan anyone who's worked the job before.

"He's a snorter and a snoozer.He's the great trunk line abuser.He's the man who put the sleeper on the rail.

"I'm a double-jawed hyena from the East.I'm the blazing, bloody blizzard from the States.I'm the celebrated slugger; I'm the Beast.I can snatch a man bald-headed while he waits.

"He's a double-jawed hyena!He's the villain of the scena!He can snatch a man bald-headed while he waits."

He finished with a whoop, and picking up the glass, drained it at a gulp. "Beat it, now, Ike, ol' Stork!" he cried, "an' take a bottle of bug-juice, an' our slumberin' friend, with you. So long, ol' timer! I'm a wolf, an' it's my night to howl! Slip up to the hotel an' tell the cook to shoot me down a half-dozen buzzard's eggs fried in grizzly juice, a couple of rattlesnake sandwiches, a platter of live centipedes, an' a prickly-pear salad. I'm hungry, an' I'm on my prowl!"

CHAPTER III

THE STAGE ARRIVES

The Timber City stage creaked and rattled as the horses toiled up the long slope of the Dog Creek divide. The driver dozed on his seat, his eyes protected from the glare of the hot June sun by the wide brim of his hat, opened mechanically at intervals to glance along the white, dusty trail. Inside, Winthrop Adams Endicott smiled as he noted the eager enthusiasm with which his young wife scanned the panorama of mountains and plain that stretched endlessly away to disappear in a jumble of shimmering heat waves.

"Oh, Win! Don't you just *love* it? The big black mountains with their girdles of green timber, the miles, and miles, and miles of absolute emptiness, the smell of the sage—yes, and the very rattle of this bumpy old stage!"

Endicott laughed: "I believe you do love it——"

"Love it! Of course I love it! And so do you love it! And you were just as crazy about coming as I was—only you wouldn't admit it. It's just as Tex said that day way up on top of Antelope Butte. He was speaking of you and he said: 'He'll go back East and the refinement will cover him up again—and that's a damned shame. But he won't be just the same, because the prejudice is gone. He's chewed the meat of the cow country and found it good.' I've always remembered that, and it's true—you are not just the same, dear," she reached over and took his hand in both of hers. "And, oh, Win—I'm glad—glad!"

Endicott smiled as he raised the slim hand to his lips: "Considerable of a philosopher—Tex. And cowboy par excellence. I hope we can find him. If we buy the ranch I've been counting on him to manage it."

"We've got to find him! And dear Old Bat, too! And, Win, won't it be just *grand*? We'll live out here in the summer and in the winter we'll go to New York and Florida, and we'll never, never go back to old Half-Way Between. The place fairly reeks of soap and whisky—and I don't care if their old soap does float!"

Again, Endicott laughed: "I suppose it will do us lots of good. I'll probably spend my days in the saddle and come home smelling of horses, and covered with alkali dust."

"Horses smell better than gas, anyway, and alkali dust is cleaner than coal-soot. Look, Win, quick! A family of Indians camped beside the trail—see the scrawny, sneaky-looking dogs and the ponies with their feet tied together, and the conical tepee. And, oh, on that red blanket—the darlingest little brown papoose! I can hardly wait to get into my riding clothes and gallop for miles! And, Win, dear, you've just got to promise me that if we do buy the ranch, you'll never bring a motor out here—not even a roadster—it would spoil everything!"

"Don't set your heart too strongly on buying that ranch," cautioned her husband.

"But the man said he'd sell at a reasonable figure."

"Yes, but you must remember that a 'reasonable figure', when you're talking about an outfit that runs ten thousand head of cattle mounts up into big money. It all depends upon the terms."

"Well, if he wants to sell his old ranch, he'd be foolish to haggle over a little thing like terms. Some way, I just feel it in my bones that we're going to buy. A woman has intuition—you wait and see."

"Colston was to meet us at Timber City today, and tomorrow we'll ride out and look over the ranch. Do you think you're up to a sixty-mile ride?"

"Sixty! I could ride six hundred!" The brake-shoes creaked as the driver drew his horses up for a breathing spell at the top of the divide. "See!" Alice cried, pointing far out into the foothills. "There is Timber City, with its little wooden buildings huddled against the pines exactly as it was a year ago today when we looked back at it from this very spot. And way beyond you can see the river glistening in the sun, and beyond that are the bad lands." Involuntarily she shuddered: "It's all as vivid as though it had happened yesterday—the dust storm, and the terrible thirst—only you and Tex cheated and gave me all the water."

Endicott nodded: "I don't think we'll ever forget it—it was a mighty close call for all of us." The stage descended the long slope and wound in and out among the foothills, its two occupants contenting themselves with watching the lazy wheeling of the buzzards against the blue, and the antics of the prairie dogs that scolded and chickered at the stage, only to dive incontinently into their holes at its approach. The little steepleless church loomed up before them, and Endicott glanced at his watch: "Four o'clock," he announced, "I wonder if Colston is waiting?"

"Well, if he is, he can wait a little longer," smiled Alice. "Because the first thing we do after we have removed some of this dust, will be to go right over and call on the Camerons—there's the cottage now, dear—just think, a year ago today we stood in that little corner room and Mr. Cameron pronounced the words that made us two the happiest people in the world—stop—please—Win! We're right in town! And if we hurry we can be there at the very same hour and minute we were there last year."

The stage drew up at the door of the little wooden hotel. The driver tossed his reins to the hostlers who were waiting with fresh horses, threw off the mail pouch, and lowered the express box to the ground where it was receipted for by the agent, who was also the post-master, and the proprietor of the hotel.

Endicott approached that dignitary who, mail pouch in hand, was gazing toward a little knot of men farther down the street: "I want to engage two rooms and a bath," he explained.

The man favoured him with a glance of surprise. "Goin' to stop over?" he queried.

"Yes, my wife and I shall be here over night."

"Married? What d'ye want of two rooms, then? Have 'em if you want 'em. Cost you more—'tain't none of my business. Take them two front ones—head of the stairs. Just give a hand an' we'll git yer trunk up, an' quick as the old woman gits the worsh out you c'n have a tub of water—that'll be four-bits extry, though—an' a dollar if I've got to fill it up twict." As they descended the stairs the man's eyes sought the group down the street: "Must be somethin's comin' off down to the Red Front. The boys ain't missed a mail sence the day they strung up Red Kelley, an' that's seven year ago, come August the fourth——"

"Fifth," corrected the stage driver who stood in the doorway.

"They brung Red in on the fourth, an' some of the boys hadn't got in yet, an' they didn't git in till after dark, so they helt Red over——"

"That was the third——"

"'Twasn't neither! I'd ort to know—it was the day my off leader throw'd his nigh fore shoe——"

Alice was manifesting impatience, and Endicott interrupted with a question: "Is Mr. W. S. Colston here?"

"Colston? You mean Y Bar Colston? Yer right, Slim, it was the fifth, 'cause I got a tooth pulled that same day, bein' as the dentist had rode over from Judith to see the hangin'. Why, no, Y Bar ain't here. He gits his mail an' trades over to Claggett."

"He was to meet me here today."

"Well, today ain't over yet. If Y Bar said he'd be here, he'll be here. Jest go in an' make yerselves to home. You can't count on that tub for an hour er so yet, so if you want to worsh up, go right on through an' you'll find the worsh dish on the bench beside the pump—an', if the towel's crusty from the boy's worshin' up this noon, tell the old woman I said to hang up a clean one."

"Hurry, Win!" cried the girl as she gave her face a final rub with the clean towel. "We've got just time enough to get into our riding togs. We both look like awful 'pilgrims' and besides, I want it to be just like it was last year."

A quarter of an hour later they were receiving a cordial welcome from the Reverend Cameron and his wife at the door of the little cottage beside the church. "We were speaking of you today," said the minister's wife "and wondering how your romance turned out."

"No need to ask," laughed her husband, as he followed them into the little living room.

"You see," cried Alice, pointing to the clock, "we arrived at almost the exact moment we did a year ago—" she started slightly as a volley of shots sounded down the street. "Oh!" she cried. "They're shooting someone!"

Cameron shook his head: "No," he smiled, "we've learned that it is the single shots or one and then another, that mean trouble. When they come in volleys that way it means that some cowboy is 'celebrating' down at the Red Front. When there are cowboys in town and they are singing, or racing their horses up and down the street, or shooting into the air or the ceiling, we know they're all right. Of course, one could wish that they wouldn't drink—but, if they must drink, by all means let's have the noise with it. If cowboys are drinking and silent, trouble follows as surely as night follows day."

"Maybe it's Mr. Colston," giggled Alice.

"Colston, of the Y Bar," smiled Cameron, "no I think we can eliminate Colston. Do you know him?"

Endicott shook his head: "No, except through correspondence. I was to meet him here today on business."

Cameron regarded him with sudden interest: "I heard in Lewiston, a couple of weeks ago, that the Y Bar might change hands and, frankly I will tell you that I was sorry to hear it."

"Why?" asked Endicott.

The minister frowned thoughtfully: "Well, Y Bar Colston has been a power in this country, and if the wrong man were to step into his place there might be no end of trouble."

"What kind of trouble?"

"Sheep and cattle. The Y Bar outfit has been a sort of buffer between the two factions. If a rabid cattleman stepped in it would immediately mean war, and if a weakling were to take Colston's place the result would be the same, because the sheep-men would immediately proceed to take advantage of him and encroach on the cattle range, and then the cowboys would take matters into their own hands and we'd have a repetition of the Johnson County War—sheep slaughtered by the thousands upon the range, dead cattle everywhere, herders murdered and their bodies left in the ashes of their burned camp wagons, and cowboys shot from ambush as they rode the range. I tell you, Mr. Endicott, I don't envy the man that succeeds Colston as owner of the Y Bar."

Endicott smiled: "Thank you for the tip. It may, or may not interest you to know that, if the business can be satisfactorily arranged, I myself, am about to assume that unenviable position."

"And the best of luck to you," said Cameron, heartily, as he extended his hand. "What one man has done another can do, but your job will be no sinecure. But, come, we're not going to permit you to return to the hotel for supper, because with cowboys in town the place will in all probability be uncomfortably noisy although I will say for the boys that Mrs. Endicott's presence would be a safeguard against any unseemly talk."

Endicott's objections were met by the Camerons who pointed out that the road by which Colston must enter Timber City ran right past the door and in plain view of the porch where they were accustomed to eat the evening meal.

Alice insisted upon helping Mrs. Cameron, and left to themselves Endicott skilfully led the minister to talk of the country, its needs and requirements, its advantages, its shortcomings, and its problems. Cameron was a minister in every sense of the word, a man who loved his work and who was beloved of the cattle country, and when, a couple of hours later, the ladies summoned them to the table, Endicott took his place with the realization that proprietorship of an outfit like the Y Bar, carried with it responsibilities and obligations that had nothing whatever to do with the marketing of beef on the hoof.

CHAPTER IV

Y BAR COLSTON TALKS

"There's Colston, now!" exclaimed Cameron, rising and hailing a rider who approached leading two saddled horses. The rider drew up, Cameron descended to the little white gate, and a moment later was helping the ranchman to tie his horses to the picket fence. As they approached the porch, Endicott noted the leathery gauntness of face that bespoke years on the open range, and as their hands met he also noted the hard, firm grip, and the keen glance of the grey eyes that seemed to be taking his measure. The man greeted the ladies with grave deference, and seated himself in the empty chair.

"Well, I got here, Endicott, but it was a considerable chore. Ain't as young as I was once. Time I was lettin' go, I guess. Seventy years old—an' young-hearted as any buck on the range—but along towards night, after a hard day's ride, I find myself beginin' to realize I be'n somewheres, an' the old bed-roll looks better to me than a carload of white-faces."

Instinctively, Endicott liked this man—the bluff heartiness of him, and the alert litheness of motion that belied the evidence of the white moustache and silvery white hair. "I hope I shall be half the man you are at your age," he laughed.

"You will be—if you buy the Y Bar outfit. Believe me young man, there's enough to do around that outfit to keep a man up an' jumpin' if he was a hundred an' seventy. A man just naturally ain't got time to get old!"

"Win tells me the ranch is sixty miles from here," smiled Alice, "and that's a pretty good ride for anybody."

"Pretty good ride! Young woman, if that was all the ridin' I done today I'd b'en here before breakfast. I couldn't get away till afternoon—up before daylight this mornin', rode two horses plumb off their feet huntin' the wagons—foreman quit yesterday—best blamed foreman I ever had, too. Just up an' quit cold because he took a notion. Tried every which way to get him to stay—might's well talk to a rock. Away he went, Lord knows where, leavin' me nothin' on my mind except bein' owner, manager, ranch boss, an' wagon boss, besides tryin' to sell the outfit. Confounded young whelp! Best doggone cow-hand on the range."

"Why did you have to hunt wagons, and what has a wagon boss got to do with a cattle ranch?" asked the girl.

"The wagons are the round-up—the rodeo. We're right in the middle of the calf round-up. The grub wagon an' the bed wagon makes what you might call the field headquarters for the round-up—move every day till they cover the whole range."

"How interesting!" exclaimed the girl, "I know I'm going to love it!"

"Sure is interesting," remarked the old man, drily, "with the wagons twenty or thirty miles out in the foothills, an' workin' over into the sheep country, an' eighteen or twenty knot-headed cow-hands hatin' sheep, an' no foreman to hold 'em level, an' hayin' on full tilt at the home ranch, an' the ranch hands all huntin' the shade! Yes'm, interestin's one word for it—but there's a shorter one that I'm afraid the parson, here, wouldn't recommend that describes it a heap better."

"By the way," said Endicott, "Mr. Cameron tells me that the cattle and sheep situation is a rather delicate one hereabouts. He says that you hold the respect of both factions—that you seem to have a peculiar knack in keeping the situation in hand——"

"Peculiar knack!" exclaimed the ranchman, "peculiar knack's got nothin' to do with it! Common sense, young man! Just plain common sense, an' maybe the ability to see that other folks has got rights, same as I have. The Y Bar stands for a square deal all the way around—when its own calves are branded, it quits brandin', an' it don't hold that open range means cattle range an' not sheep range. Any fair-minded man can take the Y Bar an' run it like I've run it, an' make money, an' let the other fellow make money, too. There's plenty of range for all of us if we keep our head. If you're afraid of buyin' into a war—don't buy. I can sell any day to parties I know are just layin' to get the Y Bar, an' the minute they got it, trouble would start an' there'd be hell a-poppin' all along the Mizoo. Somewhere there must be a man that'll buy that is fair-minded, an' not afraid to take holt an' run the outfit like I've run it."

Endicott flushed slightly: "I am not afraid of it. I only wanted to know——"

"An' you've got a right to know. If we deal, I'll stay with you long enough to wise you up to the whole layout. That would be no more than right. I'm considerable used to judgin' men, an' I think you can handle it. Let 'em know right off the reel that you ain't afraid of any of 'em—an' get this before you start out: A man ain't God A'mighty because he happens to run cattle, an' he ain't the Devil because he runs sheep, neither. There's cattlemen on this range I wouldn't trust as far as I could throw a bull by the tail, an' there's sheep-men can have anything I've got just on their say-so—mind you, that ain't the general run—pickin' 'em in the dark, I'd tie to a cow-man every time—but there's exceptions, as the fellow says, to every rule. If that confounded Tex hadn't quit——"

"*Tex!*" cried Alice, and Endicott smiled at the glad eagerness of the tone.

The old cattleman glanced at her in surprise: "Yes, my foreman. Best man on the range—handled men the easiest you ever saw. Never had any trouble with the sheep outfits—but just the same, there ain't a sheep-man south of the river that would care to try to put anything over on him—nor no one else, neither. There ain't any bluff an' bluster about him, he's the quietest hand you ever saw. But, somehow, lookin' into them eyes of his—a man just naturally stops to think—that's all."

"Oh, what is he like? Tell me about him! What is his name?"

"Name's Tex. That's all I know, an' that's all——"

"Tex Benton?" interrupted the girl.

The man regarded her curiously. "Maybe, or, Tex Smith, or Tex Jones, or Tex somethin else."

"I—we knew a Tex, once——"

Colston laughed: "There's lots of Texes here in the cow-country. Tryin' to find one that you didn't know no more about than that would be like me goin' East an' sayin' I knew a man by the name of John."

"How long has he worked for you?"

"He quit last evenin'. If he'd of stayed till day after tomorrow, it would have been just a year." The old man's voice had softened, and his gaze strayed to the far hills. "I made him foreman when he'd b'en with me a month," he continued after a short pause. "I can pick men." Another pause. "He—he called me 'Dad'."

"Did he know you were going to sell?" asked Endicott.

The old man shook his head.

"Then, why did he quit?" Somehow, the question sounded harsh, but the man seemed not to notice. There was an awkward silence during which the old man continued to stare out over the hills.

"He quit to get drunk," he said abruptly, and Endicott detected a slight huskiness in his tone.

Across the table, Alice gasped—and the sound was almost a sob.

Colston cleared his throat roughly, and turned his eyes to the girl: "That's the way I feel about it, young woman. I got to know him mighty well, an' I know what was in him. From the time he went to work for me till he quit, he never took a drink—an', God knows it wasn't because he didn't want one! He fought it just like he fought bad horses, an' like he'd of fought men if he'd had to—square an' open. He'd give away an advantage rather than take one. He was like that.

"I saw him ride an outlaw, once—a big, vicious killer—a devil-horse. The Red King, we called him, he's run with the wild bunch for years. Two men had tried him. We buried one where he lit. The other had folks. Tex run him a week an' trapped him at a water-hole—then, he *rode him!*" The old man's eyes were shining now, and his fist smote the table top. "Ah, that was a ride—with the whole outfit lookin' on!" Colston paused and glanced about the faces at the table, allowing his eyes to rest upon Alice who was listening eagerly, with parted lips. "Did you ever notice how sometimes without any reason, things gets kind of—of onnatural—kind of feel to 'em that's *different?* Well, this ride was like that. I've seen hundreds of bad horses rode, an' the boys all yellin' an' bettin', but this time there wasn't no bettin', an' the only sounds was the sound made by the Red King. It wasn't because they expected to see Tex killed—all of 'em had seen men killed ridin' bad horses, an' all of 'em had cheered the next man up. But, somethin' kep' 'em still, with their eyes froze on what they saw. It was uncanny—one hundred an' forty pounds of man tacklin' eleven hundred pounds of red fury. There we stood, the white alkali dust raisin' in a cloud, an' the devil-horse, crazy mad—screamin' shrill like a woman, snappin' like a wolf, frothin', strikin', kickin', buckin' twistin', sunfishin', swappin' ends, shootin' ten foot high an' crashin' down on his back—fightin' every minute with the whole box of tricks, an' a lot of new ones—an' Tex right up in the middle of him with that twisty smile on his face, like he wasn't only half interested in what he was doin'. Didn't even put a bridle on. Rode him with a hackamore—jerked that off an' give him his head—an' he rode straight up, an' raked him an' fanned him every jump. It wasn't *human.*

"For three days they fought, man an' horse, before the Red King knew his master—an' when they got through, the Red King would come when Tex whistled. For ten days he rode him, an'—there was a horse! A bay so bright an' sleek that he looked like red gold in the sunlight, mane an' tail black as ink, an' his eyes chain lightnin'—an' the sound of the thunder was in his hoofs.

"It was moonlight the night I rode home from the NL. I had just topped a ridge that juts from the foothills into the open range an' all at once I heard the thunder of hoofs ahead. I slipped into a scatterin' of bull pines at the edge an' waited. I didn't wait long. Along the ridge, runnin' strong an' smooth, like the rush of a storm wind, come a horse an' rider. Before I could make 'em out, I knew by the sound of the hoofs, what horse an' what rider. They passed close—so close I could have reached out an' touched 'em with my quirt. Then I saw what made my heart jump an' my eyes fair pop out of my head. The Red King flashed by—no saddle, no bridle, not even an' Injun twitch, mane an' tail flarin' out in the wind of his own goin', an' the white foam flyin' in chunks from his open mouth; an' on his back sat Tex, empty handed an' slick heeled. I thought I caught a glimpse of the twisty smile on his face, as he swayed on the back of the devil-horse—that, I saw—an' ten rod further on the ridge broke off in a goat-climb! I went limp, an' then—'Whoa!' The sound cracked like a pistol shot. The stallion's feet bunched under him an' three times his length he slid with the loose rock flyin' like hailstones! He stopped with his forefeet on the edge, an' his rump nearly touchin' the ground, then he whipped into shape like a steel spring an' stood there on the rim of the ridge, neck an' tail arched, head tossin' out that long black mane, red flarin' nostrils suckin' in the night air, an' a forefoot pawin' the rock. If Remington or old Charlie Russell could have seen what I saw there in the moonlight—man an' horse—the best man, an' the best horse in all the cow-country—the sky black an' soft as velvet, an' the yellow range—no one will paint it—because no one will ever see the like again. There they stood, lookin' out over the wild country. And, then Tex slipped down an' stepped slow to the Red King's head. He put up his arms an' they closed over the arched neck an' his cheek laid against the satin skin of him. For what seemed like a long time they stood there, an' then Tex stepped back an' pointed to the yellow range: 'Go on, boy!' he said, '*Go!*' An' he brought the flat of his hand down with a slap on the shiny flank. For just an instant the horse hesitated an' then he went over the edge. The loose rocks clattered loud, an' then come the sound of hoofs on the sod as the Red King tore down the valley. Tex watched him an' all of a sudden his fingers flew to his lips, an' a shrill whistle cut the air. Down in the valley the devil-horse stopped short—stopped an' whirled at the sound. Then of a sudden he reared high his forefeet pawin' the air in a fume of fury an' up out of the night come the wickedest, wildest scream man ever heard—it was a scream that got to a man. It sent cold shivers up an' down my back. The Red King had come into his own again—he was defyin' his master. He turned, then, an' the last I saw of him was a red blur in the distance.

"Then Tex turned an' started back along the ridge. I could see his face, now, an' the twisty smile on his lips. I aimed to stay hid an' never let on I'd seen—it seemed somehow best that way. But when he was right opposite me he stopped an' rolled a cigarette an' the flare of the match made my horse jump, an' the next second he was beside me with a gun in his hand, an' his face flamin' red as the coat of the devil-horse.

"'You saw it?' he says, kind of quiet.

"I shakes my head: 'Yes,' I says, 'but not intentional. I was ridin' home from the NL, an' I slipped in here to let you by.'

"Pretty soon he spoke again kind of slow: 'If it had b'en anyone else but you, Dad,' he says, 'I'd of—of—But, you understand, you savvy. He's wild—we're both wild—the Red King an' me. We'll fight like hell—for the fun of fightin'—an' then we'll go back to the wild again—an' we'll go back when we damn please—did you see him when I whistled?'

"'I saw,' I says. To tell the truth, I was kind of catchy in the throat, but I managed to blurt out, 'An' that's why you wouldn't brand him?'

"'Yes,' he says, 'that's why—' An' of a sudden, his voice went hard. 'I licked him to show him I could. But, I didn't brand him—an' if anyone ever lays an iron on him, I'll kill him as sure as hell—onless the Red King beats me to it.'" The old man paused and cleared his throat huskily, and as Alice dabbed at her eyes he noticed that her lips quivered. "An' that's the way he fought the booze—open an' above board—not takin' the advantage of stayin' away from it. He carried a half-pint flask of it all the time. I've seen him take it out an' hold it up to the sunlight an' watch the glints come an' go—for all the world like the glints on the coat of the Red King. He'd shake it, an' watch the beads rise, an' he'd pull the cork an' smell it—breathe its flavour an' its bouquet deep into his lungs—an' all the while the little beads of cold sweat would be standin' out on his forehead, like dew on a tombstone, an' his tongue would be wettin' his lips, an' his fingers would be twitchin' to carry it to his mouth. Then his lips would twist into that grin, an' he'd put back the cork, an' put the bottle in his pocket, an' ride off—*singin'*.

"When I saw him tackle that horse that no man had ever rode, I knew, somehow, that he'd ride him. An' when I'd see him pull that bottle, just tormented crazy for a drink, I knew he wouldn't take a drink. An' the same way, when he come to me yesterday an' said he was goin' to quit, I knew he was goin' to quit, an' there was nothin' more to be said. I asked him why, an' open an' above board he says: 'Because I'm goin' to get drunk.' I couldn't believe my ears at first. It turned me kind of sick—an' then I knew I loved him. All at once I saw red. You see, I knew what he didn't know I knew—about his fight with the booze. 'So, it got you at last, did it?' I says.

"He looked at me with those quiet eyes, an' the twisty smile come into his face. 'No, Dad,' he says. 'It didn't get me—an' you know it didn't get me—an' it never could. I showed it I could lick it, an' that's all there is to it. I'm goin' away now, an' get drunk as hell—deliberate—not because I have to get drunk, but because I want to.' An' as I watched the boy ride away, I remembered how it had been with the Red King—he licked him an' turned him back with the wild bunch—because he wanted to."

CHAPTER V

ALICE TAKES A RIDE

The meal proceeded in silence and at its conclusion Alice rose and stood with her hand on the back of her chair. "And Old Bat?" she asked, "Isn't there an old half-breed named Bat?"

Colston nodded gloomily: "Yes, there's Old Bat. He's been cookin' at the home ranch, but when he finds out Tex has blown the outfit I expect he'll light out after him."

"I think so too," agreed the girl, "I haven't the least doubt in the world that when we reach the ranch it will be to find Old Bat gone."

After helping Mrs. Cameron with the dishes, Alice returned to the porch where the men were deep in the discussion of business, and as she listened her eyes rested longingly upon the three saddled horses.

Colston noticed the look: "Like to take a little ride?" he smiled. "That buckskin's woman broke—I brought him a purpose when your husband wired that he was bringing you along. You've got an hour yet before dark, an' the trails out of Timber City are all main travelled ones—no danger of gettin' lost around here."

Alice shot a questioning glance at Endicott who nodded approval. "Go ahead if you want to, dear—only be sure and be back before dark."

"Oh, I'll be back before dark!" she assured him as she stepped into the yard, "I remember—" she laughed a trifle nervously, "I'm just dying to get into a saddle. No, you don't have to help me!" she called as Endicott rose from his chair. And her husband watched with a smile as she untied the horse, led him into the trail, and mounted.

At the first little rise, Alice reined in the buckskin and gazed about her, breathing deeply of the sage-laden air. In the gradually deepening twilight the Judith range loomed dark and mysterious and far to the northward, the Bear Paws were just visible against the faintly glowing sky. Before her, the white trail wound among the foothills in its long climb to the divide, and beyond the little town it flattened away toward the Missouri. Over that trail just one year ago she had ridden in company with her two lovers. Her heart swelled with pride of the man who had won her. "But I love Tex, too," she murmured, and blushed at the words, "I do! Nobody could help loving him. He's—he's—well, he's just Tex!" Her glance strayed to the distant reaches beyond the great river and she shuddered slightly as she thought of the bad lands that lay between her and the fast dimming mountains, and of Long Bill Kearney and his flat-boat ferry. A mile beyond the town a dark patch of pines loomed distinctly. It was there she had said good-bye to the Texan, and——. Her lips moved: "The cherry blossoms are in bloom over there—and the dear little blue and white prairie flowers—" Impulsively, she started her horse, and skirting the town, came out onto the trail beyond and urged him into a run.

She drew up at the little creek that came tumbling out of the woods, and peered, half fearfully, half expectantly, among the tree-trunks. "It isn't dark yet. And, it's only a little way," she thought, and dismounting, tied the buckskin to a low hanging limb, and plunged into the woods. "Here are the cherry blossoms, the same as a year ago, and yes, there is the big rock!" She stepped around the boulder, and stood upon the edge of the tiny glade. "A year ago," she breathed, with a catch at her throat, "and it seems like yesterday! He stood there with his cheek resting against his horse's neck, staring out over his beloved range—and, then he told me that Win hadn't killed Purdy. Right here on this spot at that moment I was the happiest woman in the world—and I've been the happiest woman in the world ever since, until—until—" The words faltered, and she stamped her foot angrily: "Oh, why does he have to drink? And today, of all days!" Her eyes rested upon the little prairie flowers that carpeted the glade and stooping, she picked a huge bouquet as the darkness gathered and when she stood erect with her hands full of blossoms the big rock at the edge of the glade was hardly distinguishable in the dusk. With a little cry, half surprise, half fright, she hastened toward it. The woods were darker than the glade and for a moment she stood peering into the thicket through which she must pass to reach her horse, while foolish terrors of the dark crowded her mind and caused little creepy chills to tickle the roots of her hair. She glanced at the flowers in her hand, "If I only hadn't stopped to pick them," she faltered, "if I were only out on the trail—" And then she pulled herself together with a laugh—a forced, nervous laugh, but it fulfilled its purpose. "You're a little fool, Alice Endicott, to be afraid of the dark! And you, a prospective rancher's wife! What would people say if they knew that Mrs. Y Bar Endicott was afraid to go a quarter of a mile through a perfectly peaceful patch of woods just because it was after sundown?" Resolutely curbing the desire to dart fearful glances to the right, and to the left, and behind her, she kept her face to the front, and plunged into the woods following the little creek. A few minutes later she gained the trail, and untying the buckskin, mounted and headed him toward the scattering lights of Timber City.

At the edge of the town she drew up abruptly. A volley of shots rang out, and she could see the thin streaks of flame that leaped out from the crowd of men that were collected in front of the saloon. Her first thought was to skirt the town and arrive at the rectory as she had left it. But once more she upbraided herself for her foolish fear. "Mr. Cameron said when they came in volleys they were harmless," she reassured herself, "and I may as well get used to it now as later." She urged her horse forward and as she reached the edge of the crowd a man raised his gun and sent a shot crashing through the window of the Red Front. Other shots followed, and Alice saw that the building was in darkness. Something in the attitude of the men caused her to draw up and regard them closely. Very few of them were cowboys, and they were not shooting into the air. Also, there was nothing in their demeanour that savoured of any spirit of jollification. They seemed in deadly earnest. More shots—streaks of thin red flame, and a tinkling of glass. This time the shots were answered from within the building, the crowd surged to one side, and those who were unable to get out of the line of fire dropped swiftly to the ground and wriggled away on their bellies. A tall man with a huge drooping moustache came toward her: "Better git along. This here ain't no place fer women folks."

"What's the matter?" asked Alice.

"You better pull there in front of the livery barn. You might git hit. They's a ring-tailed desperado in the Red Front, an' he's mighty permiscuous about his shootin'."

"Why don't they arrest him?" asked the girl. The man had walked beside her, and seating himself upon the edge of the horse trough, began deliberately to reload his pistol.

"Arrest him," he drawled, "that's jest what we aim to do. But first we got to git him in shape to arrest. He's imbibed to the point which he won't listen to no reason whatever—an' shoot! He's a two-handed gunman from hell—beggin' yer pardon, mom—I didn't aim to swear—but, them Texicans—when they gits lickered up. I'd sooner try to handle a oncontented grizzly——"

"Texan!" cried the girl. "Did you say he is a Texan? Who is he? What's his name?"

The man regarded her gravely: "Seems to me he did say—back there in the saloon, when he was holdin' kangaroo court. The rookus hadn't started yet, an' he says——"

Alice had thrown herself from her horse, and stood before the man, the wild flowers clutched tightly in her hand. "Was it Tex?" she interrupted, impatiently.

The man nodded: "Yeh, it was Tex——"

"Tex Benton?"

The man scratched at his head: "Seems like that's what he said. Anyways, he claimed he was here a year ago, an' he aimed to git drunk on account of some kind of an anniversary, or somethin'—an' he will, too, if he drinks up all them fines———"

Alice interrupted by clutching the man's arm and shaking it vigorously. "Oh, tell them to stop shooting!" she cried. "They'll kill him! Let me go in to him! I can reason with him."

The man regarded her with sudden interest: "D'you know him?"

"Yes, yes! Hurry and tell them to stop shooting!"

"You wait here a minute, an' I'll git Hod Blake, he's the marshal." The man disappeared and a moment later came toward her with another man, the two followed by a goodly part of the crowd.

The tall man stepped to the girl's side: "This here's Hod," he announced by way of introduction and, "that's her."

Gun in hand, Hod Blake nodded curtly: "D'you say you know this here party?" he asked.

"Yes, that is, I think I do."

"Ike, here, says how you figgered you could go in an' make him surrender."

Alice nodded, somehow, that word surrender had an ominous sound. "He hasn't—killed anyone, has he?"

"No, he ain't killed no one—yet. He nicked Pete Barras in the arm, an' has otherwise feloniously disturbed the peace of Timber City to a extent it'll cost him a hundred dollars' fine besides damages fer shootin' up, an' causin' to git shot up, the Red Front saloon."

"And, you'd kill a man for that!" cried the girl, indignantly.

"I'll tell a hand, we'll kill him! Anyone that starts gun-play in Timber City's got to go on through with it."

"You're cowards!" exclaimed the girl. "How many of you are there against one man?"

"That don't make no difference. We got the law on our side, an' he ain't on his'n. He come in here a-huntin' trouble—an' he got it. An' he'll pay his fine, an' settle up with Pete Barras, or we'll plant him—one."

Alice thrust the flowers into the bosom of her soft shirt and regarded the man coldly: "If all of you brave gun-fighters are afraid to go in there and get him, I'll go. I'm not afraid."

Ike Stork warned her: "You better keep out of it, mom. He's lickered up an' liable to shoot sudden."

"I'm not afraid," repeated the girl.

Hod Blake shrugged: "Go ahead if you want to. Tell him we'll git him, sure, if he don't give himself up. An' s'pose you git shot, fer yer trouble, you got any folks to notify?"

Alice glanced at him coldly: "My husband is up at Mr. Cameron's with Mr. Colston, you might mention it to him, if you think of it," she answered scornfully. "Get me a light."

Match in one hand, candle in the other, the girl advanced to the front of the saloon, while the crowd remained at a respectful distance. The door of the building stood open, but the interior was screened from the street by a heavy partition of rough planking around which one must pass to gain access to the bar. At the doorway the girl paused and her figure leaped sharply into view in the bright flare of the match. The flame dimmed as she held it to the wick of the candle, then brightened as she stood with white face and tight-pressed lips, framed in the black recess of the doorway. For a long time, as tense seconds are measured, she stood wondering at the sudden silence. She knew that the eyes of the crowd were upon her as it waited just beyond the circle of her candlelight—and her shoulders stiffened as she realized that not a man among them would dare stand where she stood with a lighted candle in her hand. She felt no fear, now. It seemed the most natural, the most matter-of-fact thing in the world that she should be standing thus in the doorway of the Red Front saloon, with a crowd of armed men in the darkness behind her, and in the darkness before her—what? What if the man behind that rough plank wall were not Tex—her Tex? What if—? It seemed suddenly as if icy fingers reached up and clutched her heart. She felt her knees tremble, and the candle swayed in her hand until it threw moving shadows on the plank wall. Thoughts of Win crowded her brain. What would Win think of her? What could he think, if the man behind that screen were not Tex, and would shoot the second she came into range? What would everyone think? She was a fool.

"Douse yer light an' crawl back!" She recognized the rough half contemptuous voice of Hod Blake. And the next instant she thought of the roar of guns, the acrid smell of burned powder, and the thin red streaks of flame that had pierced the night like swift arrows of blood. They would kill him. "He's the best man among them all," she sobbed, and closing her eyes, held the candle at arms length before her, and walked slowly toward the black opening at the end of the plank screen.

There was a crashing report. Alice opened her eyes—in darkness. "Tex!" she cried, frantically, "Tex, strike a light!"

CHAPTER VI

AT THE RED FRONT

When Ike Stork had disappeared through the door of the Red Front dragging the unconscious form of the bartender with him, the Texan poured himself a drink, set a quart bottle before him upon the bar, rummaged in a drawer and produced a box of cartridges which he placed conveniently to hand, reloaded his guns, and took another drink.

A report sounded in the street and a bullet crashed through the window and buried itself in a beer keg. The Texan laughed: "Fog 'er up, ol' hand, an' here's yer change!" Reaching over the top of a keg, he sent a bullet through the window. The shot drew a volley from the street, and the big mirror behind the bar became a jangle of crashing glass.

"Barras'll have to get him a new lookin' glass," he opined, as he shook the slivers from his hat brim. "The war's on—an' she's a beaut! If ol' Santa Anna was here, him an' I could lick the world! This red licker sure is gettin' to my head—stayed off of it too long—but I'm makin' up for lost time. Whoopee!"

"Oh, I'm a Texas cowboy,Far away from home,If I ever get back to TexasI never more will roam."

"Hey, in there!" The song ceased abruptly, and, gun in hand the Texan answered.

"There ain't no hay in here! What do you think this is, a cow's hotel? The livery barn's next door!"

"They ain't no outlaw goin' to run Timber City while I'm marshal!"

"Put 'er here, pardner!" answered the Texan. "You run Timber City an' I'll run the Red Front! Come on in an' buy a drink, so I can get my change!"

"You're arrested fer disturbin' the peace!"

"Come an' get me, then. But come a-shootin'!"

"You can't git away with it. I got twenty men here, an' everyone packin' a gun!"

"You've got me, then," mocked the Texan. "I've only got two guns. Run 'em in in a bunch. I can only take care of a dozen, an' the rest can get me before I can reload."

"Yer kickin' up an awful stink fer a dollar an' four bits."

"'Tain't the money, it's the principle of the thing. An' besides, I aimed to pull a hell-winder of a jamboree—an' I'm doin' it."

"You ain't helpin' yer case none by raisin' a rookus like this. Come out an' give yerself up. All there is agin you is a fine an' a little damages."

"How much?"

"We'll make it fifty dollars' fine, an' you'll have to talk to Pete Barras about the damages."

The Texan laughed derisively: "Guess again, you short horn! I've got more money than that!"

"You comin' out, or I got to go in there an' git you?"

"I ain't comin' out, an' you ain't comin' in here an' get me," defied the cowboy; "you ain't got the guts to—you an' your twenty gun-fighters to boot! Just you stick your classic profile around the corner of that wall an' I'll shoot patterns in it!"

"You can't git away. We've got yer horse!"

"If I was a posse I'd surround you an' string you up for a bunch of horse-thieves!"

"What you goin' to do about it?"

"I'm standin' pat—me. What you goin' to do?"

"Come on out, hands up, an' submit to arrest before you git in too deep."

"There ain't a marshal in Montana can arrest me!"

"What's yer name?"

"Hydrophobia B. Tarantula! I'm a curly wolf! I can't be handled 'cause I'm full of quills! I've got seventeen rattles an' a button, an' I'm right now coiled!"

"Yer drunk as hell," growled the marshal, "wait till you git sober an' you won't feel so damn hard."

"You're goin' to miss some sleep waitin', 'cause there's seventeen quarts in sight, without countin' the barrel goods an' beer."

For answer the exasperated marshal sent a bullet crashing into the wall high above the Texan's head, and the shot was immediately followed by a volley from the crowd outside, the bullets slivering the woodwork, or burying themselves harmlessly in the barricade of beer-kegs.

"This saloon's gettin' all scratched up, the way you ruffians are carryin' on," called the Texan, when the noise had subsided, "but if it's shootin' you want, divide these here up amongst you!" Reaching around a keg, he emptied a gun through the window, then reloaded, and poured himself another drink.

"The main question is," he announced judicially to himself, as he contemplated the liquor in the glass, "I've drunk one quart already, now shall I get seventeen times drunker'n I am, or shall I stay drunk seventeen times as long?" He drank the liquor and returned the glass to the bar, "guess I'll just let Nature take her course," he opined, and glanced about him quizzically. "I mistrusted this wasn't goin' to be no prosaic jubilee, but what I'm wonderin' is, how's it goin' to come out? 'Tain't likely anyone'll get hurt, 'cause they can't hit me, an' I don't want to hit them. But, this is goin' to get monotonous sometime an' I'll want to leave here. They've got my horse, an' it's a cinch I ain't goin' away afoot. Guess I'll have to borrow one like Ol' Bat did down to Las Vegas an' get plumb out of the country. An' there's another reason I can't linger to get venerable amongst my present peaceful surroundin's. When Ol' Bat finds I've quit the outfit he'll trail me down, just as sure as I'm goin' to take another drink, an' when he does, he'll———"

Once more the voice of the marshal sounded from without: "Hey, young feller, I'm willin' to go half way with you———"

"Half of nothin's nothin'!" replied the Texan, "I ain't goin' nowhere!"

"You better listen to reason an' give yerself up. If you do we let you off with a hundred dollar fine, an' damages—if you don't, I'm goin' to charge you with shootin' to kill, an' send you up to Deer Lodge fer a year. You got just one minute to think it over. It's gettin' dark an' I ain't had no supper."

"Me neither. You go on ahead an' get yours first, an' then hurry back an' let me go."

"I ain't foolin'! What you goin' to do?"

"Shoot to kill—if that's what I'm charged with," and the marshal leaped back as a bullet sung past his head.

As darkness gathered the crowd poured volley after volley into the saloon and the Texan replied sparingly, and between shots he drank whisky. It was dark inside the building and the cowboy could see the flash of the guns in the street. Suddenly the bombardment ceased.

"Wonder what they're up to now," he muttered, peering between the kegs. He was finding it hard to concentrate his thoughts, and passed a hand across his forehead as if to brush away the cobwebs that were clogging his brain. "I've got to out-guess 'em!" He shook himself fiercely: "Le's see, if they rush me in the dark, some of 'em's due to fall down cellar where Ike left the trap open, an' some of 'em's goin' to get mixed up with bottles an' beer-kegs—if I don't shoot they won't know where I am, an' while they're ontanglin' themselves maybe I can slip away in the dark."

A light flared suddenly beyond the wooden partition, flickered a moment, and burned steadily. The Texan's eyes widened as his hands closed about the butts of his guns: "Goin' to burn me out, eh?" he sneered, and then, with a smile, laid the two guns on the bar, and watched the glow that softened the blackness about the edges of the screen. "They can't burn me without burnin' up their whole damn little wooden town," he speculated, "but what in the devil do they want with a light?" With the words on his lips, the light moved, and once more he reached for his guns. A candle appeared around the end of the partition that formed the doorway. The Texan fired and the room was plunged into darkness. And then—through the inky blackness, thick with the pungent powder smoke, sounded a cry— a jerky, stabbing cry—a cry of mortal fear—a woman's cry—*that* woman's cry: "*Tex—Tex! Strike a light!*"

The Texan reeled as from a blow, the gun dropped from his nerveless fingers and thudded upon the floor. He leaned weakly against the back bar. He was conscious that his eyes were staring—straining to pierce the blackness in the direction of the sound—and yet, he knew there was nothing there! His mouth went dry and he could distinctly hear his own breathing. He pulled himself jerkily erect and clawed the edge of the bar. His groping hand closed about an object hard and cylindrical. It was the quart bottle of whisky from which he had filled his glass. Suddenly, he shuddered. "It's the booze," he thought, "it's got me—at last—I'm—I'm *bugs*!" The bottle slipped through his fingers and rolled along the bar and the air became heavy with the fumes of the liquor that splashed unheeded from its mouth. He passed his hand across his brow and withdrew it slippery and wet with sweat.

"*Christ!*" Thickly the word struggled from between the dry lips. He stooped, his hand groping for the gun, his fingers closed uncertainly upon the butt, and as he straightened up, the muzzle swung slowly into line with his own forehead. And in that instant a light puff of cool air fanned his dripping forehead. The gun stopped in its slow arc. The lids closed for an instant over the horribly staring eyes. The shoulders stiffened, and the gun was laid gently upon the bar—for, upon that single puff of night air, delicate, subtile—yet unmistakably distinguishable from the heavy powder smoke and the reeking fumes of the whisky, was borne a breath of the wide open places. The man's nostrils quivered. Yes, it was there—the scent of the little blue and white prairie flowers—her flowers. Instantly his brain cleared. A moment before he had been hopelessly drunk: now, he was sober. It was as though the delicate scent had entered his nostrils and cleansed his brain, clearing it of the befuddling fog, and leaving it, wholesome, alert, capable. Poignantly, with the scent of those flowers, the scene of a year ago leaped into memory, when he had stooped to restore them to her hands—there in the tiny glade beside the big boulder.

"Alice!" he cried, sharply.

"Tex!" The name was a sob, and then; "Oh, please—please strike a light! I'm—I'm—afraid!"

For just an instant the Texan hesitated, a match between his fingers, and his voice sounded strangely hard: "A light, now, will mean they'll get me! But—if you're real, girl, I'll trust you—If you ain't—the quicker they shoot, the better!" There was a scratching sound, a light flared out, and candle outstretched, the girl came swiftly to the bar, and as he held the match to the wick, the Texan's eyes gazed wonderingly into the eyes of blue.

CHAPTER VII

THE TEXAN "COMES A-SHOOTIN'"

Alice Endicott gazed searchingly into the Texan's flushed face and wondered at the steadiness of his eyes. "They—they said you were drunk," she faltered.

The cynical smile that she remembered so well twisted the man's lips: "They were right—partly. I was headed that way, but I'm cold sober, now."

"Then leave your guns here and come with me. You must submit to arrest. They'll fine you and make you pay for the damages and that will be all there'll be to it."

The Texan shook his head: "No. I told that marshal he couldn't arrest me, an' he can't."

Alice's heart sank. "Please—for my sake," she pleaded. "If you haven't got the money———"

"Oh, I've got the money, all right—a whole year's wages right here in my pocket. It ain't the money, it's the principle of the thing. I made my brag, an' I've got to see it through. They might *get* me, but they'll never arrest me."

"Oh, please———"

Tex interrupted her sharply, and the girl was startled at the gleam that leaped suddenly from the grey eyes: "What are you doing here? Has he—didn't you an' Win—hit it out?"

"Oh, yes! Yes! Win is here———"

"An' he let you come in alone—an' stayed outside———"

"No—he doesn't know. He's up at the Camerons. I went for a ride, and coming back I saw the crowd, and when they told me the man in here was a Texan, somehow, I just knew it was you."

The gleam faded from the man's eyes and he regarded her curiously; "But, what are you doin' in Timber City—you an' Win?"

"Why, it's our anniversary! We wanted to spend it here where we were married. And besides we've got the grandest scheme. Win wants to see you. Come on, give yourself up, and pay their old fine."

"I won't be arrested," repeated the Texan stubbornly, "an' don't count me in on any scheme with you an' Win." Once more his eyes blazed, and his words came low and tense: "Can't you see—I haven't forgot. I don't reckon I ever will forget! I loved you then, an' I love you now———"

"Don't, don't, Tex! You haven't tried to forget. How many girls have you known since—a year ago?"

"None—an' I don't want to know any! There ain't any more like you———"

Alice interrupted him with a laugh: "Don't be a fool! I know loads of girls—and they're all prettier than I am, and they've got lots more sense, too. Please don't spoil our anniversary this way. There are twenty men out there, and they're all armed, and they've sworn to kill you if you don't give yourself up."

"They better start in killin', then." Throwing back his shoulders, he struck the bar with his fist. "I'll tell you what I'll do—an' that's all I'll do. You go back an' tell 'em I'll pay my fine, an' a reasonable amount of damages if they'll leave my horse outside and let me go away from here. It ain't because I'm afraid of 'em," he hastened to add, "not a man of 'em—nor all of 'em. But, if you want it that way, I'll do it."

"But, we don't want you to go away!" cried the girl. "Win wants to see you."

The cowboy shook his head: "I'm goin' away—an' far away," he answered, "I don't know what his scheme is, an' I don't want to know. We'd all be fools to tackle it. If that plan suits you, go ahead—no arrest—I'll just pay my fine an' go. An' if it don't suit you, you better go back to Win. This is no place for you anyhow. Let 'em go ahead with their killin', if they think they can get away with it."

For a moment the girl hesitated, then, picking up her candle from the bar, she started slowly toward the door. "If I can only get word to Win and Mr. Colston," she thought, "I can delay things until they get here."

"Well, what'd he say?" growled Hod Blake, stepping from among his retainers.

The tone angered the girl and she glanced contemptuously into the eyes that stared boldly at her from beneath the wide hat-brim: "He said that you can't arrest him," she answered defiantly, "and if you knew him as well as I do, you'd know he told the truth."

"Oh-ho, so he's got a record, has he?" leered the marshal. "Mebbe they'll be more to this here business than just pickin' up a plain drunk—little reward money, mebbe—eh?"

"No, no!" cried the girl, "not that! It's just his—his pride. He will never submit to arrest."

"He won't, eh? Well, then he'll shove up the posies!"

"He'll go away peaceably if you give him the chance. He offered to pay his fine and the damages to the saloon, if you'll allow him to ride away unmolested."

"Oh, he will, will he?" sneered the marshal. "It wouldn't take no mind reader to tell that he's goin' to pay them fine an' damages—peaceable or onpeaceable, it don't make no difference to me. But, about lettin' him ride off without arrestin' him—they ain't nothin' doin'. I said I'd arrest him, an' I will—an' besides, I aim to hold him over a spell till I can find out if they ain't a reward out fer him. If they ain't nothin' on him what's he anxious to pay up an' git out fer?"

"Oh, can't you listen to reason?"

"Sure, Hod," urged Barras, jumping at the Texan's offer, "listen to reason. He ain't done nothin' to speak of. Let him pay up an' git."

"You shet yer mouth!" snapped the marshal. "They's reason enough in what I said. If they ain't nothin' on him it ain't goin' to hurt him none to hold him over a few days. It'll do him good. Give him a chanct to sober up."

"He's as sober as you are, now," flashed the girl angrily, "an' if he was as drunk as he could get, he'd have more sense than you'll ever have."

"Kind of peppery, ain't you? Well, you c'n go back an' tell him what I said. He c'n take it or leave it. An' while yer gone, I'll jest slip around an' put a couple of more boys guardin' the back door."

The man turned on his heel and disappeared into the darkness. Glancing about in desperation, Alice saw the tall man who had first spoken to her, still seated upon a corner of the horse trough, a little apart from the crowd. She hastened to his side: "Will you do something for me?" she asked, breathlessly.

With a dexterous contortion of his nether lip, the man gathered an end of his huge moustache into the corner of his mouth: "What would it be?" he asked noncommittally.

"Hurry to Mr. Cameron's and tell my husband and Mr. Colston to come down here quick!"

"Y Bar Colston?" he asked, with exasperating deliberation.

"Yes. Oh, please hurry!"

His left eyelid drooped meaningly, as he audibly expelled the moustache from between his lips, and jerked his head in the direction of the saloon, "Y'ain't helpin' his case none by draggin' Y Bar into it," he opined. "Hod hates Y Bar on account he trades over to Claggett. Hod, he runs the main store here besides bein' marshal."

"Oh, what shall I do!"

Making sure they were out of earshot, the man spoke rapidly. "They ain't only one way to work it. You hustle back an' tell him to slip down cellar an' climb up the shoot where they slide the beer-kaigs down. It opens onto the alley between the livery barn an' the store. Hod ain't thought of that yet, an' my horse is tied in the alley. Tell him to take the horse an' beat it."

For an instant the girl peered into the man's eyes as if to fathom his sincerity. "But why should you sacrifice your horse?"

The man cut her short: "I'll claim his'n, an' it's about an even trade. Besides, he done me a good turn by not shootin' me in there when he had the chanct, after I tried to help Barras hold him. An' I'm one of these here parties that b'lieves one good turn deserves another."

"But," hesitated the girl, "you were shooting into the saloon at him. I saw you."

"Yup, I was shootin', all right," he grinned, "but he'd of had to be'n ten foot tall fer me to of hit him. It wouldn't of looked right fer me not to of be'n a-shootin'."

"But, won't they shoot him when he tries to get away?"

The grin widened: "They won't. Tell him to come bustin' right out the front way on the high lope, right into the middle of 'em. I know them *hombres* an' believe me, it's goin' to be fun to see 'em trompin' over one another a-gittin' out of the road. By the time they git in shootin' shape, he'll be into the dark."

"But, they'll follow him."

"Yes, mom. But they ain't goin' to ketch him. That horse of mine kin run rings around anything they've got. Better hurry now, 'fore Hod thinks about that beer-kaig shoot."

"Oh, how can I thank you?"

"Well, you might set up a brass statoo of me acrost from the post office—when the sun hit it right it would show up clean from the top of the divide."

Alice giggled, as the man extended his hand: "Here's a couple more matches. You better run along, now. Jest tell that there Texas cyclone that Ike Stork says this here play is the best bet, bein' as they'll starve him out if a stray bullet don't find its way between them kaigs an' git him first."

She took the matches and once more paused in the doorway and lighted her candle. As she disappeared into the interior, Ike Stork shifted his position upon the edge of the horse trough and grinned broadly as his eyes rested upon the men huddled together in the darkness in front of the saloon.

The girl crossed to the bar, and reading the question in the Texan's eyes, shook her head: "He won't do it," she said, "he's just as mean, and stubborn, and self-important and as *rude* as he can be. He says he's going to arrest you, and he's going to hold you for a few days in jail to see if there isn't a reward offered for you somewhere. He thinks, or pretends to think, that you're some terrible desperado."

The cynical smile twisted the Texan's lips: "He'll be sure of it before he gets through."

"No, no, Tex! Don't shoot anybody—please! Listen, I've got a plan that will get you out of here. But first, you've got to promise that you will see Win. We've set our hearts on it, and you *must*."

"What's the good?"

"Please, for my sake, promise me."

The man's eyes devoured her. "I'd do anything in the world for your sake," he said, simply. "I'll promise. Tell Win to drift over to Claggett day after tomorrow, an' I'll meet him somewhere along the trail."

"Surely? You won't disappoint us?"

The man regarded her reproachfully: "You don't think I'd lie to you?"

"No, forgive me, I—" she paused and looked straight into his eyes, "and, will you promise me one thing more?"

"Tell me straight out what it is, an' I'll tell you straight out what I'll do."

"Promise me you won't drink any more until—until after you've seen Win."

The Texan hesitated: "It's only a couple of days. Yes, I'll promise," he answered, "an', now, what's your plan?"

Alice glanced toward the door, and leaned closer: "It really isn't my plan at all," she whispered, "but there's a man out there with a big, drooping faded-looking moustache, he said you did him a good turn by not shooting him, or something——"

"Ike Stork," grinned the Texan.

Alice nodded: "Yes, that's his name, and he said to tell you it was the best bet, whatever that is."

"I get him. Go on."

"Well, he says there's some kind of a chute that they slide the beer-kegs down into the cellar with, and for you to go down and climb up the chute. It will let you out into the alley between this building and the livery stable. The marshal hasn't thought of posting any guards there, and Ike's horse is tied in the alley, and you're to take him and make a dash out the front way, right through the crowd. He says they'll all fall over each other and be so scared that they won't think to shoot till you've had a chance to get away."

As the girl talked she could see that the Texan's eyes twinkled and when she finished, his shoulders were shaking with silent mirth: "Good old Ike!" he chuckled. "You tell him I say he's a bear!"

"He said it would be fun to see them trample over each other getting out of the way."

"I'll sure see that he gets his money's worth," grinned the Texan.

A troubled look crept into the girl's face: "You won't—*hurt* anyone?" she asked.

The man shook his head: "Not onless some of 'em don't get out of the road. Might knock down a few with the horse, but that won't hurt 'em to speak of. It wouldn't pain me none to knock that marshal about half ways down the street—not for anything he's done to me, but because I've got a hunch he talked pretty rough to you."

"Oh, I hope it's all right," whispered the girl, "do you really think it will work?"

"Work! Of course it'll work! I've got it all pictured out right now. It's a peach! Just you get off to one side far enough so's not to get caught in the rush, an' you'll see some fun. Tell Ike not to forget to put up an awful howl about losin' his cayuse, just to make the play good."

"Do you think he's really sincere—that it isn't just a trick to get you out where they can shoot you? How long have you known this Ike Stork?"

"Dead sure." The Texan's tone was reassuring, "known him a good half-hour. You ought to seen those eyes of his when he thought I was goin' to shoot him—never flinched a hair. He's a good man, told me to hurry up an' make a job of it."

The girl held out her hand: "Good-bye, Tex—till day after tomorrow."

The cowboy took the hand and pressed it fiercely: "You're goin' to be there, too? That'll make it harder—but—all right."

"Remember," smiled the girl, "what I said about there being loads of other girls."

"Too bad you hadn't been born in the West, so Win would never known you—then—maybe———"

"What shall I tell our friend the marshal?" interrupted the girl.

The Texan grinned: "Just tell him not to order any extra meals sent down to the jail on my account. An', here, tell him the drinks are on the house," he handed the girl a quart bottle of whisky. "That'll keep 'em from gettin' restless before the show starts."

Candle in one hand, bottle in the other, the girl made her way to the door. As she stepped out into the night, she was hailed roughly by the marshal: "Well, what'd he say, now?"

"He said," answered the girl, scornfully, "that you were not to order any extra meals sent down to the jail on his account. And he sent you this and asked me to tell you that the drinks were on the house." She extended the bottle which the marshal eagerly grasped despite the strenuous objections of Pete Barras who clamoured for the return of his property.

"Ain't I had hell enough fer one day?" demanded the bartender, "what with gittin' shot in the arm, an' gittin' tried to be held up fer four dollars of Sam's debts, an' gittin' laid out cold with a spittoon, an' gittin' my glasses an' bottles all busted, an' gittin' my place all shot up, an' my merrow shot to hell, an' my kegs all shot holes in, without all you's hornin' in an' drinkin' up what little I got left? As the feller says, where do I git off at?"

"S'pose you dry up an' let me talk," retorted the marshal. "They ain't no one payin' *you* nawthin' to maintain law an' order in this town."

"If they was I'll be damned if I wouldn't maintain it, 'stead of millin' around drinkin' up other folks' whisky———"

"Look a-here Pete Barras, this makes twict, now, you've ondertook to tell me my business. You shet yer yap, 'er you don't draw no damages when we corral that outlaw in yonder. I ain't so sure you didn't start the rookus, nohow. Besides, the boys needs a little drink, an' we'll charge this here bottle up along with the rest of the damages an' make him pay 'em."

"Y'ain't caught him yet. Where do I git off at if you don't ketch him?"

Ike Stork, grinning huge enjoyment over the altercation, managed to motion Alice to his side: "Better git over to yer cayuse," he cautioned. "He's pretty near had time to make it into the alley, an' when he comes, he'll come a-shootin'. Guess I'll jest keep the squabble a-goin', they all seem right interested," he indicated the crowd that had edged close about the two principals. And Alice smiled as she mounted her horse to hear the renewed vigour with which retort met accusation after the redoubtable Mr. Stork had contributed his observations from the side lines. The girl's eyes were fixed upon the black mouth of the alley, now, and with each passing minute she found it harder and harder to restrain her impatience. Would he never come? What if the window had been guarded unknown to Stork? What if Stork's horse had broken loose or been moved by someone passing through the alley? What if—a bloodcurdling yell split the darkness. And with a thunder of hoofs, an indistinguishable shape whirled out of the alley. A crash of shots drowned the thunder of hoofs as from the plunging shape darted thin red streaks of flame. Straight into the crowd it plunged. For a fleeting instant the girl caught a glimpse of bodies in confused motion, as the men surged back from its impact. Above the sound of the guns shrill cries of fear and hoarse angry curses split the air.

As Ike Stork had predicted, the Texan had "come a-shootin'."

CHAPTER VIII

THE ESCAPE

Alice had pressed forward until her horse stood at the very edge of the seething mêlée. Swiftly, objects took definite shape in the starlight. Men rushed past her cursing. The marshal lay upon the ground shrieking contradictory orders, while over him stood the outraged Barras, reviling him for permitting his man to escape. Other men were shooting, and between the sounds of the shots the voice of Ike Stork could be heard loudly bewailing the loss of his horse. Hoof beats sounded behind her, and glancing backward, Alice could see men mounting the half-dozen horses that stood saddled before the store and the livery barn. As a man, already in the saddle, urged the others to hurry he raised his gun and fired in the direction the Texan had taken.

"They'll kill him!" thought the girl. "No matter how fast his horse is, those bullets fly faster!" Another shot followed the first, and acting on the impulse of the moment, with the one thought to save the Texan from harm, she struck her horse down the flank and shot out into the trail behind the fleeing cowpuncher. "They won't dare to shoot, now," she sobbed as she urged her horse to his best, while in her ears rang a confusion of cries that she knew were directed at her. Leaning far forward, she shouted encouragement to her straining animal. In vain her eyes sought to pierce the darkness for a glimpse of the Texan. Her horse took a shallow ford in a fountain of spray. A patch of woods slipped behind, and she knew she was on the trail that led to the Missouri, and the flat-boat ferry of Long Bill Kearney. She wondered whether Tex would hold to the trail, or would he leave it and try to lose his pursuers among the maze of foothills and coulees through which it wound? Maybe he had turned into the patch of timber and was even now breathing his horse in the little wild flower glade. If so, her course was plain—to keep on at top speed and lead his pursuers as far as possible along the trail. Dimly, she could hear the thunder of hoofs in her wake. She wondered how long it would be before they overtook her.

On and on she sped, her thoughts racing wildly as the flying feet of her horse. "What would Win think? What would the horsemen behind her say when at last they overtook her? Maybe they would arrest her!" The thought terrified her, and she urged her horse to a still greater burst of speed. Presently she became aware that the hoof beats behind had almost died away. Fainter and fainter they sounded, and then—far ahead, on top of a knoll silhouetted against the star-dotted sky, she saw the figure of a horseman. Instantly it disappeared where the trail dipped into a coulee, and with a thrill of wild exhilaration she realized that her horse had run away from the pursuers, and not only that, he was actually closing up on the Texan despite the boast of Ike Stork that his animal could run rings around any others.

She topped the rise, and half way across a wide swale, caught another glimpse of the horseman. The man pulled up, sharply. There were two horsemen! She had almost come up to them when suddenly they crashed together. She distinctly heard the sound of the impact. There was a short, sharp struggle, and as the horses sprang apart, one of the saddles was empty, and a rider thudded heavily upon the ground. Then, faintly at first, but momentarily growing louder and more distinct, she heard the rumble of pursuing hoofs. She glanced swiftly over her shoulder and when she returned her eyes to the front one of the riders was disappearing over the rim of the swale, and the other was struggling to his feet. For only an instant the girl hesitated, then plunged straight down the trail after the fleeing rider. As she passed the other a perfect torrent of vile curses poured from his lips, and with a shudder, she recognized the voice of Long Bill Kearney. The interruption of the headlong flight had been short, but it had served to cut down their lead perceptibly. The sounds of pursuit were plainer even than at first and glancing over her shoulder as she reached the rim of the swale, she could see horsemen stringing down into the depression. Topping the ridge she was surprised to find the Texan only a short distance ahead. He was plying his quirt mercilessly but the animal moved slowly, and she could see that he limped. Swiftly she closed up the distance, and as she rode, she became conscious of a low hoarse rumbling, a peculiar sound, dull, all pervading, terrifying. Glancing ahead, beyond the figure of the rider, a cry escaped her. The whole world seemed to be a sea of wildly tossing water. The Missouri! But surely, not the Missouri as she had remembered it—this wild roaring flood! The river they had crossed a year ago on Long Bill's flat-boat had been a very commonplace stream, flowing smoothly between its banks. But, this——

As she caught up to the horseman, he whirled, gun in hand. "Tex!" she screamed.

The gun hand dropped, and the man stared at her in amazement. "What are you doing here?"

"I came—they had horses and were going to kill you—I rode in between so they wouldn't shoot——"

"Good God, girl——"

"Hurry!" she cried, frantically, "they're close behind."

"Horse went lame," he jerked out as he plied quirt and spurs. "Got to make the ferry. Long Bill says the river's broke all records. He's runnin' away. Left his flat-boat tied to a tree. It's only a little ways. You go back! I can make it. Had to knock Bill down to keep him from blockin' my game. Once on that boat, they can't follow."

"But, they're almost here—" Even at the words, a horseman topped the ridge, and with a yell to his followers, plunged toward them.

The Texan scowled darkly: "Go back! They'll never say I hid behind a woman's skirts!"

"I won't go back! Oh, hurry, there's the boat! Two more minutes, and we'll be there! Turn around and shoot! It'll hold 'em!"

"I won't shoot—not when they can't shoot back!"

The foremost horseman was almost upon them when they reached the flat-boat. He was far in advance of the rest, and as the Texan swung to the ground the report of a six-gun rang loud, and a bullet sang over their heads.

The bullet was followed by the sound of a voice: "Shoot, you fool! Keep a-shootin' till you pile onto the boat, an' I'll shoot back. Them hounds back there ain't hankerin' fer no close quarters with you—I told 'em how good you was with yer guns." And Ike Stork followed his words with two shots in rapid succession.

"Good boy, old hand!" grinned the Texan, "how's that!" Six shots cut the air like the reports of an automatic, and Ike, swerving sharply, galloped back in a well-feigned panic of fear. It was the work of a moment to get the Texan's horse aboard, and Alice followed with her own.

The man stared. "Get back!" he cried, "I'm goin' across! Go back to Win!"

"They'll shoot if I don't stay right here! Ike can't hold 'em but a few minutes, at best. They'd have you at their mercy. This boat moves slowly."

The Texan took her roughly by the arm. "You go back!" he roared. "Can't you see it won't do? You can't come! God, girl, can't you see it? The touch of you drives me crazy!"

"Don't be a fool! And I won't see you shot—so there! Oh, Tex, it's you who can't see—I do love you—like a sister. I always think of you as my big brother—I never had a real one."

The Texan backed away. "I don't want no sister! What'll folks say? This big brother stuff won't go—by a damn sight!" Hoof beats sounded nearer, and a stream of curses floated to their ears.

"There comes that horrible Long Bill," cried the girl, and before the Texan could make a move to stop her, she seized an ax from the bottom of the boat and brought it's keen edge down upon the mooring line. The flat-boat shuddered and moved, slowly at first, then faster as it worked into the current. The Texan gazed dumbfounded at the rapidly widening strip of water that separated them from the shore. But he found scant time to stare idly at the water. All about them it's surface was clogged with floating debris. The river had risen to within a foot of the slender cable that held the boat on its course, and the unwieldy craft was trembling and jerking as uprooted trees and masses of flotsam caught on the line, strained it almost to the point of snapping and then rolled under by the force of the current, allowed the line to spring into place again. Slowly, the boat, swept by the force of the flood, worked out into the stream, adding its own weight to the strain on the line. The craft shuddered as a tree-trunk struck her side, and seizing a pole, the man shoved her free. The rushing water sucked and gurgled at the edge of the boat, and Alice stepped nearer to the Texan. "We're moving, anyway," she said, "we can't see the shore, now. And the voices of the men have died away."

"We can't see, because it's cloudin' up, an' we can't hear 'em because the river's makin' such a racket. With the pull there is on the boat, we ain't ever goin' to get her past the middle—if I could, I'd work her back right now where we come from."

"They'd shoot you!"

"If they did it would only be me they'd get—the river won't be so particular."

"You mean—we're in danger?"

"Danger!" The naïve question angered the cowboy. "Oh, no we ain't in any danger, not a bit in the world. We're just as safe as if we was sittin' on a keg of powder with the fuse lit. There's nothin' in the world can hurt us except this little old Mizoo, an' it wouldn't think of such a thing——"

"Don't try to be sarcastic, Tex, you do it very clumsily."

"Maybe I do, but I ain't clumsy at guessin' that of all the tight places I've ever be'n in, this is the tightest. How far can you swim?"

"Not a stroke."

"So can I."

"Anyway, it's better than being lost in a dust storm—we won't shrivel up and die of thirst."

"No, we won't die of thirst, all right. But you an' me have sure stumbled into a fine mess. What'll Win think, an' what'll everyone else think? If we go under, they'll never know any different, an' if we do happen to get across, it'll be some several days before this river gets down to where we can get back, an' I can see from here what a lovely time we're goin' to have explainin' things to the satisfaction of all parties concerned."

"You seem to be a born pessimist. We're not going under, and what's to prevent us from waiting out here until the men on the bank go away, and then going back where we started from?"

A flash of lightning illumined the horizon and the Texan's voice blended with a low rumble of thunder. "With the force of water the way it is," he explained, "we can't move this boat an inch. It'll carry to the middle on the slack of the line, an' in the middle we'll stay. It'll be uphill both ways from there an' we can't budge her an inch. Then, either the line'll bust, or the river will keep on risin' till it just naturally pulls us under."

"Maybe the river will start to fall," ventured the girl.

"Maybe it won't. We've had enough rain this spring for four summers already—an' more comin'."

"We'll get out someway." The Texan knew that the words were forced. And his heart bounded with admiration for this girl who could thus thrust danger to the winds and calmly assert that there would be a way out. A nearer flash of lightning was followed by louder thunder. "Sure, we'll get out," he agreed, heartily. "I didn't mean we wouldn't get out. I was just lookin' the facts square in the face. There ain't any jackpot that folks can get into that they can't get out of—somehow."

"Oh, does something awful always happen out here?" the girl asked almost plaintively. "Why can't things be just—just normal, like they ought to be?"

"It ain't the country, it's the folks. Get the right combination of folks together, an' somethin's bound to happen, no matter where you're at."

Then the storm struck and the girl's reply was lost in the rush of wind and the crash of thunder, as flash after blinding flash lighted the surface of the flood. They had reached midstream. The boat had lost its forward motion and lay tugging at the taut line as the water rushed and gurgled about it. The rain fell in blinding torrents causing the two horses to huddle against each other, trembling in mortal fear. The drift was thicker in the full sweep of the current, and the Texan had his hands full warding it off the boat with his pole. By the lightning flashes Alice could see his set, tense face as he worked to keep the debris from massing against the craft. A heavy object jarred against the cable, and the next moment the two gazed wide eyed at a huge pine, branches and roots thrashing in the air, that had lodged against the line directly upstream. For a few moments it held as the water curled over it in white masses of foam. Then the trunk rolled heavily, the roots and branches thrashing wildly in the air, and the whole mass slipped slowly beneath the cable. It struck the boat with a heavy jar that canted it at a dangerous angle and caused the terrified horses to struggle frantically to keep their feet.

"Quick!" roared the Texan, "get to the upper side, before they smash you!" In vain he was pushing against the trunk of the tree, exerting every atom of power in his body to dislodge its huge bulk that threatened each moment to capsize the clumsy craft. But he might as well have tried to dislodge a mountain. The frightened animals were plunging wildly, adding the menace of their thrashing hoofs to the menace of the river. Vainly the Texan sought to quiet them but the sound of his voice was drowned in the roar of thunder, the swishing splash of rain, and the gurgle of water that purled among the roots and branches of the pine. Suddenly the lame horse reared high, pawed frantically for a moment and with an almost human scream of terror, plunged over the side. Alice reached swiftly for the flying bridle reins of her own animal and as her hand closed upon them he quieted almost instantly. Relieved of the weight of the other horse, the boat shifted its position for the worse, the bottom canting to a still steeper angle. A flash of lightning revealed the precariousness of the situation. A few inches more, and the water would rush over the side, and both realized that she would fill instantly.

It is a peculiar vagary of the human mind that in moments of greatest stress trivialities loom large. Thus it was that with almost certain destruction staring him in the face, the Texan's glance took in the detail of the brand that stood out plainly upon the wet flank of the girl's horse. "What you doin' with a Y Bar cayuse?" he cried. "With Powder Face?" and then, the boat tilted still higher, he felt a splash of water against his foot, and as he reached out to steady himself his hand came in contact with the handle of the ax. Seizing the tool, he sprang erect, poised for an instant upon the edge of the boat which was already awash, and with the next flash of lightning, brought its blade down upon the wire cable stretched taut as a fiddle gut. The rebound of the ax nearly wrenched it from his grasp, the boat shifted as the cable seemed to stretch ever so slightly, and the Texan noted with satisfaction that the edge was no longer awash. Another flash of lightning and he could see the frayed ends where the severed strands were slowly untwisting. Another blow, and the cable parted. With a jerk that nearly threw the occupants into the river the boat righted herself, the flat bottom striking the water with a loud splash. Before Alice realized what had happened she saw the high flung tree-roots thrash wildly as the released tree rolled in the water. She screamed a warning but too late. A root-stub, thick as a man's arm struck the Texan squarely on top of the head, and without a sound he sank limp and lifeless to the bottom of the boat.

CHAPTER IX

ON THE RIVER

For a moment the girl sat paralysed with terror as her brain grasped the full gravity of her position. The wind had risen, and blowing up river, kicked up waves that struck the boat with sledgehammer force and broke over the gunwales. Overhead the thunder roared incessantly, while about her the thick, black dark burst momentarily into vivid blazes of light that revealed the long slash of the driving rain, and the heaving bosom of the river, with its tossing burden of uprooted trees—revealed, also her trembling horse, and the form of the unconscious Texan lying with face awash in the bottom of the boat. His hat, floating from side to side as the craft rocked in the waves, brushed the horse's heels, and he lashed out viciously, his iron-shod hoofs striking the side of the boat with a force that threatened to tear the planking loose.

The incident galvanized her into action. If those hoofs had struck the Texan? And if he were not already dead, suppose he should drown in the filthy water in the bottom of the boat? Carefully, she worked the frightened animal to the farther end of the boat, and swiftly made her way to the limp form of the cowboy. She realized suddenly that she was numb with cold. Her hat, too, floated in the bottom of the boat, and her rain-soaked hair clung in wet straggling wisps to her neck and face. Stooping over the injured man she twisted her fingers into the collar of his shirt and succeeded in raising his face clear of the water. Blood oozed from a long cut on his forehead at the roots of his hair, and on top of his head she noticed a welt the size of a door knob. With much effort she finally succeeded in raising him to a sitting posture and propping him into a corner of the boat, where she held him with her body close against his while she bathed his wound and wiped his eyes and lips with her rain-soaked handkerchief. Opening her shirt, the girl succeeded in tearing a strip from her undergarments with which she proceeded to bandage the wound. This proved to be no small undertaking, and it was only after repeated failures that she finally succeeded in affixing the bandage smoothly and firmly in place. The storm continued with unabated fury and, shivering and drenched to the skin, she huddled miserably in the bottom of the boat against the unconscious form of the man.

Added to the physical discomfort came torturing thoughts of their plight. Each moment carried her farther and farther from Timber City—from Win. When the lightning flashed she caught glimpses of the shore, but always it appeared the same distance away. The boat was holding to the middle of the stream. She knew they must have drifted miles. "What would Win say?" over and over the same question repeated itself in her brain, and step by step, she reviewed the events of the night. "I did the right thing—I know I did!" she muttered, "they would have killed him!" And immediately she burst into tears.

Inaction became unbearable, and shifting the body of the Texan so that his head would remain clear of the ever deepening wash in the bottom of the boat, she seized the pole and worked frantically. But after a few moments she realized the futility of her puny efforts to deviate the heavy craft a hair's breadth from its course. The tree-root that had knocked the Texan unconscious had descended upon the boat, and remained locked over the gunwale, holding the trunk with its high-flung tangle of roots and branches close alongside, the whole structure moving as one mass.

She discarded the pole and tried to arouse the unconscious man, shaking and pounding him vigorously. After a time his head moved slightly and redoubling her efforts, she soon had the satisfaction of seeing his eyes open slowly. His hand raised to his bandaged head, and dropped listlessly to his side. Placing her lips close to his ear to make herself heard above the roar of the storm, she begged and implored him to rouse himself. He evidently understood, for he moved his arms and legs and shifted his body into a more comfortable position. "I—don't—remember—" the words came in a low, faltering voice, "what—happened."

"When you cut the cable that root hit you on the head," she explained, pointing to the root-stub that held the boat firmly against the trunk of the tree.

He nodded his understanding, and in the illumination of the almost continuous flashes of lightning stared at the root, as if trying to collect his scattered wits. The boat jerked unsteadily, hesitated, jerked again and the branches and uplifted roots of the tree swayed and thrashed wildly. He struggled to his knees, and holding to the girl's arm raised himself unsteadily to his feet where he stood swaying uncertainly, his eyes fixed on the thrashing branches. His vitality returned with a rush. His eyes narrowed as he pointed out the danger, and his voice rang strong above the storm: "Where's the ax?"

Stooping, the girl recovered it from the water at her feet. Instantly, it was seized from her hand, and staggering to the root, the Texan chopped at it with blows that increased in vigour with each successive swing. A few moments sufficed to sever it, and springing to one side, the man drew the girl to the bottom of the boat, while above them the branches thrashed and tore at the gunwales. A moment later the craft floated free, and placing his lips to her ear, the Texan explained: "They stick down as far as they do up, an' when we pass over a shallow place they drag along the bottom. If we'd struck a snag that would have held the tree, it would have been 'good-night' for us. That root would have ripped down through the bottom, and all there'd be'n left of us is two strings of bubbles. We're lucky."

Alice shuddered. "An' now," continued the cowboy, "we've got to bail out this old tub. What with the water that rolled in over the edge, and what's rained in, we'll have a boatful before long."

"Why, there's barrels of it!" cried the girl. "And we haven't anything to bail with!"

The Texan nodded: "There's barrels of it all right. I saw a fellow empty a barrel with a thimble, once—on a bet. It took him a considerable spell, but he did it. My boots hold considerable more'n a thimble, an' we can each take one an' go to it."

"But, wouldn't it be better to try and reach shore?"

"Reach shore?" With a sweep of his arm the man indicated the surface of the turgid flood. Following the gesture, Alice realized the utter futility of any attempt to influence the course of the clumsy craft. The wind had risen to a gale, but the full fury of the electrical storm had passed. Still continuous, the roar of the thunder had diminished to a low rumbling roll, and the lightning flashed pale, like ghost lightning, its wan luminescence foreshortening the range of vision to include only the nearer reaches of wild lashing water upon whose surface heaved and tossed the trunks and branches of trees over which the whitecapped waves broke with sodden hiss. The shore line with its fringe of timber had merged into the outer dark—an all-enveloping, heavy darkness that seemed in itself a *thing*—a thing of infinite horror whose evil touch was momentarily dispelled by the paling flashes of light. "Oh, where are we? Where are we going?" moaned the girl.

"Down river, somewhere," answered the Texan, with an attempt at cheerfulness. The man was industriously bailing with a boot. He tossed its mate to the girl. "Bail," he urged, "it gives you somethin' to think about, an' it's good exercise. I was about froze till I got to heavin' out this water. We ain't so bad, now. We're bound to get shoved ashore at some bend, or the wind'll blow us ashore. Looks to me as if she was widenin' out. Must of overflowed some flat." Mechanically she took the boot and, following the example of the Texan, began to bail out. "Rain's quit, an' this wind'll dry us out when we get the boat emptied so we don't have to sit in the water. My shirt's most dry already."

"The wind has changed!" cried the girl. "It's blowing crosswise of the river, now."

"More likely we've rounded a bend," opined the Texan. "I don't know the river below Claggett."

"If we're blown ashore, now, it will be the wrong shore."

"Most any old shore'd look good to me. I ain't what you might call aquatic by nature—I ain't even amphibious." Alice laughed and the sound was music to the Texan's ears. "That's right, laugh," he hastened to say, and the girl noticed that the cheerfulness was not forced, "I've never heard you laugh much owin' to the fact that our acquaintance has be'n what you might call tribulations to an extent that has be'n plumb discouragin' to jocosity. But, what was so funny?"

"Oh, nothing. Only one would hardly expect a cowboy, adrift in the middle of a swollen river to be drawing distinctions between words."

"Bailin' water out of a boat with a boot don't overtax the mental capacity of even a cowboy to absolute paralysis."

"You're certainly the most astonishing cowboy I've ever known."

"You ain't known many——"

"If I'd known a thousand—" The sentence was never finished. The boat came to a sudden stop. Both occupants were thrown violently to the bottom where they floundered helplessly in their efforts to regain their feet. "What happened?" asked the girl, as she struggled to her knees, holding fast to the gunwale. "Oh, maybe we're ashore!" Both glanced about them as a distant flash of lightning threw its pale radiance over the surface of the flood. On every side was water—water, and the tossing branches of floating trees. The Texan was quieting the terrified horse that crouched at the farther end of the boat, threatening momentarily to become a very real menace by plunging and lashing out blindly in the darkness.

"Struck a rock, I reckon," said the cowboy. "This cayuse'll be all right in a minute, an' I'll try to shove her off. Must be we've headed along some new channel. There hadn't ought to be rocks in the main river."

The clumsy craft shifted position with an ugly grating sound as the current sucked and gurgled about it, and the whitecapped waves pounded its sides and broke in white foam over the gunwales. The Texan took soundings with the pole. "Deep water on three sides," he announced, "an' about a foot down to solid rock on the other. Maybe I can climb out an' shove her off."

"No! No!" cried the girl, in a sudden panic of fear. "You can't swim, and suppose something should happen and the boat moved off before you could climb into it? You'd be washed off the rock in a minute, and I—I couldn't stand it alone!"

"The way she's millin' around on the rock, I'm afraid she'll rip her bottom out. She's leakin' already. There's more water in here now, than when we started to bail."

"Most of it splashed in over the side—see, when the waves break."

"Maybe," assented the Texan, carelessly, but in the darkness he stooped and with his fingers located a crack where the planking had been forced apart, through which the river water gushed copiously. Without a word he stepped to the girl's saddle and took down the rope. "We've got to get off here," he insisted, "where'd we be if some big tree like the one that knocked me cold would drift down on us?" As he talked he passed the loop of the rope over his head and made it fast about his shoulders, and allowing ten or twelve feet of slack, knotted it securely to a ring in the end of the boat. "There, now I can get onto the rock an' by using the pole for a crow-bar, I can pry us off, then if I get left I'll just trail along on this rope until I can pull myself in."

The man's first effort resulted only in breaking a couple of feet from the end of his lever, but finally, by waiting to heave on his bar at the moment a wave pounded the side, he had the satisfaction of seeing the craft move slowly, inch by inch toward the deeper water. A moment later the man thanked his stars that he had thought of the rope, for without warning the boat lifted on a huge wave and slipped from the rock where it was instantly seized by the current and whirled down stream with a force that jerked him from his feet. Taking a deep breath, he clutched the line, and easily pulled himself to the boat, where the girl assisted him over the side.

They were entirely at the mercy of the river, now, for in the suddenness of their escape from the rock, the Texan had been unable to save the pole. Groping in the water for his boot he began to bail earnestly, and as Alice attempted to locate the other boot her hand came in contact with the inrushing stream of water. "Oh, it *is* leaking!" she cried in dismay. "I can feel it pouring through the bottom!"

"Yes, I found the leak back there on the rock. If we both bail for all we're worth maybe we can keep her afloat."

Alice found the other boot and for what seemed interminable hours the two bailed in silence. But despite their efforts, the water gained. Nearly half full, the boat floated lower and more sluggishly. Waves broke over the side with greater frequency, adding their bit to the stream that flowed in through the bottom. At length, the girl dropped her boot with a sigh that was half a sob: "I can't lift another bootful," she murmured; "my shoulders and arms ache so—and I feel—faint."

"Just you prop yourself up in the corner an' rest a while," advised the Texan, with forced cheerfulness, "I can handle it all right, now." Wearily, the girl obeyed. At the bow and stern of the square-ended boat, the bottom curved upward so that the water was not more than six or eight inches deep where she sank heavily against the rough planking, with an arm thrown over the gunwale. Her eyes closed, and despite the extreme discomfort of her position, utter weariness claimed her, and she sank into that borderland of oblivion that is neither restful sleep, nor impressionable wakefulness.

It may have been minutes later, or hours, that the voice of the Texan brought her jerkily erect. Vaguely she realized that she could see him dimly, and that his arm seemed to be pointing at something. With a sense of great physical effort, she managed to follow the direction of the pointing arm, and then he was speaking again: "It's breakin' daylight! An' we're close to shore!" Alice nodded indifferently. It seemed, somehow, a trivial thing. She was conscious of a sense of annoyance that he should have rudely aroused her to tell her that it was breaking daylight, and that they were close to shore. Her eyes closed slowly, and her head sank onto the arm that lay numb and uncomfortable along the gunwale.

The Texan was on his feet, eagerly scanning his surroundings that grew momentarily more distinct in the rapidly increasing light. The farther shore showed dimly and the man emitted a low whistle of surprise. "Must be a good four or five miles wide," he muttered, as his eyes took in the broad expanse of water that rolled between. He saw at a glance that he was well out of the main channel, for all about him were tiny islands formed by the summits of low buttes and ridges while here and there the green tops of willows protruded above the surface of the water swaying crazily in the current.

"Some flood!" he muttered, and turned his attention to the nearer bank. The boat floated sluggishly not more than fifty or sixty feet from the steep slope that rose to a considerable height. "Driftin' plumb along the edge of the bench," he opined, "if I only had the pole." He untied the rope by which he had dragged himself aboard from the rock, and coiled it slowly, measuring the distance with his eye. "Too short by twenty feet," he concluded, "an' nothin' to tie to if I was near enough." He glanced downward with concern. The boat was settling lower and lower. The gunwales were scarcely a foot above the water. "She'll be divin' out from under us directly," he muttered. "I wonder how deep it is?" Hanging the coiled rope on the horn of the saddle he slipped over the edge, but although he let down to the full reach of his arms his feet did not touch bottom and he drew himself aboard again. The boat was moving very slowly, drifting lazily across a bit of slack water that had backed into the mouth of a wide coulee. Fifty yards away, at the head of the little bay formed by the backwater, the Texan saw a bit of level, grass-covered beach. Glancing helplessly at his rope, he noticed that the horse was gazing hungrily at the grass, and in an instant, the man sprang into action. Catching up his boots he secured them to the saddle by means of a dangling pack string, and hastily uncoiling the rope he slipped the noose over the horn of the saddle. The other end he knotted and springing to the girl's side shook her roughly. "Wake up! Wake up! In a minute it'll be too late!" Half lifting her to her feet he hastily explained his plan, as he talked he tore the brilliant scarf from his neck and tied it firmly about his own wrist and hers. Making her take firm hold about his neck he seized the knotted rope with one hand, while with the other he reached for the ax and brought the handle down with a crash against the horse's flank. The sudden blow caused the frightened animal to leap clean over the low gunwale. He went completely out of sight, but a moment later his head appeared, and snorting, and thrashing about, he struck out for shore. When the slack was out of the line the Texan threw his arm about the girl's waist, and together they leaped over the side in the wake of the swimming horse. Even with the small amount of slack that remained, the jerk when the line pulled taut all but loosened the Texan's hold. Each moment seemed an eternity, as the weight of both hung upon the Texan's one-handed grip. "Hold for all you're worth!" he gasped, and he felt her arms tighten about him, relinquished the hold on her waist and with a mighty effort gripped the rope with the hand thus freed. Even with two hands it was no mean task to maintain his hold, for the current slight as it was, swung them down so the pull was directly against it. The Texan felt the girl's grasp on his neck weaken. He shouted a word of encouragement, but it fell on deaf ears, her hands slipped over his shoulders, and at the same instant the man felt the strain of her weight on his arm as the scarf seemed to cut into the flesh. The Texan felt himself growing numb. He seemed to be slipping—slipping—from some great height—slipping slowly down a long, soft incline. In vain he struggled to check the slow easy descent. He was slipping faster, now—fairly shooting toward the bottom. Somehow he didn't seem to care. There were rocks at the bottom—this he knew—but the knowledge did not worry him. Time enough to worry about that when he struck—but this smooth, easy slide was pleasant. Crash! There was a blinding flash of light. Fountains of stars played before his eyes like fireworks on the Fourth of July. An agonizing pain shot through his body—and then—oblivion.

A buckskin horse, with two water-soaked boots lashing his flanks and trailing a lariat rope from the horn of his saddle, dashed madly up a coulee.

The pack string broke and the terrifying thing that lashed him on, fell to the ground with a thud. The run became a trot, and the trot a walk. When the coulee widened into a grassy plain, he warily circled the rope that dragged from the saddle, and deciding it was harmless, fell eagerly to eating the soggy buffalo grass that carpeted the ground.

While back at the mouth of the coulee lay two unconscious forms, their bodies partly awash in the lapping waves of the rising river.

CHAPTER X

JANET MCWHORTER

The Texan stirred uneasily. Vaguely, he sensed that something was wrong. His head ached horribly but he didn't trouble to open his eyes. He was in the corral lying cramped against the fence where the Red King had thrown him, and with bared teeth, and forefeet pawing the air, the Red King was coming toward him. Another moment and those terrible hoofs would be striking, cutting, trampling him into the trodden dirt of the corral. Why didn't someone haze him off? Would they sit there on the fence and see him killed? "Whoa, boy—Whoa!" In vain he struggled to raise an arm—it was held fast, and his legs were pinned to the ground by a weight! He struggled violently, his eyes flew open and—there was no Red King, no corral—only a grassed slope strewn with rocks against one of which his head rested. But why was he tied? With great effort he rolled over. The weight that held his legs shifted, and he found that one of his arms was free. He sat up and stared, and instantly recollection of the events of the night, brutally vivid, crowded his brain. There was no slow, painful tracing step by step, of the happenings of the past twelve hours. The whole catenation in proper sequence presented itself in one all-embracing vision—a scene painted on canvas, rather than the logical continuity of a screen picture.

The unconscious form of the girl lay across his legs. Her temple, and part of her cheek that lay within range of his vision were white with the pallor of death, and the hand that stretched upward toward his own, showed blue and swollen from the effect of the tightly knotted scarf. Swiftly the man untied the knots, and staggering to his feet, raised the limp form and half-carried, half-dragged it to a tiny plateau higher up the slope. Very gently he laid the girl on the grass, loosened her shirt at the throat, and removed her wet boots. Her hands and feet were ice cold, and he chafed them vigorously. Gradually, under the rubbing the sluggish blood flowed. The blue look faded from her hand and a slight tinge of colour crept into her cheeks. With a sigh of relief, the Texan grasped her by the shoulder and shook her roughly. After a few moments her eyelids fluttered slightly, and her lips moved. The shaking continued, and he bent to catch the muttered words:

"Win——"

"Yeh, Win'll be 'long, directly. Come, wake up!"

"Win—dear—I'm—so—sleepy."

She was asleep again as the words left her lips and the man, squatting on his heels, nodded approval. "That's what I wanted to know—that she ain't drowned. If there'd been any water in her lungs she'd have coughed."

He stood up and surveyed his surroundings. At the water's edge, not a hundred feet below the spot where the horse had dragged them against the rocks, the flat-boat lay heavily aground. Relieved of its burden, it had been caught in the slowly revolving back current that circled the tiny bay, and had drifted ashore. Removing the scarf from his wrist, he knotted it into place and descended to the boat where he fished his hat from the half-filled hull. The handle of the ax caught his eye and searching his pockets, he examined his supply of matches, and cast the worthless sticks from him with an oath: "Heads plumb soaked off, or I could build her a fire!"

As he ascended the bank the sun just topped the rim of the bench. Its rays felt grateful to the chilled man as he stood looking down at the sleeping girl. "It'll dry her, an' warm her up, while I'm huntin' that damn cayuse," he muttered. "The quicker she gets to some ranch house, the better it'll be. I wish I knew where I'm at."

Once more he descended to the water's edge, and searched the ground. It was but the work of a moment to pick up the trail of the galloping horse, and he followed it up the coulee, making his way gingerly in his stockinged feet among the loose stones and patches of prickly pears. "Wish I'd left my boots in the boat, but I figured old Powder Face would stop when he got to shore instead of smashin' us again' the rocks an' lightin' out like the devil was after him—he's old enough to know better. An' I wonder how in hell she come to be ridin' him? Powder Face is one of Dad's own special horses."

The coulee wound interminably. The cowboy glanced at his feet where a toe protruded from a hole in his sock, and seating himself on a boulder he removed the socks and crammed them into his pocket. "Wouldn't be nothin' left of 'em but legs in a little bit," he grumbled, and instinctively felt for his tobacco and papers. He scowled at the soggy mass and replaced them. "Ain't got a match even if I did dry the tobacco. I sure feel like I'd died an' went to hell!"

He continued along the coulee limping painfully across stretches of sharp stones and avoiding the innumerable patches of prickly pears with which the floor of the valley was dotted. Rounding a sharp spur of rock that protruded into the ravine, he halted abruptly and stared at his boots which lay directly in his path. He grinned as he examined the broken thong. "I've be'n cussin' busted pack-strings all my life," he muttered, "but this particular string has wiped out the whole score again' 'em." Removing his leather chaps, he seated himself, drew on his socks, and inserted a foot into a boot. In vain he pulled and tugged at the straps. The wet leather gripped the damp sock like a vise. He stood up and stamped and pulled but the foot stuck fast at the ankle of the boot. Withdrawing the foot, he fished in his hip pocket and withdrew a thin piece of soap from the folds of a red cotton handkerchief. Once again he sat down and proceeded to rub the soap thickly upon the heels and insteps of his socks and inside of his boots, whereupon, after much pulling and stamping, he stood properly shod and drew on his chaps.

A short distance farther on, a cattle trail zigzagged down the steep side of the coulee. The Texan paused at the foot of it. "Reckon I'll just climb up onto the bank an' take a look around. With that rope trailin' along from the saddle horn, that damn cayuse might run his fool head off."

From the rim of the coulee, the man gazed about him, searching for a familiar landmark. A quarter of a mile away, a conical butte rose to a height of a hundred feet above the level of the broken plain, and the Texan walked over and laboriously climbed its steep side. He sank down upon the topmost pinnacle and studied the country minutely. "Just below the edge of the bad lands," he muttered. "The Little Rockies loom up plain, an' the Bear Paws an' Judiths look kind of dim. I'm way off my range down here. This part of the country don't look like it had none too thick of a population." In vain his eyes swept the vast expanse of plain for the sight of a ranch house. He rose in disgust. "I've got to find that damn cayuse an' get *her* out of this, somehow." As he was about to begin the descent his eye caught a thin thread of smoke that rose, apparently from a coulee some three or four miles to the eastward. "Maybe some nester's place, or maybe only an' Injun camp, but whatever it is, my best bet is to hit for it. I might be all day trailin' Powder Face. Whoever it is, they'll have a horse or two, an' believe me, they'll part with 'em." He scrambled quickly down to the bench and started in the direction of the smoke, and as he walked, he removed the six-gun from its holster and after wiping it carefully, made sure that it was in working condition.

The Texan's course lay "crossways of the country," that is, in order to reach his objective he must needs cross all the innumerable coulees and branches that found their way to the Missouri. And as he had not travelled far back from the river these coulees were deep and their steep sides taxed his endurance to the utmost. At the bottom of each coulee he drank sparingly of the bitter alkali water, and wet the bandage about his throbbing head. After each climb he was forced to rest. A walk of three or four miles in high-heeled riding boots assumes the proportions of a real journey, even under the most favourable circumstances, but with the precipitous descents, the steep climbs, and the alkali flats between the coulees, which in dry weather are dazzling white, and hard and level as a floor, now merely grey greasy beds of slime into which he sank to the ankles at each step, the trip proved a nightmare of torture.

At the end of an hour he figured that he had covered half the distance. He was plodding doggedly, every muscle aching from the unaccustomed strain. His feet, which burned and itched where the irritating soap rubbed into his skin, had swollen until the boots held them in a vise-like grip of torture. At each step he lifted pounds of glue-like mud which clung to the legs of his leather chaps in a thick grey smear. And each step was a separate, conscious, painful effort, that required a concentration of will to consummate.

And so he plodded, this Texan, who would have cursed the petty mishap of an ill-thrown loop to the imminent damnation of his soul, enduring the physical torture in stoic silence. Once or twice he smiled grimly, the cynical smile that added years to the boyish face. "When I see her safe at some ranch, I'll beat it," he muttered thickly. "I'll go somewhere an' finish my jamboree an' then I'll hit fer some fresh range." To his surprise he suddenly found that the mere thought of whisky was nauseating to him. His memory took him back to a college town in his native State. "It used to be that way," he grinned, "when I'd get soused, I couldn't look at a drink for a week. I reckon stayin' off of it for a whole year has about set me back where I started."

He half-climbed, half-fell down the steep side of a coulee and dipped his aching head in the cool water at the bottom. With a stick he scraped the thick smear of grey mud from his chaps and boots, and washed them in the creek. He rose to his feet and stood looking down into a clear little pool. "By God, I can't go—like that!" he said aloud. "I've got to stay an' face Win! I've got to know that he don't think there's anything—wrong—with her!"

Instead of climbing the opposite slope, he followed down the coulee, for he had seen from the edge that it led into a creek valley of considerable width, above the rim of which rose the thin grey plume of smoke. Near the mouth of the coulee he crawled through a wire fence. "First time a nester's fence ever looked good to me," he grinned, and at a shallow pool, paused to remove the last trace of mud from his chaps, wash his face and hands, box his hat into the proper peak, and jerk the brilliant scarf into place.

"She can rest up here till I find Win," he said aloud, and stepped into the valley, trying not to limp as he picked his way among the scattered rocks. "Sheep outfit," he muttered, as he noted the close-cropped grass, and the stacked panels of a lambing pen. Then, rounding a thicket of scrub willows, he came suddenly upon the outfit, itself.

He halted abruptly, as his eyes took in every detail of the scene. A little dirt roofed cabin of logs, a rambling straw thatched sheep shed, a small log barn, and a pole corral in which two horses dozed dreamily. The haystacks were behind the barn, and even as he looked, a generous forkful of hay rolled over the top of the corral fence, and the horses crossed over and thrust their muzzles into its fragrant depths. A half-dozen weak old ewes snipped half-heartedly at the short buffalo grass, and three or four young lambs frisked awkwardly about the door-yard on their ungainly legs.

Another forkful of hay rolled over the corral fence, and making his way around the barn, the Texan came abruptly face to face with Miss Janet McWhorter. The girl stood, pitchfork in hand, upon a ledge of the half-depleted haystack and surveyed him calmly, as a startled expression swiftly faded from her large, blue-black eyes. "Well you're the second one this morning; what do *you* want?"

The Texan noticed that the voice was rich, with low throaty tones and also he noticed that it held a repellent note. There was veiled hostility—even contempt in the peculiar emphasis of the "you." He swept the Stetson from his head: "I'm afoot," he answered, simply, "I'd like to borrow a horse."

The girl jabbed the fork into the hay, gathered her skirts about her, and slipped gracefully from the stack. She walked over and stood directly before him. "This is McWhorter's outfit," she announced, as if the statement were a good and sufficient answer to his plea.

The cowboy looking straight into the blue-black eyes, detected a faint gleam of surprise in their depths, that her statement apparently meant nothing to him. He smiled: "Benton's my name—Tex Benton, range foreman of the Y Bar. And, is this Mrs. McWhorter?"

"The Y Bar!" exclaimed the girl, and Tex noticed that the gleam and surprise hardened into a glance of open skepticism. "Who owns the Y Bar, now?"

"Same man that's owned it for the last twenty years—Mr. Colston."

"You must know him pretty well if you're his foreman?"

"Tolerable," answered the man, "I've been with him most every day for a year."

A swift smile curved the red lips—a smile that hinted of craft rather than levity. "I wonder what's worrying him most, nowadays—Mr. Colston, I mean."

"Worryin' him?" The Texan's eyes twinkled. "Well, a man runnin' an outfit like the Y Bar has got plenty on his mind, but the only thing that right down worries him is the hair on his head—an' just between you an' me, he ain't goin' to have to worry long."

The air of reserve—of veiled hostility dropped from the girl like a mask, and she laughed—a spontaneous outburst of mirth that kindled new lights in the blue-black eyes, and caused a fanlike array of little wrinkles to radiate from their corners: "I'll answer your question now," she said. "I'm Mrs. Nobody, thank you—I'm Janet McWhorter. But what are you doing on this side of the river? And how's Mr. Colston?"

"He's just the finest ever," replied the cowboy, and the girl was quick to note the deep feeling behind the words. "An' I—two of us—were tryin' to cross on the Long Bill's ferry from Timber City, an' the drift piled up again' us so we had to cut the cable, an' we got throw'd into shore against the bench three or four miles above here."

"Where's your friend? Is he hurt?" Her eyes rested with a puzzled expression upon the edge of the white bandage that showed beneath the brim of his hat.

The Texan shook his head: "No, not hurt I reckon. Just plumb wore out, an' layin' asleep on the bank. I've got to go back."

"You'll need two horses."

The man shook his head: "No, only one. We had our horses with us. We lost one in the river, an' the other pulled us ashore, an' then beat it up the coulee. I can catch him up all right, if I can get holt of a horse."

"Of course you can have a horse! But, you must eat first———"

"I can't stop. There'll be time for that later. I'm goin' to bring—my friend back here."

"Of course you're going to bring him back here! But you are about all in yourself. Three or four miles through the mud and across the coulees in high-heeled boots, and with your head hurt, and sopping wet, and no breakfast, and—I bet you haven't even had a smoke! Come on, you can eat a bite while I fix up something for your friend, and then you can tackle some of Dad's tobacco. I guess it's awful strong but it will make smoke—clouds of it!"

She turned and led the way to the house and as the Texan followed his eyes rested with a suddenly awakened interest upon the girl. "Curious she'd think of me not havin' a smoke," he thought, as his glance strayed from the shapely ankles to the well-rounded forearms from which the sleeves of her grey flannel shirt had been rolled back, and then to the mass of jet black hair that lay coiled in thick braids upon her head. He was conscious that a feeling of contentment—a certain warm glow of well-being pervaded him, and he wondered vaguely why this should be.

"Come right on in," she called over her shoulder as she entered the door. "I'll have things ready in a jiffy?" As she spoke, she slid a lid from the top of the stove, jammed in a stick of firewood, set the coffee-pot directly on to the fire, and placed a frying pan beside it. From a nail she took a slab of bacon and sliced it rapidly. In the doorway the Texan stood watching, in open admiration, the swift, sure precision of her every move. She glanced up, a slice of bacon held above the pan, and their eyes met. During a long moment of silence the man's heart beat wildly. The girl's eyes dropped suddenly: "Crisp, or limber?" she asked, and to the cowboy's ears, the voice sounded even richer and deeper of tone than before.

"Limber, please." His own words seemed to boom harshly, and he was conscious that he was blushing to the ears.

The girl laid the strips side by side in the pan and crossed swiftly to a cupboard. The next moment she was pouring something from a bottle into a glass. She returned the bottle and, passing around the table, extended the half-filled tumbler. The liquid in it was brown, and to the man's nostrils came the rich bouquet of good whisky. He extended his hand, then let it drop to his side.

"No, thanks," he said, "none for me."

She regarded him in frank surprise. "You don't drink?" she cried. "Why—oh, I'm glad! I hate the stuff! Father—sometimes—Oh, I hate it! But, a cowboy that don't drink! I thought they all drank!"

The Texan stepped to her side and, reaching for the glass, set it gently upon the table. As his hand touched hers a thrill shot through his veins, and with it came a sudden longing to take the hand in his own—to gather this girl into his arms and to hold her tight against his wildly throbbing heart. The next moment he was speaking in slow measured words. "They all do—me along with the rest. But, I ain't drinkin' now."

CHAPTER XI

AT THE MOUTH OF THE COULEE

The girl's eyes flashed a swift glance into his, and once more raised to the bandage that encircled his head, then, very abruptly, she turned her back toward him, and busied herself at the stove. A plate of sizzling bacon and a steaming cup of coffee were whisked onto the table and, as the cowboy seated himself, she made up a neat flat package of sandwiches.

As Tex washed down the bacon and bread with swallows of scalding coffee, she slipped into an adjoining room and closed the door. Just as he finished she reappeared, booted and spurred, clad in a short riding skirt of corduroy, her hands encased in gauntleted gloves, and a Stetson set firmly upon the black coiled braids. A silk scarf of a peculiar burnt orange hue was knotted loosely about her neck.

Never in the world, thought the man as his eyes rested for a moment upon the soft, full throat that rose from the open collar of her shirt, had there been such absolute perfection of womanhood; and his glance followed the lithe, swift movements with which she caught up the package of lunch and stepped to the door. "I'm going with you," she announced. "Father's up at the lambing camp, and I've fed all the little beasties." A lamb tumbled awkwardly about her legs and she cuffed it playfully.

As the Texan followed her to the corral, his thoughts flashed to Alice Endicott lying as he had left her beside the river—flashed backward to the moment of their first meeting, to the wild trip through the bad lands, to their parting a year ago when she had left him to become the bride of his rival, to the moment she had appeared as an apparition back there in the saloon, and to the incidents of their wild adventure on the flat-boat. Only last night, it was—and it seemed ages ago.

Thoughts of her made him strangely uncomfortable, and he swore softly under his breath, as his glance rested upon the girl who had stooped to release a rope from a saddle that lay beside the corral gate. She coiled it deftly, and stepping into the enclosure, flipped the noose over the head of a roman-nosed roan. The Texan stared. There had been no whirling of the rope, only a swift, sure throw, and the loop fastened itself about the horse's throat close under his chin. The cowboy stepped to relieve her of the rope, but she motioned him to the other animal, a gentle looking bay mare. "I'll ride Blue, you take the mare," she said.

He surveyed the roan dubiously: "He looks snorty. You better let me handle him."

She shook her head: "No, I've ridden him before. Really, I'm quite a twister. You can help saddle him, though."

The saddling proved to be no easy task. The animal fought the bit, and shied and jumped out from under blanket a half-dozen times before they finally succeeded in cinching him up. Then, Tex saddled the mare, and led both horses through the gate. Outside the corral, the girl reached for the roan's reins but the man shook his head. "I'll ride him, you take the bay."

The girl stared at him while the slow red mounted to her cheeks. There was a note of defiance in her tone as she answered: "I tell you I am going to ride him. I've ridden him, and I'll show him that I can ride him again."

The Texan smiled: "Sure, I know you can ride him—I knew that when I saw you catch him up. But, what's the use? He's got a bad eye. What's the use of you takin' a chance?"

The girl hesitated just a moment: "You're in no condition to ride him, you're hurt, and all tired out——"

The cowboy interrupted her with a laugh: "I ain't hurt to speak of, an' since I got that coffee inside me, I'm good for all day an' then some."

"Whose horse is Blue? And what right have you to tell me I can't ride him?"

"Whose horse he is, don't make any difference. An' if I ain't got the right to tell you not to ride him, I'll take the right."

"Well, of all the nerve! Anybody would think you owned the earth!"

The Texan regarded her gravely: "Not much of it, I don't. But, I'm goin' to own more——"

"More than the earth!" she mocked.

"Yes—a whole heap more than the earth," he answered, as his steady grey eyes stared straight into her own stormy, blue-black ones. Then, without a word, he extended the reins of the mare, and without a word, the girl took them and mounted.

As the cowboy swung into the saddle, the blue roan tried to sink his head, but the man held him up short, and after two or three half-hearted jumps the animal contented himself with sidling restlessly, and tonguing the bit until white, lathery foam dripped from his lips.

As the girl watched the animal the resentment died from her eyes: "That's the littlest fuss I ever saw Blue kick up," she announced.

The Texan smiled: "He's on his good behaviour this mornin'."

"He saw it was no use," she replied, quickly. "Horses have got lots of common sense."

The two headed up the little used trail that led upward to the bench by way of a shallow coulee. When they gained the top the man pointed toward the west: "The coulee we're hittin' for is just beyond that little butte that sets out there alone," he explained. "We better circle away from the river a little. The coulees won't be so deep back aways, an' I've got to catch up that cayuse. He hit straight back, an' the way his tracks looked, he sure was foggin' it."

They rode side by side at a sharp trot, the Texan now and then casting a glance of approval at the girl who rode on a loose rein "glued to the leather." A wide alkali bed lay before them, and the pace slowed to a walk. "Your partner," began the girl, breaking the silence that had fallen upon them, "maybe he will wake up and start out to find you."

The Texan glanced at her sharply: Was it his own imagination, or had the girl laid a significant emphasis upon the "He." Her eyes did not meet his squarely, but seemed focussed upon the edge of the bandage. He shook his head: "I reckon not," he replied shortly.

"But, even if he did, we could easily pick up his trail," persisted the girl.

"Dead easy." The man was battling with an impulse to tell the girl that his companion upon the river was a woman. The whole thing was so absurdly simple—but was it? Somehow, he could not bring himself to tell this girl— she might not understand—she might think—with an effort he dismissed the matter from his mind. She'll find out soon enough when we get there. He knew without looking at her that the girl's eyes were upon him. "Heavy goin'," he observed, abruptly.

"Yes."

Another long silence, this time broken by the Texan: "I don't get you quite," he said, "you're different from—from most women."

"How, different?"

"Why—altogether different. You don't dress like—like a nester's girl—nor talk like one, neither."

The girl's lips smiled, but the man could see that the blue-black eyes remained sombre: "I've been East at school. I've only been home a month."

"Learn how to rope a horse, back East? An' how to ride? It's a cinch you never learnt it in a month."

"Oh, I've always known that. I learned it when I was a little bit of a girl—mostly from the boys at the Y Bar."

"The Y Bar?"

"Yes, we used to live over on Big Box Elder, below the Y Bar home ranch. Father ran sheep there, and Mr. Colston bought him out. He could have squeezed him out, just as well—but he bought him out and he paid him a good price—that's his way."

The Texan nodded. "Yes, that would be his way."

"That was four years ago, and father sent me off to school. I didn't want to go a bit, but father promised mother when she died—I was just a little tike, then—and he promised her that he would give me the best education he could afford. Father's a Scotchman," she continued after a moment of silence, "he's sometimes hard to understand, but he always keeps his word. I'm afraid he really spent more than he can afford, because—he moved over here while I was away and—it isn't *near* as nice as the old outfit. I hate it, here!"

The Texan glanced up in surprise at the vehemence of her last words: "Why do you hate it?" he asked. "Looks to me like a likely location—plenty range—plenty water———"

"We're—we're too close to the bad lands."

The man swept the country with a glance: "Looks like there ought to be plenty room. Must be five or six miles of range between you an' the bad lands. Looks to me like they lay just right for you. Keeps other outfits from crowdin'."

"Oh, it isn't the range! You talk just like father does. Any place is good enough to live in if there's plenty of range—range and water—water and range—those two things are all that make life worth living!"

The man was surprised at the bitterness of her voice. The blue-black eyes were flashing dangerous lights.

"Well, he can build a bigger house," he blundered.

"It isn't the house, either. The little cabin's just as cozy as it can be, and I love it! It's the neighbours!"

"Neighbours?"

"Yes, neighbours! I don't mean the nesters—they're little outfits like ours. They're in the same fix we are in. But the horse-thieves and the criminals that are hiding out in the bad lands. There's a sort of understanding—they leave the money here, and father brings out their supplies and things from town. In return, they keep their hands off our stock."

"Well, there's no harm in that. The poor devils have got to eat, an' they don't dare to show up in town."

"Oh, I suppose so," answered the girl, wearily, as though the subject were an old one, covering the same old ground. "But, if I had my way, they'd all be in jail where they belong. I hate 'em!"

"An' you thought I was one of 'em?" grinned the man.

She nodded: "Of course I did—for a minute. I thought you're wanting to borrow a horse was just the flimsiest kind of an excuse to steal one."

"You don't know, yet—for sure."

The girl laughed: "Oh, yes I do. I didn't think you were, when I told you that this was McWhorter's ranch. The name didn't mean anything to you, and if you were a horse-thief, it would have meant 'hands off.' Then, to make sure, I asked you what Mr. Colston's chief worry was? You see if you were a horse-thief you might know Y Bar, but you'd hardly know him well enough to know about how he fusses over that little bald spot."

Tex laughed: "Little bald spot just about reaches his ears now. Top of his head looks like a sheep range."

"There you go," flashed the girl, "you mighty cattlemen always poking fun at the sheep. We can't help it if the sheep eat the grass short. They've got just as much right to eat as the cattle have—and a good deal better right than your old horse-thieves that you all stick up for!"

The Texan regarded her with twinkling eyes: "First thing we know, we'll be startin' a brand new sheep an' cattle war, an' most likely we'd both get exterminated."

Janet laughed, and as the horses plodded across the sodden range with the man slightly in advance, she watched him out of the corner of her eye. "He's got a sense of humour," she thought, "and, he's, somehow, different from most cowboys—and, he's the best looking thing." Then her eyes strayed to the bandage about his head and her brows drew into a puzzled frown.

They had dipped down into a wide coulee, and the Texan jerked his horse to a stand, swung to the ground, and leaned over to examine some tracks in the mud.

"Are they fresh?" asked the girl. "Is it your horse?"

A moment of silence followed, while the man studied the tracks. Then he looked up: "Yes," he answered, "it's his tracks, all right. An' there's another horse with him. They're headin' for the bad lands." He swung into the saddle and started down the coulee at a gallop, with the bay mare pounding along in his wake.

The little plateau where he had left Alice Endicott was deserted! Throwing himself from the saddle, the Texan carefully examined the ground. Here also, were the tracks of the two horses he had seen farther up the coulee, and mingled with the horse tracks were the tracks of high-heeled boots. The man faced the girl who still sat her bay mare, and pointed to the tracks on the ground. "Someone's be'n here," he said, in a low, tense voice.

"Maybe your partner woke up and caught his horse, or maybe those are your own tracks——"

The man made a swift gesture of dissent: "Well, then," uttered the girl in a tone of conviction, "that horrible Purdy has been along here——"

"Purdy!" The word exploded from the Texan's lips like the report of a gun. He took a step toward her and she saw that his eyes stared wide with horror.

"Yes," she answered, with a shudder, "I loathe him. He was at the ranch this morning before you came—wanted to see father——"

A low groan from the lips of the Texan interrupted her. With a hand pressed tightly to his brow, he was staggering toward his horse.

CHAPTER XII

IN TIMBER CITY

On the porch of the Cameron cottage, Endicott and Colston, absorbed in business, talked until the ends of their cigars made glowing red spots in the darkness. The deal by which Endicott became sole proprietor of the Y Bar outfit was consummated, and Colston's promise to have the papers drawn up in the morning was interrupted by a furious volley of shots from the direction of the Red Front. Colston smiled: "NL rodeo probably camped near here an' the boys run in to wake up the town!"

Endicott glanced swiftly about him: "But, my wife!" he exclaimed, "Where is she? She promised to return before dark, and—why, it must have been dark for an hour!"

Colston noting the look of genuine alarm on the man's face, sought to reassure him: "Oh, well, she probably got interested in the scenery and rode a little farther than she intended. She'll be along directly——"

"Something may have happened—an accident——"

"Not much chance of that. Powder Face is woman broke, an' gentle as any cayuse can get. About that lower range I was tellin' you—where the Wilson sheep are creepin' in—" With merely the barest pretence of listening, Endicott rose, opened the screen door, tossed his cigar into the yard, and began pacing up and down the porch. At each turn he paused and peered out into the darkness.

The older man got up and stood beside him: "There's nothin' to worry about, my boy. An' that's one of the first things you'll learn—not to worry. A dozen things can happen to delay anyone, an' they're hardly ever serious. If it'll ease your mind any, we'll ride down town, maybe she stopped to take in the excitement, an' if she ain't there we'll ride out on the trail a piece."

The scattering shots that followed the volley had ceased and as the two proceeded down the sandy street in silence, a light appeared suddenly in the Red Front, from whose doors issued a babble of voices as of many men talking at once. Dismounting, Colston and Endicott entered to see Barras standing upon the bar in the act of lighting the second of the two huge swinging lamps. "Looks like there'd been a battle," grinned Colston, eyeing the barricade of kegs, the splintered mirror, and the litter of broken glass.

"I'll tell a hand it was a battle!" vouchsafed a bystander. "That there Texian, onct he got a-goin', was some ructious! He made his brag that he was a wolf an' it was his night to howl. An', believe me! He was a curly wolf! An' he howled, an' by God, he prowled! An' he's prowlin' yet—him an' his woman, too."

"Texan!" cried Colston.

"Woman!" shouted Endicott. "What woman?"

"What woman d'ye s'pose?" growled Barras, glaring wrathfully from the bar. "I don't know what woman. His woman, I guess—anyways they got plumb away after we had him all *see*rounded, an' all over but the shoutin'—an' all on account of Timber City's got a marshal which his head's solid bone plumb through, like a rock; an' left the keg shoot wide open fer him to beat it!"

"If you're so damn smart, why didn't you think of the keg shoot?" retorted the representative of law and order. "You know'd it was there an' I didn't."

"You lie! Unless you've fergot a whole lot sence—" A crash of thunder drowned the irate bartender's voice.

"Hold on, Pete, don't git to runnin' off at the head an' say somethin' yer sorry fer———"

"You'd be the one to be sorry, if folks know'd———"

"Talkin' don't git you nothin'. You listen here. We'll git this party yet. If the boys that took after him don't bring him in, I'll post a reward of a hundred dollars cash money out of my own pocket fer him———"

"Post it, then," snapped Barras, somewhat mollified, "git it on paper—" Another, louder clap of thunder followed a vivid lightning flash and wild with apprehension, Endicott forced his way to the bar and interrupted the quarrel: "What did this woman look like? Where is she?"

A dozen men, all talking at once answered him: "Good looker—" "Wore bran' new ridin' outfit—" "Rode a blaze-face buckskin—" "Said she knowed him—" "Went right in—" "Tried to dicker with Hod an' git him off—" The marshal pushed through the crowd to Endicott's side: "An' what's more, when he come bustin' out of the alley an' rode off down the trail she follered right in behind so we didn't dast to shoot; er we'd of got him. If you want to know what I think, they're a couple of desperadoes that figgered on stickin' up the express box over to the hotel, bein' as the payroll fer the Rock Creek mine come in today, only he got drunk first an' queered the game. An' what I want to know," the man continued, thrusting his face close to Endicott's, "is who the hell you be, an'———"

The hotel keeper interrupted importantly: "Him an' the woman come in on the stage an' wanted a couple rooms an' changed into them ridin' outfits, an' slipped out an' didn't show up fer supper! I mistrusted they was somethin' suspicious—they wanted a bath—an' the old woman usin' the tubs——"

"An' bein' as we couldn't git you all," broke in the marshal, drawing his gun, and at the same time pulling back his coat and displaying a huge badge, "we'll jest take what we kin git. Yer under arrest, an' fer fear you might be as handy with yer guns as yer pardner, you kin stick up yer hands——"

"Hold on!" Colston's words boomed above the voices of the men who had surged forward to hold Endicott.

"It's Y Bar Colston!" someone cried, and all eyes turned to the speaker. The marshal eyed him sullenly as the men made way for him.

The ranchman was smiling: "Don't go makin' any mistakes, Hod," he said, "let me make you acquainted with Mr. Endicott, of Cincinnati, Ohio, owner of the Y Bar."

"The Y Bar!"

"Yes. I sold out to him this evenin'—lock, stock, an' barrel."

The marshal dropped his gun into its holster and eyed Endicott shrewdly: "Sorry I got you wrong," he mumbled, extending his hand. "Blake's my name. Glad to meet you. I run the store here. Carry the biggest stock between Lewiston an' the Mizoo. Where do you figger on doin' yer tradin'?"

Endicott made a gesture of impatience: "I haven't figured at all. But this woman—my wife? How long has she been gone? Which way did she go? And why——?"

"Be'n gone pretty clost to an' hour. Went down the trail to the Mizoo. You kin search me fer why, onless it was to keep us from shootin' after that hell-roarin' Texian. She said she know'd him. Who is he, an' what's she so anxious he don't git shot fer?"

Before Endicott could reply, hoof-beats sounded on the trail, and in the doorway a man yelled "They're comin' back!" Disregarding the rain which fell in torrents the crowd surged into the street and surrounded the horsemen who drew up before the door.

"They didn't git 'em!" "Where'd they go?" Eager questions were hurled in volleys.

As the men dismounted the light from the windows glistened on wet slickers. Ike Stork acted as spokesman, and with white face and tight-pressed lips, Endicott hung on every word. "Got to the river," he explained, as he shook the water from his hat, "an' piled onto Long Bill's ferry, an' cut 'er loose. We didn't dast to shoot on account of the woman. We couldn't see nothin' then till the storm broke, an' by the lightnin' flashes we seen the boat in the middle of the river—an' boys, she's some river! I've be'n a residenter in these parts fer it's goin' on twenty year, an' I never seen the like—bank-full an' trees an' bresh so thick you can't hardly see no water. Anyways, there they was an' all to onct there come a big flash, an' we seen a pine with its roots an' branches ra'red up high as a house right on top of 'em. Then, the cable went slack—an' when the next flash come, they wasn't no boat—only timber an' bresh a-tearin' down stream, it looked like a mile a minute."

"And they were both on the boat?" Endicott's words came haltingly, and in the lamplight his face looked grey and drawn.

Ike Stork nodded: "Yes, both of 'em—an' the two horses."

"Isn't there a chance? Isn't it possible that they're—that the boat is still afloat?"

"We-ell," considered Ike, "I wouldn't say it's plumb onpossible. But it would be like ketchin' a straight-flush in the middle in a pot that had be'n boosted to the limit—with a full deck, an' nothin' wild."

Endicott turned away as the crowd broke into a babble of voices. Colston took him gently by the arm, but the younger man shook his head: "No, I— I want to think," he whispered, and with a nod of understanding the ranchman proceeded slowly toward the hotel. As Endicott passed from the glare of light thrown by the windows of the Red Front, Ike Stork managed to pass close to him. "They're a-floatin'," he whispered, "I seen 'em a flash or two afterwards. But the others didn't, an' they ain't no use spittin' out all you know. If anyone kin make 'er, them two will—they're game plumb through."

"You mean—" cried Endicott—but Ike Stork had mingled with the crowd.

At the door of the Red Front, Barras was importuning the marshal: "Gwan over to the printin' office an' git out that reward. I'm a-goin' to git paid fer these here damages."

"I hain't a-goin' to pay out no reward fer no drownded man!"

Endicott shuddered, and paused as the bartender's next words reached his ears: "If he's drownded the river'll take him farther than what them hand bills will git to. An' if he hain't, I want them damages."

Endicott hurried toward the two who stood slightly apart from the crowd: "If you are offering a reward," he said, "I will add a thousand for information concerning my wife."

"A thousand!" exclaimed the marshal, "dead or alive?"

Endicott nodded: "Yes," he answered, "dead or alive," and turning abruptly, walked slowly up the street entirely unheeding the shadowy form that kept pace with him in the darkness.

The storm ceased as suddenly as it had broken, and at the outskirts of the town the man paused and sank onto a boulder with his head in his arms. Minutes passed as he sat thus, too dazed to think. He was conscious of a dull pain in his heart, and his brain felt numb and pinched as though an iron band were being drawn tighter and tighter about his skull. Gradually his mind began to function. The words of Ike Stork recurred to him: "They're floatin'. If anyone kin make 'er through, them two will." Very possibly his wife was alive—but, where? Why had she ridden after this Texan, and why was she on the river with him? Methodically, step by step, the man retraced the events of their year of married life. They had been wondrously happy together. They had often spoken of the Texan—had wondered what had become of him. They had both written to him, addressing their letters to Wolf River, but all the letters had come back stamped "Return to writer." He remembered that she had been disappointed, but so had he. Was it possible that *all* the letters had not been returned? He remembered how eager she had been to spend their anniversary in Timber City. She had talked of it for months. And he remembered how she had urged him to buy a ranch and live at least part of the time in the West. And when he had got in touch with Colston through a real estate broker, he remembered how enthusiastic she had been over the prospect. How they had planned and planned, until she had imparted to him a goodly share of her enthusiasm. Was her love all for the West? Could it be that the Texan—? Surely, her previous experience had hardly been one that should have engendered any great love for the cattle country. He thought with a shudder of Purdy, of the flight in the night, and the subsequent trip through the bad lands. The one pleasant memory in the whole adventure had been the Texan—Tex, the devil-may-care, the irresponsible, the whimsical. And yet, withal, the capable, the masterful. He recollected vividly that there had been days of indecision—days when her love had wavered between himself and this man of the broad open spaces. Long before this adventure of the wilds Endicott had known her,—had loved her—and she had never taken him seriously.

With the suddenness of a blow, came the thought that when she did choose him—when finally she yielded to his pleading and consented to become his wife, it was because he had unexpectedly shown some of the attributes that were the inborn heritage of the Texan. Could it be that his great love for her had found no answering chord in her heart? If she had loved the Texan, why had she married him? Could it be that she did not even now take him seriously? Was her love so shallow a thing that it must be fanned into a flame by the winds of high adventure? He knew that the commonplaces of society bored her to extinction. Had the humdrum existence of civilization palled on her until her heart in very desperation had turned to her knight of the boundless plains. Had she deliberately planned this journey in order to be once more with the Texan? Had their meeting—their flight, even, been prearranged? Endicott groaned aloud, and the next moment a hand was placed on his shoulder. He leaped to his feet and peered into the face that stood vaguely outlined in the darkness.

"*Oui*, A'm t'ink you don' 'member Ol' Bat."

"Bat! Bat!" cried the man, "remember you! I guess I do remember you!" He seized a leathery hand in his own. "I'd rather see you, now, than any man in the world. What do you make of it, Bat? Tell me—what has happened?"

"*Oui*, A'm t'ink dat 'bout tam' A'm com' 'long. A'm t'ink you feel pret' bad, *non*? A'm com' 'long w'en de men com' back for no kin ketch Tex."

"You heard what they said?"

"*Oui*, A'm hear dat."

"Do you think they're alive?"

"*Oui, bien!* A'm stan' clos' I kin git beside de hoss, an' A'm hear dat man say de boat floatin' off, an' he ain' gon' spit 'bout dat. You com' 'long Ol' Bat—we fin' um."

Endicott thrust his face close and stared straight into the half-breed's eyes: "Have you been with Tex all the time—this past year?"

"*Oui*, him wagon boss on Y Bar, an' me, A'm cook."

"Would you have known it if he had been writing letters? Has he ever talked about—about—my wife?"

"*Non*, he ain' git lettaire. He don' talk 'bout dat 'oman. He lov' her too mooch———"

"*What!*" Endicott grasped the half-breed's arm and shook him roughly.

"*Oui*, he lov' dat 'oman so bad he ain' talk 'bout dat."

"You mean, you think they've planned it all out to run away together?"

Bat regarded the other gravely: "W'at you t'ink?" he asked, abruptly.

Endicott found it strangely hard to answer the direct question: "I—I don't know what to think."

"W'at you t'ink?" insisted the half-breed.

"What can I think?" cried the man in desperation. "She planned to be here today—and she met him here—and they are gone! What do you think?"

The half-breed answered slowly and very directly: "Me, A'm t'ink, you pret' mooch, w'at you call, de Godam fool. You lov' dat 'oman. You be'n marry wan year—an' you ain' know dat 'oman. You de gran' pilgrim. Me, A'm know dat 'oman. Ol' Bat, she tell Tex way back on Antelope Butte, dat tam, dat ain' hees 'oman—dat de pilgrim 'oman. Dat 'oman, he lov' you—Ol' Bat, know dat. Tex, she ain' belief dat," he paused and shrugged, expressively. "W'at de hell! She mar' de pilgrim, lak A'm say. An' Tex she feel ver' bad. She ain' drink no booze for wan' year—becos' she t'ink, w'en she feel lak dat, de booze she git heem—an' she would. A'm know 'bout dat, too. A'm know Tex. A'm know he gon' git drunk today, sure as hell. So A'm com' long tonight an' git heem hom'. He lov' dat oman too mooch. Dat hurt heem lak hell een here." The old half-breed paused to tap his breast, and proceeded. "He ain' wan' see dat 'oman no more. She com' 'long, w'at you call, de haccident. Me, A'm ain' know how dat com' dey gon'—but no mattaire. Dat all right. Dat good 'oman an' Tex, he good man, too. He ain' harm dat 'oman—he got de good heart. A'm ain' say dat Tex she ain' got not'in' to do wit' 'omans. But she know de good 'oman—an' she lov' dat good 'oman—an' dat 'oman she safe wit' Tex lak she wit' de own modder. You come 'long now wit' Ol' Bat, an' git de hoss, we gon' fin'. Mebbe-so tomor', mebbe-so nex' week—dat mak' no differ'. You fin' out dat all right." Old Bat ceased abruptly and started off and as Endicott followed him blindly through the dark, his eyes burned hot, and scalding tears coursed down his cheeks and dropped unheeded to the ground.

CHAPTER XIII

A MAN ALL BAD

Jack Purdy had turned horse-thief. And because chance had thrown him in with one of the strongest gangs of horse-thieves that ever operated the range, he had prospered.

A year and a week had elapsed since the countryside turned out to help Wolf River celebrate the opening of her bank. At that celebration the Texan had openly insulted him before the eyes of all cow-land. And, before the eyes of all cow-land he, a reputed gunman, hesitated with his hand on his gun, and every man and woman who waited in breathless expectancy for him to shoot, knew that he was afraid to shoot—knew that he was a coward. Only the pilgrim's girl did not know. She thought he had done a brave thing to ignore the insult, and that night she rode with him, and upon the rim of the bench, as they paused to look down upon the twinkling lights of the little town Purdy committed the unpardonable sin of the cattle country. He attacked her—dragged her from her horse. And then the pilgrim came. Purdy heard the sound of the furious hoof-beats, and grinned evilly as he watched the man dismount clumsily when he came upon the two horses grazing with empty saddles. When the pilgrim was almost upon him he flung the girl to the ground and drew his gun. There was a blinding flash—and Purdy knew no more until, hours afterward Sheriff Sam Moore and two of three sworn deputies were loading his "corpse" into a spring wagon. Then he sat up suddenly and Sam Moore and his deputies fled gibbering into the dark, while Purdy drove the team back to Wolf River. Swaggering into the dance hall, he found that the news of his demise at the hand of the pilgrim had preceded him—found, also, a marked lack of enthusiasm over his escape from death. Some countenances registered open disappointment, and the men whom he invited to drink, evinced a sudden absence of thirst. He sought to dance, but the women who occupied the chairs along the walls invented excuses, reasonable or preposterous according to the fertility of their imagination. So Purdy, a sullen rage in his heart, returned to the bar and drank alone. As he called for the third drink, the bartender eyed him truculently: "Just spread a little change, Purdy. Yer owin' fer two, now."

The sullen rage flared into swift anger and the cowpuncher's hand dropped to his gun: "What the hell's loose with you? What's the matter with everyone here? Ain't I good fer the drinks?"

The bartender stared straight into the blazing eyes: "You ain't good fer nothin' in Wolf River. After Tex showin' you up this afternoon but 'special what happened later. Folks knows what you tried to pull off up there on the bench. Reports was that the pilgrim had bumped you off but you don't notice no crêpe hangin' around nowheres, do you? An' when you turn up alive an' kickin' you don't notice 'em gittin' out no brass band about it, do you? An' I'm givin' you a tip—if I was you I'd right now be kickin' up a cloud of white dust a hell of a ways from Wolf River. Jest cast yer eyes around an' you'll see that there's a bunch of live ones missin'. Well, they're goin' to come driftin' back in a little, an' it's dollars to buffalo chips that when they do they'll start in an finish up the job the pilgrim botched."

Purdy's face went suddenly pale in the lamplight. The hand dropped limp from the gun-butt, and as he glanced swiftly about the room he moistened his lips with his tongue. There was a distinct whine in his voice as he forced his eyes to meet the other's steady gaze: "I didn't do nothin'. They—they can't do it."

"Can't do it—hell! A tree's a tree, ain't it? An' a rope's a rope?"

Purdy swayed heavily against the bar: "Give me a drink?" he begged, "jest one—I'm broke."

Without a word the other poured a full glass of liquor and pushed it toward him. Purdy reached for it, and part of the contents slopped upon his trembling fingers before the glass left the bar. Seizing it with both hands, he drained it at a gulp, and hurriedly made his way the length of the hall. In the doorway he paused and swept the room with a glance of malignant hate: "To hell with you!" he cried, shrilly, "to hell with you all!" And staggering down the steps, mounted the first horse he came to and fled wildly into the dark. All night he rode, with rage in his heart toward all men, a rage that found vent in wild raving and cursing and gradually fixed itself into a sullen hate—a smouldering savage hatred that included all mankind and womankind, but centred with abysmal brutishness upon the Texan, the pilgrim, the pilgrim's girl, and strangely enough, upon the bartender who had warned him to flee.

At daylight he entered the cabin of a nester who had not yet returned from the celebration, and according to the custom of the country cooked himself a meal and ate it. Then, in defiance of the custom of the country, he proceeded to make up a pack of provisions, helping himself liberally from the limited store. And not only provisions he took, but cooking utensils as well, and a pair of heavy blankets from the bed. He found savage satisfaction in scattering things about the room, in wantonly destroying provisions he could not use, and leaving the place in the wildest confusion. The owner, he recollected, was one of those who had refused to drink with him in the dance hall. The insane rage flared out anew. He even thought of burning the shack, but feared that the smoke would betray him before he could get away. "Won't drink with me, eh?" he muttered, and ground his heel into the face of a cheap photograph of a smiling baby girl. He had stopped overnight in this cabin once and heard the story of how the little two-year-old had toddled out and been bitten by a rattlesnake, and of the little grave beneath the tree in front of the house. He laughed, harshly: "Too good to drink with me!" and deliberately spat tobacco upon the faded little red shoe that had stood beside the picture. Then he secured his pack behind the cantle of his saddle, mounted, and rode away, leaving the dishes unwashed and the door wide open.

It was broad daylight when Purdy left the cabin, and he suddenly realized that he was riding a stolen horse. He had ridden the horse hard and it was becoming tired. Also he realized that he was packing the loot from the cabin. He cursed himself for a fool, for well he knew what would happen if he were caught—now. He should have been careful to leave no trail, and should at this moment be "holed up" in some coulee or patch of timber to wait for darkness. But he dared not camp within miles of the violated cabin. He was approaching the Bear Paws, and swinging sharply to the west, decided to skirt the mountains and strike into the foothills where there are no nesters and no trails. He must push on. The bad lands were only thirty miles away and if his horse held out he should reach them in the early afternoon. He breathed easier. The nester would not reach his cabin till evening.

There was a telephone at the TU and the TU lay between him and the bad lands. He must either swing in close to the mountains, or take a chance on the open bench. He chose the mountains, and toward noon passed a solitary sheepherder seated on the crest of a conical butte with his band of freshly sheared sheep spread out below him like an irregular patch of snow. The man motioned him in, but Purdy slipped swiftly into a coulee and came out a mile below. Later, a lone rider cut his trail, and from the shelter of a cottonwood thicket, Purdy watched him pass. He wanted to talk with him. Maybe he had a bottle and Purdy needed a drink. The man was idly twirling the end of his rope and singing a song as he rode. He seemed carefree, even gay. The song that he sang was a popular one on the cattle range, grossly obscene, having to do with the love intrigues of one "Big Foot Sal."

Purdy felt suddenly very much alone. Here was one of his kind with whom he would like to pass the time of day—smoke with him and if circumstances permitted, drink with him, and swap the gossip of the range. Instead, he must skulk in the thicket like a coyote until the man passed. A great wave of self-pity swept over him. He, Jack Purdy, was an outcast. Men would not drink with him nor would women dance with him. Even at this moment men were riding the range in search of him, and if they caught him—he shuddered, cold beads of sweat collected upon his forehead, involuntarily his fingers caressed his throat, and he loosened the collar of his shirt. Every man's hand was against him. His anger blazed forth in a volley of horrible curses, and he shook his gloved fist at the back of the disappearing rider. He rode on. "Damn 'em all!" he muttered, the sullen hatred settling itself once more upon him. "Wait till I get to the bad lands, an' then—" Purdy had no definite plan further than reaching the bad lands. His outfit had worked the range to the northward of Milk River, and he knew little of the bad lands except that they furnished a haven of refuge to men who were "on the run." He was "on the run," therefore he must reach the bad lands.

It was late in the afternoon when he rode unhesitatingly into the treeless, grassless waste of dry mud and mica studded lava rock, giving no heed to the fact that water holes were few and far between and known only to the initiated. Darkness found him following down a dry coulee into which high-walled, narrow mud cracks led in a labyrinth of black passages. His horse's head was drooping and the animal could not be forced off a slow walk. No spear of grass was visible and the rock floor of the coulee was baked and dry. Purdy's lips were parched, and his tongue made an audible rasping sound when he drew it across the roof of his mouth. The dark-walled coulee was almost pitch black, and he shivered in the night chill. His horse's shod feet, ringing loudly upon the rock floor, shattered a tomb-like silence. It seemed to Purdy that the sound could be heard for miles and he shuddered, glanced furtively about him, and pulled up to listen for sounds of pursuit. He spurred his horse viciously and the animal walked slowly on. He glanced upward. The walls of the coulee were steep and high, and far above him, little stars twinkled. Suddenly his heart ceased to beat. He felt weak and flabby and there was a strange chill at the pit of his stomach. He could have sworn that a face looked down at him from the clean-cut rim of the coulee. The next moment it was gone. He proceeded a quarter of a mile, again looked upward, and again he saw the face. His nerveless fingers closed about the butt of his gun and drew it from its holster, but his hand shook so that he thrust back the gun in disgust. They were after him. It was the posse, or perhaps the nester whose cabin he had plundered—and he hoped it was the posse. But, why didn't they shoot? Why didn't they come down and get him, instead of hanging along the edge of the coulee like buzzards, waiting for him to die of thirst. Twice more within the next half-hour he saw the face, and each time it disappeared.

Something seemed to snap inside his head and he spurred his horse in a perfect frenzy of rage. "Damn you!" he shrilled, and his voice rang hollow and thin, "damn you, come and get me! Shoot me! String me up! But, for

Christ's sake, give me a drink! I stole the horse to make a getaway. I gutted the nester's cabin! An' if it hadn't be'n for the pilgrim, I'd—" A man stood directly in front of him—two men. They were very close and one of them held a gun. Purdy could see the starlight gleam faintly upon the barrel.

"Put 'em up!" The words were not loudly spoken, but somehow they seemed deadly in earnest. Purdy's hands raised shakily:

"Damn you!" he screamed, "damn you all! Damn the world!"

"Coverin' quite a bit of territory, young feller. Better save up yer cussin' till you know yer hurt. Take his bridle reins, Bill, an' we'll be gittin' to camp." The other caught up the reins and once more the coulee rang to the measured tread of hoofs.

"Give me a drink," mumbled Purdy, thickly. "Water—whisky——"

"We've got 'em both. Jest hold on about five minutes an' we'll fix you out."

"An' then string me up," the words came with difficulty and the man in front laughed shortly.

"Well, mebbe not. I'm guessin' young feller, mebbe you've lit luckier'n what you think."

They turned abruptly into a side coulee, and a few moments later the spokesman ordered Purdy to dismount. He staggered weakly, and the man supported him while the other took the horse and disappeared. After a few steps Purdy braced up, and relieving him of his gun the man bade him follow. They seemed to be in a cave. Purdy glanced upward and could see no stars. The darkness was intense, and he placed his hand on the man's shoulder. They turned a sharp corner and another and found themselves in a blaze of light. Three men lounged about an open fire, and the light from two coal-oil lamps lighted the interior of what seemed to be a large room. Cooking utensils were ranged neatly along the wall near the fire, and beyond, Purdy could see rolls of bedding. The man who conducted him in tendered him a tin cup of water and Purdy gulped it greedily to the last drop and extended the cup for more. "Better wait a bit an' let that soak in," advised the man, "they's plenty an' you kin have all you want." The other three men looked on in silence, and when Purdy had drained two more cupfuls of water, one of them motioned him to be seated. Another handed him tobacco and papers, and as he rolled a cigarette, Purdy glanced about with a distinct air of relief. This was no posse. There was an air of permanency about the camp, and as he glanced into the faces of the men he recognized none of them.

When he had returned the tobacco and lighted his cigarette, one of the men addressed him directly. Purdy noticed that he was a squat man, and that the legs of his leather chaps bowed prodigiously. He was thick and wide of chest, a tuft of hair protruded grotesquely from a hole in the crown of his soft-brimmed hat, and a stubby beard masked his features except for a pair of beady, deep-set eyes that stared at Purdy across the glowing brands of the dying fire. He tossed his cigarette into the coals and spoke abruptly:

"What you doin' down here? Where you headin'?"

Purdy glanced into the eyes that seemed to flash menacingly as a brand flared feebly. Then he lied: "Headin' fer south of the Mizoo. Got a job down there."

"Who with?"

"Don't know the name. It's out of Lewiston. Feller come through couple of days ago an' said they was short-handed."

"Cow outfit?"

"Yup."

"That why yer ridin' a Circle J horse? An' why you snuck into the brush back yonder an' laid low while Pete, here, rode past a-singin' 'Big Foot Sal'?" The man's eyes were still upon him, and Purdy knew that he had been caught in his lie. He glanced toward the man called Pete, and recognized the leisurely rider of the afternoon. The man who had conducted him in laughed, and Purdy was surprised that the sound held a note of genuine amusement:

"An' is that why you cussed me an' Bill when we was keepin' cases on you comin' down the coulee, an' wound up by cussin' the whole world, an' invitin' us to string you up?"

Purdy was at loss for words. He felt the blood mounting to his face, and he cleared his throat uncertainly.

"D'you know who I am?" The squat man questioned.

Purdy shook his head.

"Grimshaw's my name—Cass Grimshaw."

"Cass Grimshaw! The—" Purdy stopped abruptly in confusion.

The other laughed shortly: "Go ahead an' say it. It won't hurt my feelin's none. I'm the party—Cass Grimshaw, the horse-thief."

Purdy stared open-mouthed, for the man had uttered a name that in the cattle country was a name to conjure with. Cass Grimshaw, and the Grimshaw gang were notorious for their depredations throughout Montana and half of Wyoming. For two years they had defied the law and resisted all efforts to break them up. One or two of their number had been killed in fights with posses, but the gang remained intact, a thorn in the side of the Stock Association, and the sheriffs of many counties. Purdy continued to stare and again Grimshaw broke the silence: "Total rewards on all of us is thirty-two hundred. On me, personal, takin' Association, State, an' County, it's two thousan' even money. Figurin' on collectin'?"

Purdy gasped. What kind of a man was this? As a matter of fact, he had been thinking of those rewards. He had forgotten his own crimes and was picturing himself riding into Wolf River with a squat, bow-legged body dangling across the front of his saddle.

"Hell—no!" he managed to blurt out, "I'm—I'm a horse-thief, myself!"

CHAPTER XIV

THE INSURGENT

And so Purdy had joined the Grimshaw gang, and had prospered. Raids were planned and, under the leadership of the crafty Cass Grimshaw whole bands of horses were run across the line and disposed of, and always the gang returned to the bad lands unbroken. For nearly a year things went well, and then came a change. Where absolute unity of purpose, and unswerving loyalty to their leader were essential, dissension crept in—and Purdy was at the bottom of it.

The first intimation of discord came to Cass Grimshaw one night in the hang-out where the six sat smoking. Purdy casually mentioned that it was getting along towards shearing time and that the Wolf River bank ought to be heavily stocked with cash. The leader blew a double plume of smoke from his nostrils and abruptly asked:

"Well, what if it is?"

"Oh, nothin'," Purdy answered with a show of indifference, "only—I was just thinkin'."

"Thinkin', mebbe, to slip over an' pull a hold-up?"

"Well, they's more *dinero* in one haul there than they is in a half a dozen horse raids. Pete, here, he says he knows about handlin' soup."

"Be'n talkin' it over, eh?" there was a sneer in Grimshaw's voice. "Figure because you've helped pull off a few good horse deals, you're a regular outlaw? Want to tackle banks, an' express boxes? The horse game's got too slow, eh? Tired of follerin' my lead?"

Purdy interrupted with a gesture of impatience: "Hell—no! We thought, maybe, you'd———"

"Thought I'd turn bank robber, eh? Thought I'd quit a game where I hold all the aces, an' horn in on one where I don't hold even a deuce to draw to? Bitin' off more'n he c'n chaw has choked more'n one feller. Right here in Choteau County they's some several of 'em choked out on the end of a tight one, because they overplayed their hand. I'm a horse-thief—an' a damn good one. You fellers is good horse-thieves, too—long as you've got me to do yer thinkin'. My business is runnin' off horses an' sellin' 'em—an' I ain't holdin' up no banks fer a side line. If I ain't able to pull a bank job, how in hell be you forty-dollar-a-month cow hands goin' to do it? So don't go lettin' me hear any more of that talk." He paused and looked his hearers over with narrowed eyes: "An' if any of you feel like trying it on yer own hook—if you don't git away with it, the sheriff'll git you—an' if you do, I'll git you—so, take yer pick."

There was no more talk of bank robbery. Grimshaw planned a horse raid that was successful, but the heart of the leader was troubled and always he kept close watch on Purdy. And Purdy gave him no grounds for suspicion, nevertheless he was busy with his own thoughts, and way back in his brain was an ever present vision—the vision of a squat, bow-legged man, dangling limp across the front of his saddle.

The next friction between them came one evening when Grimshaw announced that there was a new nester over on Red Sand Creek.

"Is he—right?" asked Bill.

The leader nodded: "Yeh, it's Cinnabar Joe, that used to tend bar in the Headquarters saloon in Wolf River. Him an' that there Jennie Dodds that used to work in the hotel's got married an' filed along the crick, 'bout four mile above McWhorter's."

Purdy laughed harshly: "Cinnabar, eh? Well, when the time comes, I'll just naturally tap him fer his pile. I've got somethin' on that bird. He's mine."

Cass Grimshaw eyed Purdy coldly: "I said *he's right*. D'you git that? Meanin' that him, an' his stock, an' his wife, an' everything he's got is safe an' sound fer as this gang's concerned. He ain't in on nothin'—same as McWhorter. Only—he don't know nothin'—see? An' if any of us wants anythin' an' he's goin' to town—all right."

"But, I've be'n aimin' to make him come acrost for over a year, an'———"

"An', now you c'n fergit it! Friends is worth more'n enimies, anyways you look at it—'special,' in our business. That makes jest eighty-three ranches, big an little, that the Grimshaw gang counts friends. That's why we git away with it. They's be'n times when most any of 'em could of said the word that would of got posses on to us—an' I've made it right with all of 'em. We don't owe none of 'em nothin'. Why they's plenty of sheriffs, much as they want to git me, wouldn't bushwhack me—not fer all the reward money they is, 'cause they know they's be'n times when I could of got 'em easy, an' didn't. I don't hold it agin' 'em. My rule is never kill a posse man or a sheriff onless it gits right down to you an' him fer it. They're doin' their duty accordin' to law—an' the laws has got to be uphelt—er this would be a hell of a country to live in—fer most folks." The man ceased speaking and Purdy maintained silence. The subject of Cinnabar Joe was never mentioned again.

It was not long, however, before Purdy once more fell in the way of Grimshaw's displeasure. He came into the hang-out late one evening. The five were playing poker upon a blanket spread upon the floor between the swinging lamps, but instead of joining them, Purdy seated himself with his back to the wall, rolled a cigarette, and smoked in silence. A few deals went around, bets were made, and pots raked in. Grimshaw shuffled the deck slowly with a sidewise glance toward Purdy: "They say McWhorter's gal's to home," he announced, casually. Purdy said nothing. Grimshaw dealt, picked up his hand, examined it minutely, and tossed the cards onto the blanket. "How about it, Purdy?"

"You seem to know," answered the other, surlily.

"Yes," answered the leader, without even glancing in his direction, "I generally know what's goin' on in the bad lands, an' out of 'em fer a ways. Mighty good lookin', they say." No answer from Purdy, and a deal or two went by. Again Grimshaw tossed away his cards: "Ain't she good lookin', Purdy?"

Purdy scowled: "Well, what if she is? What you drivin' at? If you got somethin' to say, why the hell don't you say it?"

Grimshaw cleared his throat: "They ain't never no good comes from mixin' up with women—in our business. If they're good women they ain't goin' to have no truck with such as us, nohow—an' if they ain't, they'll double-cross you sure as hell sometime or other. I've read where most of the crooks an' outlaws that's caught, is caught 'cause they was stuck on some woman—either the woman double-crossed 'em, or the sheriffs or officers watches the woman, an' nabs the man when he goes to see her. 'Twas a woman got Billy the Kid caught—an' I could name some more right here in Montana."

"Guess ridin' over to git McWhorter to fetch me out some tobacco from town ain't goin' to hurt none."

"No. Only McWhorter won't be goin' to town till after lambin', an' it looks like he could remember tobacco with one tellin', instead of six in ten days."

Purdy's anger flared up: "Keep pretty close cases, don't you? Whose business is it if I was over there sixteen times? I ain't in jail, am I?"

"No—not yet, you ain't." Grimshaw's voice was low and hard. The game had ceased, and the four others were watching the two. "An', by the way things is framin', I don't expect you'll ever git there." There was something ominous in the man's words, and Purdy shifted uncomfortably.

"I didn't s'pose it mattered what a man done—between jobs," he muttered.

"It don't—so long as he leaves women alone, an' don't do nothin' that puts this gang in bad."

"I never told her nothin' about the gang. I ain't goin' to marry her."

"I know damned well you ain't. She despises you because yer a horse-thief." Grimshaw's voice suddenly dropped lower, "an', if she know'd what I know—an' what all Wolf River knows she'd know that yer horse-thievin' is the best thing about you."

Purdy laughed nastily: "Cinnabar Joe spilled a mouthful, did he? I fell down on that job—maybe I'll have better luck, next time."

Grimshaw nodded: "Mebbe you will. But, McWhorter's like Cinnabar Joe, an' all the rest that's friends of mine—he's safe, an' his stock's safe, an' By God, his *girl's* safe!" The leader paused and allowed his eyes to travel slowly over the faces of his five companions, "That goes—an' whatever else I say goes." And Purdy, watching narrowly from the corner of his eye, saw that, of the other four only Bill's eyes stood Grimshaw's gaze unflinching, and in the dim shadow his lips twisted into a sardonic grin. What Purdy did not see was that Grimshaw had seen exactly what he saw, and not only that, he had seen Purdy's smile, but with a perfectly impassive face, the leader spread his blanket and stretched himself upon the floor.

CHAPTER XV

PURDY MAKES A RIDE

Purdy's altercation with Grimshaw occurred on the night Alice Endicott and the Texan spent on the river. A raid on a bunch of Flying A mares had been planned for the following night, and early in the morning Grimshaw and the man called Bill, pulled out to the northward to locate the mares, while the other outlaws separated to skirmish the surrounding country and make sure that the coast was clear. Purdy's patrol took him into the vicinity of Red Sand Creek, and as he rode the outlaw smiled grimly: "Grimshaw's busted," he muttered, "this one job an' he's through. It'll be the Purdy gang, then—an', believe me, we ain't goin' to stop at runnin' off a few head of horses. This country's lousy with money, just layin' around for someone to reach out an' take it—an' I'm the bird c'n do it! They'll be four of us, an' that's a-plenty. We'll clean up the Wolf River bank, an' the Zortman gold stage, an' the Lewiston bank, an' a train or two—then it's me for South America—an' to hell with 'em all!" He pulled up abruptly and sat gazing down upon the buildings of McWhorter's ranch. The cabin door opened, a woman stepped out, emptied a pan of dishwater, and entered the cabin again. "So, my pretty," sneered the man, "you carry yer nose high. Yer too good for a horse-thief, eh? If you had your way McWhorter would have a posse camped on the ranch till they'd wiped us out. Guess I'll just slip down an' give you one more chanct. When Purdy's boss of the gang you won't be so damn *safe*! I ain't afraid of losin' no friends. Friends never got me nothin'. Damn the nesters! There won't be no deals when I'm runnin' the gang. It'll be every man for himself an' the devil take the hindmost. If a nester's got anything I want I'll reach out an' take it—nesters, or banks, or railroads—they all look alike to me. An' if McWhorter's huzzy don't throw in with me willin', she'll come along unwillin'. I'll break her. I'll take the snap out of them eyes, an' the sneer offen them red lips—she's the purtiest thing I've laid eyes on sence—sence Wolf River—an' I'm goin' to have her!" He swung down into the creek bed, spurred his horse into a run, and pulled up before the door with a flourish, heedless of the fact that one of his horse's hoofs ground a tiny lamb into the dirt. The door flew open and Janet McWhorter appeared. Her eyes rested for a moment on the little dead lamb, deep red mounted to her cheeks, and when she met Purdy's glance, her eyes blazed. The man laughed, and reaching into his pocket, tossing her a gold piece: "What's lambs worth?" he asked, "that had ought to pay for two or three of 'em. Why didn't the fool thing git out of the way?"

"You brute!" The girl's voice trembled with passion, and snatching the coin from the ground she hurled it into his face.

Purdy caught it in a gloved hand, and again he laughed: "Plenty more of these yeller boys where this come from," he announced flipping the shining disk into the air and catching it, "I'm goin' away fer a few days, jest you say the word, an' when I come back I'll bring you a—a diamon' ring—diamon' as big as yer thumb nail—I'll treat you swell if you'll let me."

The girl cuddled the dead lamb in her arms: "I despise you! I utterly loathe you!"

"Purtier'n ever when yer mad," he opined. "I'll make you mad sometimes jest for fun———"

"Some day I think I'll kill you," she spoke in a low, level tone and her eyes stared directly into his.

Purdy laughed loudly: "That's a good one. Here, do it now." He drew a gun from its holster and grasping it by the barrel, extended the butt toward the girl. She shrank into the doorway still clutching the lamb. The man returned the gun to its place and leaned forward in the saddle, "If you'll be reasonable—listen: You throw in with me, an' I'll quit the horse game. I've got a-plenty, an' we'll go somewhere's an' buy us an outfit—bigger outfit than this, too—an' we'll settle down. I never liked the business, nohow. I was forced into it when I was young, an' I've always wanted to get out—with a good woman to—to kind of help a feller along———"

The girl laughed harshly. "Don't try that on me—you can't get away with it. I'll tell you once and for all, I despise you. I wouldn't trust you as far as I would a rattlesnake. You are the most loathesome creature in the world. You're nothing but a low-down horse-thief, and you never will be anything but a horse-thief, till somebody shoots you—then you'll be a carrion." Her eyes were blazing again, and Purdy actually winced at her words. "If you were dying of thirst I'd pour alkali dust down your throat. Do I make myself plain? Do you understand now thoroughly just what I think of you? Because if you don't I'll go on and explain———"

"Oh, I guess I git you, all right," sneered Purdy, "from what you mentioned I gather you ain't seriously considerin' me for a husban'. Well, you've had yer say—next time it'll be my turn. Them was hard words, but some day you'll eat 'em—an' when you've got 'em et, you'll sing a different tune. Where's McWhorter?"

"Lambing camp," she answered shortly, and disappeared into the cabin slamming the door behind her.

Purdy sat for a moment staring at the door, then whirled his horse, and rode away. The girl's words had thrown him into a terrible rage: "This time a week from now, you'll wish to God you hadn't spoke 'em," he muttered, and, avoiding the lambing camp, swung toward the river. "Kill me some day, will she? She meant it, too. She's a hell-cat!"

He headed up stream, following the shore of the swollen river, muttering, cursing, plotting as he rode. And so he came to the high bluff that overlooked the mouth of a broad coulee. He paused on the rim of the bluff and stared out over the raging flood. Something directly below him caught his eye, and he glanced downward. A water-logged craft, which he recognized as Long Bill Kearney's ferry boat, lay grounded against the narrow strip of sloping beach that lay between the foot of the bluff and the river. At the same instant an object lying part way up the slope caught his eye and instinctively he jerked his horse back, swung to the ground and, crawling to the rim of the bluff looked cautiously over the edge. For a long time he stared downward at the motionless form of a woman. Her face was not visible but he could see that she wore a riding costume, and a hat of approved cowboy pattern. In vain his eyes searched the beach, and the bluff, and even the river. "Crossin' on Long Bill's ferry an' the cable busted," he muttered, "but, it's a cinch she wasn't crossin' alone—an' it's a cinch they ain't no one else around—onless they're up the coulee. Maybe whoever was along got drownded—anyhow, I'm goin' to find out—an' if she's all alone—" the man grinned—"maybe she won't be so damned uppity as McWhorter's gal." He sprang into the saddle, and, after a careful survey of the bluff and the surrounding bench, headed away from the river and came to the coulee a half-mile back from its mouth at a point where the sides allowed easy descent.

Once in the coulee Purdy again headed for the river, riding slowly, with a hand on the butt of his gun. Rounding an abrupt bend, he drew up sharply. Not fifty yards from him, a blaze-faced buckskin, saddled and bridled, with a lariat rope trailing from the saddle horn, was cropping grass. His eyes surveyed every nook and cranny of the coulee for signs of the rider, but seeing none he approached the horse which raised its head and nickered friendly greeting. He loosened his rope, but the horse made no effort to escape, and riding close the man reached down and secured the reins which he made fast to the horn of his own saddle and dismounted. "Yer a plumb gentle brute," he muttered as he coiled the trailing rope and secured it in place, "Y Bar brand—that's over somewhere across the river." Again he grinned, evilly: "Looks like they come from the other side, in which case, providin' they don't no men-folks show up in the next few minutes er so, things looks purty favourable for yours truly. With the river like it is, an' the ferry gone, they can't no one bother from the other side, an' by the time they find out she's missin', they'll think she got drownded along with the rest. Things is sure framin' my way, now," he grinned, as he swung into the saddle and, leading the buckskin, headed down the coulee with his thoughts centred on the woman who lay on the little grassed slope at its mouth. "Be hell if she was dead," he growled, "be just my luck—but if she is, I'll cache her in a mud crack somewheres an' maybe her friends from acrost will stick up a reward, an' I'll make Cinnabar Joe or Long Bill go an' collect it an' fork it over."

Proceeding cautiously, Purdy rode down the coulee, and at its mouth, dismounted and proceeded directly to the motionless form. Swiftly he stooped and lifted the hat-brim that had pushed forward over her face, then with an oath he leaped erect and jerking his gun from its holster, glared wildly about him. But save for the two horses, and a buzzard that wheeled high in the blue above, there was no living, moving thing within his range of vision, and the only sounds were the soft rattle of bit-chains as the horses thrashed lazily at pestering flies, and the sullen gurgle of the swollen river. Again he swore. His lips drew into a snarl of hate as his glance once more sought the face of the woman. In his eyes the gleam of hot desire commingled with a glitter of revenge as his thoughts flew swiftly to Wolf River—the Texan's open insult and the pilgrim's swift shot in the dark. Here, helpless, completely in his power to do with as he pleased, lay the woman who had been the unwitting cause of his undoing! Vengeance was his at last, and he licked his lips in wolfish anticipation of the wrecking of that vengeance. The thought of revenge was more sweet in that he never anticipated it. The Texan had disappeared altogether, and he had heard from Long Bill that the girl had married the pilgrim in Timber City, and that they had gone back East. But if so, what was she doing here—alone?

Swiftly the man scanned the ground for tracks, but found none. The bootless feet of the Texan had left no mark on the buffalo grass. Only one horse had gone up the coulee—and he had that horse. Whoever had been with her when the ferry cable broke, had certainly not landed with her at the mouth of the coulee. "Pilgrim's prob'ly fell out an' drownded—an' a damned good job—him an' his horse, too—prob'ly the horse got to raisin' hell an' jerked him into the river—Long Bill, too, most likely—I'll swing around by his shack an' see if they's anything there I want. But, first off, I got to take care of this here lady—silk stockin's an' all an' the quicker I git to the bad lands with her the better—it ain't no cinch that the pilgrim, or Long Bill didn't make shore somewheres else, an' if they did they'll be huntin' her." After a vain attempt to rouse the girl Purdy led the buckskin close and throwing her over the saddle bound her firmly in place with the rope. Then, leading the buckskin, he rode rapidly up the coulee and coming out on the bench headed up the river for the bad lands only a few short miles away.

CHAPTER XVI

BIRDS OF A FEATHER

Purdy did not hit for the subterranean hang-out of the gang. Instead, after entering the bad lands, he continued on up the river for a distance of several miles, being careful to select footing for the horses among the rock ridges and coulees that would leave no trail—no trail, at least, that any white man could pick up and follow. Two hours later with five or six miles of trailless bad lands behind him he dismounted and, climbing a rocky eminence, carefully surveyed his surroundings. An object upon the river caught his attention, and after a moment's scrutiny he made out a man in a skiff. The boat was close in shore and the man was evidently scanning the bank. He was still a half-mile above, and clambering hastily down, Purdy led the horses into a patch of scrub a few hundred yards from the river. Loosening the rope, he allowed the body of the unconscious girl to slip to the ground. He secured her feet and hands with a few quick turns of the rope, hobbled the horses, and hastening to the bank concealed himself in a bunch of willows. "If it's the pilgrim," he muttered, "—well, it's my turn now." He drew the gun from its holster and twirled the cylinder with his thumb. The boat approached slowly, the man resting on his oars except at such times as it was necessary to force the light craft out of the clutch of backwaters and eddies. Not until he was nearly opposite did Purdy see his face: "Long Bill," he growled, and returning the gun, wriggled from the willows and hailed him. Long Bill shot his boat into a pool of still water and surveyed the man on the bank.

"That you, Purdy?" he drawled.

"Yeh, it's me. What's yer hurry?"

Long Bill pondered. He had no wish to run ashore. In the skiff were upwards of a hundred of the dodgers hastily struck off at the Timber City printing office, which proclaimed the reward for the Texan and the thousand-dollar reward for information concerning the whereabouts of Alice Endicott. Long Bill was canny. He knew the river and he had figured pretty accurately the probable drift of the ferry boat. He expected to come upon it any time. And he wanted that reward for himself. The hundred dollars offered for the Texan did not interest him at all, but if he could find out what had become of the girl, he could, with no risk to himself, claim the larger reward. Why acquaint Purdy with the fact of the reward? Purdy had a horse and he would ride on ahead and scour the bank. Of course, later, if he should fail to find the boat, or if its occupants had escaped, he would distribute the bills. He wanted to see the Texan caught—he owed him a grudge anyway.

"I got to be goin' on down—got some business below," he answered.

"Huntin' yer ferry?"

Long Bill glared at the questioner. Purdy must have found the flat-boat or he would not have known it was missing. And if he had found the boat, he must know something of its occupants. He could not know of the reward, however, and acting on the theory that half a loaf is better than none, Long Bill reached for his oars and pulled ashore.

"That's what I'm a-huntin'," he answered, "saw any thin' of her?"

Purdy nodded: "She's layin' up agin' the mouth of a coulee, 'bout two mile or so this side of Red Sand."

Long Bill removed his hat, scratched his head, and stared out over the river. Finally he spoke: "See her clost up?"

"Yup. Went right down to her."

Another pause, and with a vast show of indifference Long Bill asked: "Anyone in her?"

"No."

"Any tracks around—like anyone had be'n there?"

"Not none except what I made myself. Look a-here, Bill; what you so damned anxious to find that ferry fer? It would cost you more to haul it back upstream than what it would to build you a new one."

"Sure they wasn't no one there? No one could of got off her an' struck back in?"

"Not onless they could of flew," opined Purdy, "how'd she come to bust loose?"

Long Bill burst into a tirade of profanity that left him breathless. "I'll tell you how come she bust loose," he roared, when he had sufficiently recovered to proceed, "that damned son of a—of a Texian stoled her—him an' the pilgrim's woman!"

"Texan!" cried Purdy, "d'ye mean Tex—Tex Benton?"

"Who the hell d'ye s'pose I mean? Who else 'ud have the guts to steal the Red Front saloon, an' another man's woman, an' my ferry all the same day—an' git away with it? Who would?" The infuriated man fairly screamed the words, "Me—or you—not by a damn sight! You claim to be a horse-thief—my Gawd, if that bird ever turned horse-thief, in a year's time horses would be extincter than what buffaloes is! They wouldn't be *none* left fer *nobudy—nowheres*!"

It was some moments before Purdy succeeded in calming the man down to where he could give a fairly lucid account of the happenings in Timber City. He listened intently to Long Bill's narrative, and at the conclusion the ferryman produced his dodgers: "An' here's the rewards—a hundred fer Tex, an' a thousan' fer information about the woman."

Purdy read the hand-bill through twice. Then for several minutes he was silent. Finally, he turned to Long Bill. "Looks like me an' you had a purty good thing—if it's worked right," he said with a wink.

"Wha' d'ye mean?" asked the other with sudden interest.

"I mean," answered Purdy, "that I've got the woman."

"Got the woman!" he repeated, "where's Tex?"

Purdy frowned: "That's what I don't know. I hope he's drownded. He never landed where she did. They wasn't no tracks. That's the only thing that's botherin' me. I don't mind sayin' it right out, I ain't got no honin' to run up agin' him—I don't want none of his meat."

"Course he's drownded, if he never landed," cried Long Bill, and taking tremendous heart from the thought, he continued: "I hain't afraid of him, nohow—never was. I hain't so damn glad he drownded neither. If I'd of run onto him, I'd of be'n a hundred dollars richer. I'd of brung him in—me!"

"You'd of played hell!" sneered Purdy, "don't try to put yer brag over on me. I know what you'd do if you so much as seen the colour of his hide—an' so do you. Le's talk sense. If that there pilgrim offered a thousan' first off—he'll pay two thousan' to git his woman back—or five thousan'."

Long Bill's eyes glittered with greed: "Sure he will! Five thousan'—two thousan' five hundred apiece——"

Purdy fixed him with a chilling stare: "They wasn't nothin' mentioned about no even split," he reminded, "who's got the woman, you or me?"

Long Bill glared angrily: "You didn't know nothin' about the reward till I come along. An' who's got to do the dickerin'? You don't dast to show up nowheres. You'd git nabbed. They's a reward out fer you."

Purdy shrugged: "When we git the five thousan', you git five hundred. Take it or leave it. They's others can do the dickerin'."

Long Bill growled and whined, but in the end he agreed, and Purdy continued: "You listen to me. We don't want no mistakes about this here. I'll write a note to the pilgrim an' sign Tex's name to it, demandin' five thousan' fer the return of the woman. You take the note to him, an' tell him Tex is hidin' out in the bad lands, an' they ain't a show in the world to git the woman without he pays, because Tex will kill her sure as hell if he goes to gittin' any posses out. Then you fetch him over here—this place is good as any—today a week, an' we'll give him his woman."

"What if he won't come? What if he thinks we're double-crossin' him?"

Purdy shrugged: "If he wants his woman bad enough, he'll come. It's his only chanct. An' here's another thing: Before you hit back acrost the river, you spread them bills around all the ranches an' on all the trails around here. They ain't no one else can horn in on the big reward 'cause I've got the woman, an' if the Texan should of got to shore, it's just as well to have everyone huntin' him."

"I ain't got no horse," objected the ferryman.

"Drift down the river till you come to a coulee with two rock pinnacles on the left hand side. Go up it till you come to a brush corral, there's two horses in there, an' a saddle an' bridle is cached in a mud crack on the west side. Saddle up one of 'em, an' be sure you put him back or Cass Grimshaw'll make coyote bait out of you."

As Purdy watched Long Bill disappear down the river, he rolled a cigarette: "If I c'n double-cross the pilgrim, I will," he muttered, "if I can't, back she goes to him. Five thousan' is a higher price than I'll pay fer luxeries like women. Anyhow there's McWhorter's gal left fer that. An' seein' there ain't no one else in on this but me, I'll just duck the hang-out, an' take her over to Cinnabar Joe's. Him an' his woman'll keep her safe—or he'll do time. Them's the only kind of friends that's worth a damn—the ones you've got somethin' on." And having thus unburdened himself he proceeded leisurely toward the scrub.

Alice Endicott returned slowly to consciousness. Her first sensation was one of drowsy well-being. For some minutes she lay while her brain groped in a vague, listless way to find itself. She and Win were going West—there was a ranch for sale—and ... she suddenly realized that she was uncomfortable. Her shoulders and hips ached. Where was she? She felt cold. She tried to move and the effort caused her pain. She heard a sound nearby and opened her eyes. She closed them and opened them again. She was lying upon the ground among trees and two horses stood a short distance away. The horses were saddled. She tried to raise a hand to her eyes and failed. Something was wrong. The recollections of the night burst upon her with the suddenness of a blow. The river—the lightning and drenching rain, the frantic bailing of the boat, the leap into the water with the Texan! Where was he now? She tried to sit up—and realized that her hands and feet were tied! Frantically she struggled to free her hands. Who had tied her? And why? The buckskin horse she recognized as the one she had ridden the night before. The Y Bar brand showed plainly upon his flank. But, where was she? And why was she tied? Over and over the two questions repeated themselves in her brain. She struggled into a sitting posture and began to work at the knots. The tying had been hurriedly accomplished, and with the aid of a projecting limb stub the knot that secured her wrists was loosened and she freed her hands. It was but the work of a moment to loosen the hitch about her ankles and she assayed to rise. She sank back with a moan of pain. Every muscle in her body ached and she lay still while the blood with an exquisite torture of prickling and tingling, began to circulate her numbed veins. Again she struggled to her feet and, supporting herself against a tree, stared wildly about her. Nobody was in sight. Through the trees she caught the sparkle of water.

"The river!" she breathed. A wild idea flashed into her brain. If she could find a boat she could elude the horseman who had made her a prisoner. The numbness was gone from her limbs. She took a step and another, steadying herself by means of the tree-trunks. Finding that she could walk unaided she crossed an open space, paused and glanced out over the flood with its rushing burden of drift. The thought terrified her—of being out there alone in a boat. Then came the thought of her unknown captor. Who was he? When would he return? And with the thought the terror of the water sank into insignificance beside the terror of the land. Reaching the edge of the bank she peered cautiously over. There, just at the end of a clump of willows, a boat floated lazily at the end of its painter. She could see the oars in their locks, and a man's coat upon the back seat. She was about to descend the bank when the sound of voices sent her crouching behind a bush. Through the willows she could make out the forms of two men. Even as she looked one of the men rose and made his way toward the boat. At the edge of the willows he turned to speak to the other and the terrified girl gazed into the face of Long Bill Kearney! The other she could not see, but that he was her captor she had no doubt. She felt suddenly weak and sick with horror. Whoever the other was he was a confederate of Long Bill's and she knew how Long Bill must hate her on account of the treatment he had received a year ago at the hands of Win and the Texan. In all probability they had even now murdered the Texan—come upon him weak and exhausted from his struggle with the river and murdered him in cold blood and taken her prisoner.

Stifling a sob, she turned to fly. Her trembling knees would scarce support her weight as she crossed the open space. Once in the timber she staggered toward the horses. Grasping the reins of the buckskin, she tried to lead him into the open, but he followed slowly with a curious shuffle. Her eyes flew to the hobbles, and kneeling swiftly she pulled at the thick straps that encircled his ankles. Her trembling fingers fumbled at the heavy buckles. Jerking frantically at the strap, she pushed and pulled in an endeavour to release the tongue from the hole. Minutes seemed like hours as she worked. At length she succeeded in loosening a strap and set to work on the other. Fortunately the horse was thoroughly gentle, "woman broke," as Colston had said, and he stood motionless while she tugged and jerked at his ankles. After an interminable time the other strap yielded and, throwing the hobbles aside, Alice sprang erect, grasped the reins and started for the open, her throbbing brain obsessed by one idea, to ride, ride, ride! Stumbling, tripping in her frantic haste she made her way through the scrub, the buckskin following close upon her heels. Only a few yards more and the open country stretched before her, ridge after rocky ridge as far as the eye could see. Redoubling her effort, she pushed on, tripped upon a fallen tree limb and crashed heavily to her knees. She struggled to her feet and as her eyes sought the open, stood rooted to the spot while the blood froze in her veins. Directly before her, legs wide apart, hands on hips, an evil grin on his lips, eyes leering into her own, stood Jack Purdy!

CHAPTER XVII

IN THE SCRUB

It seemed hours she stood thus, staring into those black, leering eyes. Her damp garments struck a deadly chill to her very bones. Her knees trembled so that she shook visibly, as her thoughts flashed back to that night on the rim of the bench when this man had reached suddenly out and dragged her from her horse. Her plight would have been bad enough had she fallen into the hands of Long Bill Kearney—but Purdy!

At length the man spoke: "What's yer hurry? You sure wouldn't pull out an' leave, after me savin' you from the river, would you?"

"The river," she repeated, dully, and her own voice sounded strange—like a voice she had never heard. "Where—where's Tex?" The question was not addressed to Purdy, it was merely the groping effort of a numbed brain trying to piece together its sequence of events. She did not know she had asked it. His answer brought her keenly alive to the present. He laughed, harshly:

"He's drownded—fell out of the ferry, back there in the river—him an' his horse both."

Alice did not know that the man was eyeing her keenly to detect refutation by word or look. She did not know that he was lying. The events of the night, to the moment of her plunge with the Texan into the river at the end of the lariat line, stood out in her brain with vivid distinctness. Purdy believed Tex to have drowned. She did not believe it, for she knew that if he had not reached shore, she could not possibly have reached shore. Her brain functioned rapidly. If Tex had survived he would surely come to her rescue. And, if Purdy believed him dead so much the better. She raised her hand and passed it across her eyes:

"I remember," she said, slowly.

Again the man laughed: "Oh, you do, eh? I was only guessin'! I know'd if I asked you you'd lie about it—but I know now! An' it makes things a damn sight easier fer me."

"Stand aside and let me pass!" cried the girl, "I didn't say he drowned. He'll be along here any minute—and my husband will be here, too!"

"Oh-ho, my thousan' dollar beauty!" sneered the man, "yer bluff comes in too late! If you'd of got it in first off, as soon as I said he was drownded, I might of b'lieved you—but there's nothin' doin' now. You can't scare me with a ghost—an' as fer yer husband—he'd ought to got me when he had the chanct." He advanced toward her, and the girl shrank back against her horse's shoulder. "Surely, you ain't afraid of me," he taunted, "why, it ain't only a year back sence you went ridin' with me. Remember—Wolf River, in the moonlight on the rim of the bench, an' the little lights a-twinklin' down in the valley? An' you remember how we was interrupted then—the sound of hoofs thumpin' the trail—the pilgrim come out of the dark an' shot 'fore I even know'd he had a gun. But it's different this time. Here in the bad lands there ain't no one to butt in. I've got you all to myself here. I love you now, same as I did then—only a whole heap more. Women are scarce down here. You figgered you wanted a change of men, or you wouldn't of be'n runnin' off with Tex. Well, you've got it—only you've got me instead of him. We won't hit it off so bad when you git used to my ways."

Every particle of blood receded from the girl's face and as she cowered against her horse, her eyes widened with horror. Her lips moved stiffly: "You—*you dog*!" she muttered hoarsely.

Purdy grinned: "Dog, eh? You ain't helpin' yer case none by callin' me names. Ain't you got no thankfulness in you? Here I pulled you out of the drink where you'd washed ashore—an' take you along safe an' sound—an' yer callin' me a dog!"

"I would rather be dead, a thousand times, than to be here this minute—with you!"

"Well, you ain't dead—an' you be here. An' if you don't go the limit with me, yer goin' to wish a thousan' times more that you was a damn sight deader than you ever will be! You know what I mean! An' you ain't a damn bit better than what I be, either! If you was you wouldn't of left yer man an' pulled out with Tex. I've got yer number, so you might's well throw in with me an' save yerself a whole lot of hell. I've got more'n what Tex has, anyhow—an' there's plenty more where I git mine. You might's well know it now, as later—I'm an outlaw! I was outlawed on account of you—an' it ain't no more'n right you should share it with me. I've worked on horses up to now, but I'm a-goin' to branch out! Banks an' railroad trains looks better to me! The name of Purdy's goin' to be a big name in these parts—an' then all to onct it won't be heard no more—an' you an' me'll be down in South America rollin' 'em high!" The man's voice had raised with his boasting, and as he finished, he pounded his chest with his fist.

During his speech the girl's heart shrivelled within her until it touched the lowest depths of terror and despair. She cowered against the horse, pressing her knuckles into her lips till the blood came—and, suddenly, as he finished, she felt an insane desire to laugh. And she did laugh, loudly and unnaturally—laughed and pointed a shaking forefinger into the man's face:

"You fool!" she screamed, hysterically, "*you fool!* I'm not afraid of you! You're not real! You can't be real! You remind me of comic opera!"

For a moment the man stared in surprise, and then, with an oath he grasped her roughly by the arm: "What are you laughin' at? I'm a fool, be I? I ain't real? When I git through with you, you'll think I'm real enough! An' I won't put you in mind of no comical opry neither! But, first, I'm goin' to collect that reward."

"Reward?"

"Yes—reward," snarled the man, releasing her arm with a violent push that whirled her half way around. Fumbling in his pocket he produced one of the hand-bills that Long Bill had given him. "There it is—the reward yer man stuck up for you—though what in hell he wants of you now is more'n I know. It only says a thousan' there—but I raised it to five. I'll jest hold you safe till I git my mitts on that five thousan', an' then——"

"You'll hold me safe till you get the money?" asked the girl, a gleam of hope lighting her eyes, "and then you'll turn me over to my husband? Is that all you want—the money—five thousand dollars?"

The man laughed and again his eyes leered evilly into hers: "You know what I want," he sneered, "an' what I want, I'll git—an' I'll git the money, too! Things has broke my way at last! Tex is dead. When Long Bill comes along to collect his share of the *dinero* he'll foller Tex. An' when the pilgrim rides into the bad lands with the money—well, it'll be my turn, then. You'll be a widder, an' won't have only one man after all—an' that man'll be me! An' they won't be no one a-huntin' you, neither. They'll all think you drownded along with Tex."

"You devil! You fiend!" cried the girl, "surely if there's a God in heaven, He will not let you live to do these things!"

"If there is, or if there ain't, it'll be the same," defied the man, "I ain't afraid of Him! He won't lay no hand on *me*!" More terrible even than his threats against her—more terrible than the open boast that he would murder her husband, sounded the blasphemy of the man's words. She felt suddenly weak and sick. Her knees swayed under her, and she sank unconscious at the feet of her horse.

Staring down at her, Purdy laughed aloud, and securing his own horse and the rope, lifted her into her saddle and bound her as before. Leading the two animals, he made his way into the open where he mounted and striking out at a right angle to his former course, headed for Cinnabar Joe's.

As he disappeared around a bend in a coulee, a man who had been intently watching all that transpired, rose to his feet. He was a squat man, with ludicrously bowed legs. A tuft of hair protruded from a hole in the crown of his hat. "I've seen considerable fools in my life, but when a man gits to where he thinks he kin put over a whizzer on God A'mighty an' git away with it—it's pretty close to cashin' in time fer him." He stared for a moment at his six-gun before he returned it to its holster. "There's them that's got a better right to him than me," he muttered, "but at that, my finger was jest a-twitcherin' on the trigger."

CHAPTER XVIII

THE TEXAN TAKES THE TRAIL

At the mouth of the coulee, Janet McWhorter stared in astonishment as the Texan swung into the saddle and headed the big blue roan up the ravine at a run. A moment later the bay mare was following, the girl plying quirt and spur in an endeavour to keep the flying horseman in sight. The roan's pace slackened, and the bay mare closed up the distance. The girl could see that the man was leaning far over studying the ground as he rode. Suddenly, without a moment's hesitation he turned into a side coulee, gained the bench, and headed straight for the bad lands. The pace was slower, now. The Texan rode with his eyes glued to the ground. She drew up beside him and, as she expected, found that he was following the trail of two horses. The trail was easily followed in the mud of the recent rains, and they made good time, dipping into coulees, scrambling out, crossing ridges. Purdy had evidently wasted no time in picking his trail, but had taken the country as it came, his one idea evidently had been to gain the bad lands that loomed in the near distance.

"What will he do when he gets there?" wondered the girl, as she glanced into the set face of the man who rode with his eyes on the tracks in the mud, "he can't follow him in. There won't be any trail."

True to her prediction, the Texan drew up at the edge of a black ridge that cut diagonally into the treeless, soilless waste. Since he had uttered Purdy's name at the mouth of the coulee, he had spoken no word, and now, as he faced her, the girl saw that his face looked tense and drawn. "You've got to go back," he said looking straight into her eyes, "it's a blind trail from here, an' God knows where it will lead to."

"But—you—where are you going?"

"To find Purdy." There was a steely glint in the man's eyes, and his voice grated harshly.

"But you can't find him!" she cried. "He knows the bad lands. Purdy's a horse-thief, and if you did find him there would be others. He's one of a gang, and—they'll kill you!"

The Texan nodded: "Maybe—an' then, again, maybe they won't. There's two sides to this killin' game."

"But you wouldn't have a chance."

"As long as I've got a gun, I've got a chance—an' a good one."

The spirit of perversity that had prompted her to insist upon riding the blue roan, asserted itself, "I'm going with you," she announced. "I've got a gun, and I can shoot."

"You're goin' home." The Texan spoke quietly, yet with an air of finality that brooked no argument. The hot blood mounted to the girl's face, and her eyes flashed. Her lips opened to frame an angry retort but the words were never spoken, for the Texan leaned suddenly toward her and his gauntleted hand rested lightly on her arm, "For God's sake, don't hinder—*help*!" There was no trace of harshness in the voice—only intense appeal. She glanced into his eyes, and in their depths read misery, pain, worry—the very soul of him was wrung with torture. He was not commanding now. This strong, masterful man was imploring help. A lump rose in her throat. Her eyes dropped before his. She swallowed hard, and nodded: "All right—only—promise me—if you don't find him, you'll return to the ranch tonight. You've got to eat, and Blue has got to eat. I'll have a pack ready for you to start again early in the morning."

"I promise," he said, simply. His gloved hand slipped from her sleeve and closed about her own. Once more their eyes met, once more the girl felt the hot blood mount to her cheeks, and once more her glance fell before his. And then—he was gone and she was alone upon the edge of the bad lands, listening to catch the diminishing sound of his horse's hoofs on the floor of the black coulee.

The sound died away. Minutes passed as she sat staring out over the bad lands. There was a strange ache at her throat, but in her heart welled a great gladness. What was it she had read in his eyes—during the moment of that last glance? The pain, and the worry, and the misery were still there but something else was there also—something that leaped from his heart straight to hers; something held in restraint that burst through the restraint, overrode the pain and the worry and the misery, and for a brief instant blazed with an intensity that seemed to devour her very soul. Slowly she raised the hand that had returned the firm, gentle pressure of his clasp and drew the back of it across her cheek, then with a laugh that began happily and ended in a choking sob, she turned the mare toward home.

She rode slowly, her thoughts centred upon the Texan. She had liked him from the moment of their first meeting. His eagerness to return to the aid of his friend, his complete mastery of Blue, his unhesitating plunge into the bad lands to fight against odds, all pointed to him as a man among men. "And, aside from all that," she murmured, as she reached to smooth the bay mare's mane, "There's something about him—so wholesome—so clean—" Her words trailed into silence, and as her thoughts followed him into the trailless maze of the bad lands, her fists clenched tight, "Oh, I hope he won't find Purdy. They'll kill him."

She turned the mare into the corral, and entering the cabin, prepared her solitary luncheon, and as she ate it her thoughts retraced the events of the morning. She remembered how he had looked when she had mentioned Purdy's name—the horrified tone with which he had repeated the name—and how he had recoiled from it as though from a blow. "What does he know of Purdy?" she asked herself, "and why should the fact that Purdy had ridden away with his friend have affected him so? Purdy wouldn't kill his friend—there had been no sign of a struggle there on the river bank. If the man went with Purdy, he went of his own free will—even a horse-thief couldn't steal a full grown cowpuncher without a struggle." She gave it up, and busied herself with the preparation of a pack of food for the morrow. "It seems as though I had known him for years," she murmured, "and I never laid eyes on him till this morning. But—Mr. Colston would never have made him foreman, if he wasn't all right. Anyway, anybody with half sense can see that by just looking into his eyes, and he's really handsome, too—I'll never forget how he looked when I first saw him—standing there beside the haystack with his hat in his hand and his bandaged head—" she paused and frowned at the thought of that bandage, "I'll dress his wound tonight," she murmured "but—I wonder."

From time to time during the afternoon, she stepped to the door and glanced anxiously up and down the creek. At last, just at sundown, she saw a rider pause before the gate of the corral. She flew to the door, and drew back hurriedly: "It's that horrid Long Bill Kearney," she muttered, in disappointment, "disreputable old coot! He ought to be in jail along with other denizens of the bad lands. Dad sure picked a fine bunch of neighbours—all except the Cinnabar Joes—and they say he used to be a bartender—but he's a nice man—I like him."

Long Bill rode on, and glancing out the window Janet saw a fragment of paper flapping in the wind. She hurried to the corral and removing the paper that had been secured to a post by means of a sliver of wood, read it hurriedly. The blood receded slowly from her face, and a great weight seemed pressing upon her heart. She reread the paper carefully word for word. This Texan, then, was a man with a price on his head. He was no better than Purdy, and Long Bill, and all the others. And now she knew why there was tatting on the bandage! She turned indifferently at a sound from the direction of the barn, and hurriedly thrust the paper into the bosom of her grey flannel shirt as McWhorter appeared around the corner of the haystack.

Once into the bad lands the Texan slowed the blue roan to a walk, and riding in long sweeping semicircles, methodically searched for Purdy's trail. With set face and narrowed eyes the man studied every foot of the ground, at times throwing himself from the saddle for closer scrutiny of some obscure mark or misplaced stone. So great was his anxiety to overtake the pair that his slow pace became a veritable torture. And at times his struggle to keep from putting spurs to his horse and dashing wildly on, amounted almost to physical violence.

Bitterly he blamed himself for Alice Endicott's plight. He raved and cursed like a madman, and for long periods was silent, his eyes hot and burning with the intensity of his hate for Purdy. Gradually the hopelessness of picking up the trail among the rocks and disintegrated lava, forced itself upon him. More than once in utter despair and misery of soul, he drew the six-gun from its holster and gazed long and hungrily at its blue-black barrel. One shot, and—oblivion. His was the blame. He sought no excuse—no palliation of responsibility. This woman had trusted him—had risked life and happiness to protect him from the bullets of the mob—and he had failed her—had abandoned her to a fate worse—a thousand times worse than death. Sweat stood upon his forehead in cold beads as he thought of her completely in the power of Purdy. He could never face Win—worst of all he could never face himself. Night and day as long as he should live the torture would be upon him. There could be but one end—madness—unless, he glanced again at the long blue barrel of his Colt. With an oath he jammed it into its holster. The coward's way out! The girl still lived. Purdy still lives—and while Purdy lives his work is cut out for him. Later—perhaps—but, first he must find Purdy. On and on he rode pausing now and then to scan the horizon and the ridges and coulees between, for sight of some living, moving thing. But always it was the same—silence—the hot dead silence of the bad lands. With the passing of the hours the torture became less acute. The bitter self-recrimination ceased, and the chaos of emotion within his brain shaped and crystallized into a single overmastering purpose. He would find Purdy. He would kill him. Nothing else mattered. A day—a year—ten years—it did not matter. He would find Purdy and kill him. He would not kill him quickly. Purdy must have time to think—plenty of time to think. The man even smiled grimly as he devised and discarded various plans. "They're all too easy—too gentle. I'll leave it to Old Bat—he's Injun—he'll know. An' if Bat was here he'd pick up the trail." A wild idea of crossing the river and fetching Bat flashed into his mind, but he banished it. "Bat'll come," he muttered, with conviction. "He's found out before this that I've gone an' he'll come."

As the sun sank below the horizon, the Texan turned his horse toward McWhorter's. He paused on a rocky spur for one last look over the bad lands, and raising his gauntleted fist, he shook it in the face of the solitude: "I'll get you! Damn you! *Damn you!*"

As he whirled his horse and headed him out into the open bench, a squat, bow-legged man peered out from behind a rock, not fifty feet from where the Texan had sat his horse. A tuft of hair protruded from a hole in the crown of his battered hat as he fingered his stubby beard: "Pretty damn lively for a corpse," grinned the squat man, "an' he *will* git him, too. An' if that there gal wasn't safe at Cinnabar Joe's, I'd see that he got him tonight. It looks from here as if God A'mighty's gittin' ready to call Purdy's bluff."

CHAPTER XIX

AT McWHORTER'S RANCH

Colin McWhorter was a man of long silences. A big framed, black-bearded giant of a man, he commanded the respect of all who knew him, and the friendship of few. His ranch, his sheep, his daughter were things that concerned him—the rest of the world was for others. Twice each year, on the twentieth of June and the third of December, he locked himself in his room and drank himself very drunk. At all other times he was very sober. No one, not even Janet, knew the significance of those dates. All the girl knew was that with deadly certainty when the day arrived her father would be locked in his room, and that on the third day thereafter he would unlock the door and come out of the room, shaken in nerve and body, dispose of an armful of empty bottles, resume his daily routine, and never by word or look would he refer to the matter.

These semi-annual sprees had been among the girl's earliest recollections. They had come as regularly and as certainly as the passing of the seasons, and she had come to accept them as a matter of course. Janet McWhorter stood in no fear of her father, yet never had she brought herself to venture one word of remonstrance, nor offer one word of sympathy. His neighbours accepted the fact as they accepted McWhorter—with respect. If they wondered, they continued to wonder, for so far as anyone knew nobody had ever had the temerity to seek knowledge at its fountain head.

McWhorter's habit of silence was not engendered by any feeling of aloofness—cowpunchers, sheep-men, horse-thieves, or nesters—all were welcome at his cabin, and while they talked, McWhorter listened—listened and smoked his black pipe. With Janet he was as sparing of words as with others. Father and daughter understood each other perfectly—loved each other with a strange undemonstrative love that was as unfaltering as the enduring hills.

The moment McWhorter came upon the girl at the gate of the corral he sensed that something was wrong. She had greeted him as usual but as he watched her walk to the cabin, he noted an unwonted weariness in her steps, and a slight drooping of her square shoulders. Unsaddling his horse, he turned him into the corral with the bay mare. He noted the absence of the big roan. "Been tryin' to ride Blue, an' he got away from her," he thought; "weel, she'll tell me aboot it, if so."

While Janet placed supper on the table her father washed noisily at the bench beside the door, then entered, and took his place at the table. The meal progressed in silence, and in silence McWhorter, as was his custom, helped the girl wash and dry the dishes and put them away on their shelves. This done, he filled his black pipe and seated himself in the chair. In another chair drawn close beside the big lamp, Janet pretended to read a magazine, while at every muffled night sound, her eyes flew to the window.

"Wheer's Blue," asked McWhorter, as he knocked the ashes from his pipe and refilled it.

"I loaned him to a man who came here on foot."

"From the bad lands?"

"No. From the river. He's Mr. Colston's range foreman and he and—and somebody else were crossing the river on Long Bill's ferry and the cable broke, and the boat came ashore above here."

"An' the ither—did the ither come?"

"No. That's why he borrowed Blue—to hunt for the other."

"An' ye rode wi' 'um? I see the mare's be'n rode."

Janet nodded: "Yes, I rode with him as far as the bad lands, and then—he sent me back."

McWhorter puffed for some minutes in silence: "Think you he will come here the night?"

"Yes—unless something happens."

"An' that's what's worrin' ye—that something might happen him—oot theer? What wad ye think could happen?"

"Why—why—lots of things could happen," she glanced at her father, wondering at his unwonted loquacity.

The man caught the look: "Ye'll be thinkin' I'll be talkin' o'er much," he said, "but ye've found out befoor this, when theer's words to be said I can say 'em." The man's voice suddenly softened: "Come, lass, 'tis ye're own happiness I'm thinkin' of—ye've na one else. Is he some braw young blade that rode that de'el of a Blue wi'oot half tryin'? An' did he speak ye fair? An' is he gude to look on—a man to tak' the ee o' the weemin'? Is ut so?" The girl stood at the window peering out into the darkness, and receiving no answer, McWhorter continued: "If that's the way of ut, tak' ye heed. I know the breed o' common cowpunchers—they're a braw lot, an' they've takin' ways—but in theer hearts they're triflin' gude-for-naughts, wi' na regard for God, mon, nor the de'el."

"He's not a common cowpuncher!" defended the girl hotly, she had turned from the window and stood facing the stern faced Scotchman with flushed cheeks. Then the words of the hand-bill seemed to burn into her brain. "He's—he's—if he were a common cowpuncher Mr. Colston would never have made him foreman," she concluded lamely.

McWhorter nodded gravely: "Aye, lass—but, when all is said an' done, what Colston wants—what he hires an' pays for, is cowpunchin'—the work o' the head an' hands. Gin an mon does his work, Colston wadna gi' a fiddle bow for what's i' the heart o' him. But, wi' a lass an' a mon—'tis different. 'Tis then if the heart is clean, it little matters that he whirls his loop fair, or sits his leather like a plough-boy."

"What's this nonsense," cried the girl, angrily, "—this talk about choosing a man? I never saw him till today! I hate men!"

McWhorter finished his pipe, returned it to his pocket and stepping into his own room reappeared a moment later with a pair of heavy blankets which he laid on the table. "I'm goin' to bed, for I must be early to the lambin' camp. I'm thinkin' the young mon will not return the night—but if he does, here's blankets." He stood for a moment looking down at the girl with as near an expression of tenderness as the stern eyes allowed: "My little lass," he murmured, as though speaking to himself, "I ha' made ye angry wi' my chatter—an' I am glad. The anger will pass—an' 'twill set ye thinkin'—that, an' what's here on the paper." Reaching into his pocket he drew out a hand-bill and tossed it upon the blankets. "'Tis na news to ye, bein' I mistrust, the same as the one ye concealed in ye're bosom by the corral gate—'twas seein' that loosed my tongue. For, I love ye, lass—an' 'twad be sair hard to see ye spend ye're life repentin' the mistake of a moment. A mon 'twad steal anither's wife, wad scarce hold high his ain. Gude night." McWhorter turned abruptly, and passing into his own room, shut the door.

Standing beside the table, Janet watched the door close behind her father. The anger was gone from her heart, as McWhorter had said it would go, and in its place was a wild desire to throw herself into his arms as she used to do long, long ago—to sob her heart out against his big breast, and to feel his big hand awkwardly stroking her hair, as he muttered over and over again: "Theer, theer wee lassie, theer, theer"—soothing words—those, that had eased her baby hurts and her childish heartaches—she remembered how she used to press her little ear close against his coarse shirt to hear the words rumble deep down in the great chest. He had been a good father to his motherless little girl—had Colin McWhorter.

The girl turned impulsively toward the closed door, hot tears brimming her eyes. One step, and she stopped tense and listening. Yes, there it was again—the sound of horse's hoofs. Dashing the tears from her eyes she flung open the outer door and stood framed in the oblong of yellow lamplight. Whoever it was had not stopped at the corral, but was riding on toward the cabin. A figure loomed suddenly out of the dark and the Texan drew up before the door.

"You here alone?" he inquired, stooping slightly to peer past her into the cabin, "'cause if you are, I'll go on to the lambin' camp."

"No, Dad's here," she answered, "he's gone to bed."

The man dismounted. "Got any oats?" he asked, as he turned toward the corral. "Blue's a good horse, an' I'd like him to have more'n just hay. I may ride him hard, tomorrow."

"Yes—wait." The girl turned back into the cabin and came out with a lighted lantern. "I'll go with you. They're in the stable."

Side by side they walked to the corral, where she held the lantern while the Texan stripped off the saddle. "Got a halter? I ain't goin' to turn him in with the others. They'd nose him out of his oats, or else worry him so he couldn't eat comfortable."

"Blue's never been in the stable—and he's never eaten oats. He don't know what they are."

"It's time he learnt, then," he smiled, "but, I don't reckon he'll kick up any fuss. A horse will do anything you want him to, once you get him mastered."

"Like women, aren't they?" the girl asked maliciously, as she handed him the halter.

The Texan adjusted the halter, deftly slipped the bridle from beneath it, and glanced quizzically into her face: "Think so?" he countered, "reckon I never run across any that was mastered." At the door of the stable the horse paused, sniffed suspiciously, and pulled back on the halter rope. "Just step away with the lantern so he can't see what's ahead of him, an' he'll come—won't you, Blue?"

"They wouldn't any of them come if they could see what's ahead, would they?"

The Texan peered into the girl's face but it was deep in the shadows, "Maybe not," he agreed, "I expect it's a good thing for all of us that we can't see—what's ahead." The man abruptly transferred his attention to the horse; gently slapping his neck and pulling playfully at his twitching ears. His voice dropped into a soothing monotone: "Come on, you old Blue, you. You old fraud, tryin' to make out like you're afraid. Come on—take a chance. There's oats, an' hay, an' beddin' a foot thick in there. An' a good stall to stand in instead of millin' around a corral all night." The rope slackened, and securing a firm grip on the halter, the Texan edged slowly toward the door, the horse following with nervous, mincing steps, and nostrils aquiver. From her place beside the corral, the girl watched in astonishment as man and horse passed from sight. From the black interior of the stable the voice of the Texan sounded its monotonous drone, and presently the man himself appeared and taking the lantern returned to attend to the horse. Alone in the darkness, Janet wondered. She knew the big blue roan, and she had expected a fight. A few minutes later the man reappeared, chuckling: "He's learnt what oats are," he said, "ate 'em out of my hand, first. Now he's goin' after 'em like he'd tear the bottom out of the feed box. I wonder if your Dad would sell Blue? I'll buy him, an' gentle him, an' then——"

"And then—what?" asked the girl after a moment of silence. She received no answer, and with a trace of impatience she repeated the question. "What would you do then?"

"Why—then," answered the man, abstractedly, "I don't know. I was just thinkin' maybe it ain't such a good thing after all we can't see farther ahead."

"Did you find your friend?" Janet asked abruptly, as they walked toward the house.

"No." In spite of herself, the dead tonelessness of the man's voice aroused her to sudden pity. She remembered the pain and the misery in his eyes. Perhaps after all, he loved this woman—loved her honestly—yet, how could he love honestly another man's wife? Her lips tightened, as she led the way into the house, and without a word, busied herself at the stove.

Hat in hand, the Texan stood beside the table, and as his glance strayed from the girl, it fell upon a small square of paper upon a fold of a blanket. Mechanically he glanced at the printed lines, and at the first word, snatched the paper from the table and held it to the light.

The girl turned at the sound: "Oh!" she cried, and stepped swiftly forward as if to seize it from his hand. Her face was flaming red: "Dad left it there—and then—you came—and I—I—forgot it."

The man read the last word and carefully returned the paper to the table. "I didn't aim to read your papers," he apologized, "but I couldn't help seein' my own name—an' hers—an' I thought I had the right—didn't I have the right?"

"Yes," answered the girl, "of course you had the right. Only I—we—didn't leave it there on purpose. It——"

"It don't make any difference how it come to be there," he said dully, and as he passed his hand heavily across his brow, she saw that his fingers fumbled for a moment on the bandage. "The news got around right quick. It was only last night."

"Long Bill Kearney stuck one on the corral post, and he left some at the lambing camp."

"Long Bill, eh?" The man repeated the name mechanically, with his eyes on the square of paper, while the girl pushed the blankets back and placed dishes upon the table.

"You must eat, now," she reminded him, as she filled his plate and poured a cup of steaming coffee.

The Texan drew up a chair and ate in silence. When he had finished he rolled a cigarette: "One hundred dollars," he said, as though speaking to himself, "that's a right pickyune reward to offer for a full-grown man. Why, there's over a thousand for Cass Grimshaw."

"Cass Grimshaw is a horse-thief. Apparently, horses are held in higher regard than mere wives."

Tex disregarded the withering sarcasm. He answered, evenly, "Looks that way. I suppose they figure a man could steal more of 'em."

"And now that Purdy has stolen her from you, will you continue the search, or look around for another. Surely, wives are cheap—another hundred dollars oughtn't to make any difference."

"No. Another hundred won't make any difference. Win Endicott was a fool to post that reward. It makes things look bad——"

"Look bad!" cried the girl, angrily. "Could it look any worse than it is?"

"No," agreed the Texan, "not with Purdy into it, it couldn't."

"Because, now—he'll probably claim the reward he and Long Bill—and you will have had your trouble for your pains."

"Claim the reward!" exclaimed the Texan. To the girl's surprise he seemed to grasp at the thought as a drowning man would grasp at a straw. There was a new light in his eyes and the words seemed to hold a ray of hope. "Do you suppose he would? Would he hold her safe for a thousand dollars? Prob'ly he'll try to get more!" The man talked rapidly in short jerky sentences. "How'd Long Bill cross the river? Have those two got together? Does Purdy know about the reward?"

"Long Bill was riding——"

"Purdy's horse?"

"Not the one Purdy rode today—but, I think I've seen Purdy ride that horse."

"But, why did they go on spreadin' these bills? Why didn't they keep it to themselves?" The girl shook her head, and after a few moments of silence, during which his fists opened and closed as if striving to grasp at the truth, the Texan spoke: "Maybe if they had the girl hid away safe, they wanted folks to be on the lookout for me." He pushed back his chair abruptly and as he stood up the girl indicated the blankets, and the package of food.

"Here are blankets," she said, "and there is grub for tomorrow. There is a bunk in the loft——"

The Texan gathered the things into his arms: "Never mind the bunk," he said, "I'll sleep in the hay. I'll be wanting an early start. You've helped, girl," he said looking straight into her eyes, "you've guessed wrong—but you've helped—maybe more than you know. I reckon Win wasn't such a fool with his reward after all," and before she could frame a reply, the man had opened the door and disappeared into the night.

CHAPTER XX

AT CINNABAR JOE'S

Along toward the middle of the afternoon Cinnabar Joe laid down his hammer and smilingly accepted the sandwich his wife held out to him. "You sure don't figure on starvin' me none, Jennie," he grinned as he bit generously into the thick morsel.

"Ranchin's some different from bartendin'—an' you're workin' awful hard, Joe." She surveyed the half-completed stable with critical eye: "Couple more weeks an' it'll be done!" she exclaimed in admiration, "I didn't know you was so handy. Look over to the house."

Cinnabar looked: "Gee! Curtains in the window! Looks like a regular outfit, now."

"Do you like 'em—honest? I didn't think you'd even notice they was hung." With the pride of new proprietorship, her eyes travelled over the tiny log cabin, the horse corral with its new peeled posts, and the stable which still lacked the roof: "We ain't be'n here quite two months, an' the best part is, we done it all ourselves. Why, Joe, I can't hardly believe we've really got an outfit of our own—with horses an' two hundred an' fifty head of cattle! It don't seem real. Seems like I'm bound to wake up an hear Hank roarin' to git up an' git breakfast. That's the way it ended so many times—my dream. I'm so sick of hotels I hope I'll never see another one all my life!"

"You an' me both! It's the same with bartendin'. But you ain't a-goin' to wake up. This here's *real!*"

"Oh, I hope we can make a go of it!" cried the girl, a momentary shadow upon her face, "I hope nothin' happens———"

Her husband laid his hand affectionately upon her shoulder: "They ain't nothin' goin' to happen," he reassured her, "we've got to make a go of it! What with all both of us has be'n able to save, an' with the bank stakin' us fer agin as much—they ain't no two ways about it—we've got to make good."

"Who's that?" asked the girl, shading her eyes with her hand, and peering toward the mouth of a coulee that gave into Red Sand Creek from the direction of the bad lands. Cinnabar followed her gaze and both watched a horseman who, from the shelter of a cutbank seemed to be submitting the larger valley to a most careful scrutiny.

"One of them horse-thieves, I guess," ventured, the girl, in a tone of disgust, "I wisht, Joe, you wouldn't have no truck with 'em."

"I don't have no dealin's with 'em, except to keep my mouth shut an' haul their stuff out from town—same as all the other ranchers down in here does. A man wouldn't last long down here that didn't—they'd put him out of business. You don't need to fear I'll throw in with 'em. I guess if a man can tend bar for six years an' stay straight—straight enough so the bank ain't afraid to match his pile an' shove the money out through the window to him—there ain't much chance he won't stay straight ranchin'."

"It ain't that, Joe!" the girl hastened to assure him, "I never would married you if I hadn't know'd you was square. I don't want nothin' to do with them crooks—I've got a feelin' that, somehow, they'll throw it into you."

"About the only ones there is around here is Cass Grimshaw's gang an' outside of runnin' off horses, Cass Grimshaw's on the level—everyone knows that."

"Well," replied the girl, doubtfully, "maybe they might be one horse-thief like that—but a whole gang—if they was that square they wouldn't be horse-thieves."

"What Cass says goes——"

"Look at comin', yonder!" interrupted Jennie, pointing to the lone rider, "if it ain't that low-down Jack Purdy, I'll jump in the crick!" At the mention of the name of Purdy, Cinnabar Joe started perceptibly. His wife noticed the movement, slight as it was—noted also, in one swift sidewise glance, that his face paled slightly under its new-found tan, and that a furtive—almost a hunted look had crept into his eyes. Did her husband fear this man, and if so—why? A sudden nameless fear gripped her heart. She stepped close to Cinnabar Joe's side as though in some unaccountable way he needed her protection, and together they waited for the approaching rider. The man's horse splashed noisily into the creek, lowered his head to drink, but the rider jerked viciously on the reins so that the cruel spade bit pinked the foam at the animal's lips. Spurring the horse up the bank, he stopped before them, grinning. "'Lo Cinnabar! 'Lo, Jennie! Heard you'd located on Red Sand, an' thought I'd run over an' look you up—bein' as we're neighbours."

"Neighbours!" cried the girl, in undisguised disgust, "Lord! I know'd the bad lands was bad enough—but I didn't think they was that bad. I thought you was plumb out of the country or dead, long before this!"

The man leered insolently: "Oh, you did, eh? Well, I ain't out of the country—an' I ain't dead—by a hell of a ways! I guess Cinnabar wouldn't sob none if I was dead. You don't seem tickled to death to see an' old pal."

"Sure, you're welcome here, Jack. Anyone is. Anything I can do for you?"

The man seemed to pay no attention to the words, and swinging from the saddle, threw an arm over the horn, and surveyed the outfit with a sneering grin: "Saved up enough to start you an outfit of yer own, eh? You ought to done pretty good tendin' bar for six years, with what you got paid, an' what you could knock down. Go to it! I'm for you. The better you do, the better I'll like it."

"What I've saved, I've earnt," replied Cinnabar evenly.

"Oh, sure—a man earns all he gits—no matter how he gits it. Even if it's shootin' up his old pals an' grabbin' off the reward."

Cinnabar's face went a shade paler, but he made no reply and the other turned to Jennie. "You go to the house—me an' Cinnabar wants to make medicine."

"You go to the devil!" flashed the girl. "Who do you think you are anyhow? Tryin' to order me around on my own ranch! If you've got anything to say, just you go ahead an' spit it out—don't mind me."

"Kind of sassy, ain't you? If you was mine, I'd of took that out of you before this—or I'd of broke you in two."

"If I was yourn!" cried the girl contemptuously, "if you was the last man in the world, I'd of et wolf poison before I'd be'n seen on the street with you. I've got your number. I didn't work in the hotel at Wolf River as long as I did, not to be onto your curves. You're a nasty dirty low-down skunk—an' that's the best can be said about you! Now, I guess you know how you stand around here. Shoot off what you got to say, an' then take your dirty hide off this ranch an' don't come back!"

"I guess Cinnabar won't say that," sneered the man, white with rage, "you don't hear him orderin' me off the place, do you—an' you won't neither. What I've got on him'll hold you for a while. You're holdin' yer nose high—now. But, you wait—you'll pay fer them words you said when the time comes—*an' you'll pay my way!*"

Jennie's face went suddenly white and Cinnabar Joe stepped forward, his eyes narrowed to slits: "Shut up!" he said, evenly, "or I'll kill you."

Purdy glanced into the narrowed eyes of the ex-bartender, and his own glance fell. Cinnabar Joe was a man to be reckoned with. Purdy had seen that peculiar squint leap into the man's eyes once or twice before—and each time a man had died—swiftly, and neatly. The horse-thief laughed, uneasily: "I was only jokin'. What do I care what the women say? Come on over here a piece, an' I'll tell you what I want. You asked me if there was anything you could do."

"Say it here," answered Cinnabar without taking his eyes from the man's face.

Purdy shrugged: "All right. But first let me tell you somethin' fer yer own good. Don't kill me! I've got three pals not so far from here that's in on—well, you know what. I told 'em the whole story—an' if anything happens to me—up you go—see? An' if you try to double-cross me—up you go, too. You git that, do you? Well, here's what you got to do. It ain't much. I've got a boarder fer you. It's a woman. Keep her here fer a week, an' don't let anyone know she's here. Then I'll come an' git her. That's all!"

"Who is she, an' what you goin' to do with her?"

"That ain't none of yer damn business!" snapped Purdy, "an' mind you don't try to bushwhack me, an' don't let no one know she's here, or you'll spend the rest of your life in Deer Lodge—an' me an' Jennie'll run the outfit——"

With a cry Jennie threw herself upon her husband who, unarmed, had launched himself at Purdy. "Joe! Joe! He'll kill you! He's got his guns!" she shrieked, and held on the tighter as Cinnabar struggled blindly to free himself. Purdy vaulted into his saddle and dashed across the creek. Upon the opposite side he jerked his horse to a stand, and with a wave of his hand, indicated the coulee down which he had come: "She's up there a piece on a cayuse tied to a tree. Go get her—she's had a hard ride."

Cinnabar succeeded in freeing himself from his wife's grasp, and dashed for the house. Purdy stopped speaking abruptly and spurring his horse madly, whirled and dashed for the shelter of a cottonwood grove. As he plunged into the thicket a gun cracked behind him, and a piece of bark flew from the side of a tree not a foot from his head. "The damn fool! I wonder if he knew I was lyin' about tellin' the others. He sure as hell was shootin' to kill—an' he damn near called my bluff!"

Working out of the thicket into the mouth of a deep coulee, Purdy rode rapidly into the bad lands.

Three or four miles from the hang-out of the Grimshaw gang, was a rocky gorge that had become the clandestine meeting place of the four who sought to break the yoke of Grimshaw's domination. Unlike the cave, the place was not suited to withstand a siege, but a water-hole supplied moisture for a considerable area of grass, and made a convenient place to turn the horses loose while the conspirators lay among the rocks and plotted the downfall of their chief. Purdy made straight for this gorge, and found the other three waiting.

"Where in hell you be'n?" asked one, "we be'n here sence noon." Purdy eyed the speaker with contempt: "Who wants to know?" he asked and receiving no answer, continued, "where I be'n is my business. Why don't you ask Cass where he's be'n, sometime? If you fellers are goin' to follow my lead, I'll be boss—an' where I've be'n is my own business."

"That's right," assented one of the others, in a conciliating tone. "Don't git to scrappin' amongst ourselves. What we wanted to tell you: the Flyin' A's raid is off."

"Off!" cried Purdy, "what do you mean, off?"

"Cass told me this noon. The IX rodeo has worked down this side of the mountains, an' it'll be a week before the slope's clear of riders."

Purdy broke into a torrent of curses. The Flying A horse raid, planned for that very night, was to have been the end of Cass Grimshaw. He was to have been potted by his own men—both Cass and his loyal henchman, Bill.

After a few moments Purdy quieted down. He rolled a cigarette and as he smoked his brows knitted into a frown. Finally he slapped his leg. "All right, then—he'll take it where he gits it!" The others waited. "It's this way," he explained, "we ain't got time to dope it all today—but be here tomorrow noon. Tonight everything goes as usual—tomorrow night, Cass Grimshaw goes to hell—an' it'll be the Purdy gang then, an' we won't stop at horse-runnin' neither." The men looked from one to the other, uneasily. "It's better this way anyhow," announced Purdy, "we'll bump him off, an' collect the reward. I know a feller that'll collect it—I've got somethin' on him—he's got to."

"We're all in the gang," muttered the man who had asked Purdy where he had been, "looks like if you had somethin' on someone you'd let us all in."

"Not by a damn sight! If I did, what would keep you from double-crossin' me, an' goin' after him yerselves. All you got to do is be here tomorrow noon—then we'll cut the cards to see who does the trick."

Grumbling dubiously, the men caught up their horses, and scattering approached the hang-out from different directions. As Purdy rode he scowled blackly, cursing venomously the heavens overhead, the earth beneath, and all the inhabitants thereof. "I overplayed my hand when I made Cinnabar sore," he muttered. "But he'll come around in a week. Trouble is, I've took too much on. Cass an' Bill'll git theirn tomorrow night, that'll give me time to git organized, an' horn the pilgrim out of his five thousan', an' git it over with by the twentieth when old McWhorter's due fer his lonesome jag, an' then fer three days I'll have my own way with the girl—an' when I've had her fer three days—she'll never go back!" A sudden thought struck him, and he pulled up and gazed toward Red Sand while a devilish gleam played in his narrowed eyes. "Gawd," he muttered, "drunk as he gits, the shack could burn to the ground—it's every man fer hisself—might's well play safe. An' after that comes Cinnabar's turn—an' another woman's goin' to pay fer bein' free with her tongue. Then the Wolf River bank. Damn 'em!" he cried, suddenly, "I'll clean 'em all! I'm smarter'n the whole mess of 'em. I'm a killer! I'm the last of the loboes! Cass depended on friends, but me—the name of Purdy'll chill their guts!"

CHAPTER XXI

THE PASSING OF LONG BILL KEARNEY

It was yet dark when the Texan rolled from the blankets at the edge of McWhorter's haystack, and dumped a liberal measure of oats into the blue roan's feed box. While the animal ate, the man carefully examined his outfit by the light of the waning moon. Gun, cinch, bridle, saddle, rope, each came in for its bit of careful scrutiny, and when he had finished he saddled and bridled the horse in the stall and led him out just as the first faint hint of dawn greyed the east. As he swung into the saddle, the horse tried to sink his head, but the Texan held him up, "Not this mornin', old hand," he said, soothingly, "it wastes strength, an' I've got a hunch that maybe I'm goin' to need every pound you've got in you." As if recognizing the voice of a master, the horse gave one or two half-hearted jumps, and stretched into an easy lope. As the coulee began to slant to the bench the man pulled him down to a walk which became a steady trot when the higher level was gained.

The Texan rode with a much lighter heart than he had carried on the previous day. The words of Janet McWhorter had kindled a ray of hope—a hope that had grown brighter with the dawning of the day. He even smiled as he thought of the girl back there in the cabin. "I didn't think there was her like in the world. She's—she's the kind of woman a man dreams about, an' knows all the time they ain't real—they couldn't be. Hair as black an' shiny as the wing of a crow. An' eyes! Sometimes you can see way down into 'em—like deep, clear water an' when they laugh, the surface seems to ripple an' throw back flashes of sunshine. An' there's other times, too. They can look at you hard an' grey—like a man's eyes. An' they can get black an' stormy—with lightnin' flashes instead of sunshine. There's a woman for some man—an' believe me, he better be *some man*! He'd have to be to get her." The man dreamed a jumbled, rosy dream for a mile or more. "An' she can ride, an' shoot, leastwise she packs a gun—an' I bet she can use it. I've seen these ridin', shootin' kind—lots of 'em—an' mostly, they don't sort of stack up to what a man would want to marry—makes you kind of wonder if they wouldn't expect the man to rock the cradle—but not her—she's different—she's all girl. After Win's wife—I never expected to see another one—but, shucks—she said there was more—an' she was right—partly—there's one more. I'm goin' to hunt a job over on this side—" his train of thought halted abruptly, and involuntarily, his gaze fastened upon the blue-black peaks of the Judith range to the southward across the river. His gloved hand smote his leather chaps with a crack that made the blue roan jump sidewise: "I'll be damned if I do!" he exclaimed aloud, "I'll go straight back to Dad Colston! I'll tell him the whole thing—he'll know—he'll understand an' if he'll give me my job back I'll—I'll buy me a mile of cable an' rig up Long Bill's ferry right plumb across to the mouth of Red Sand! I don't want her till I've earnt her—but there ain't no one else goin' to come snoopin' around—not onless he's a better man than I am—an' if he is, he ought to win."

At the edge of the bad lands the Texan pulled up in the shelter of a twisted bull pine that grew from the top of a narrow ridge, and banishing all thought of the girl from his mind, concentrated upon the work at hand. He knew Purdy for just what he was. Knew his base brutishness of soul—knew his insatiable greed—and it was upon this latter trait that he based his hope. Carefully he weighed the chances. He knew how Purdy must hate the pilgrim for the shooting back at Wolf River. He knew that the man's unreasoning hate would extend to the girl herself. He knew that Purdy hated him, and that if he found out through Long Bill that he had been with her, the man's hate would be redoubled. And he knew that even in the absence of any hatred on the part of Purdy, no woman would be safe in his hands. To offset unreasoning hate and bestial desire was only the man's greed. And greed would be a factor only if Purdy knew of the reward. The fact that Long Bill had ridden one of Purdy's horses added strength to the assumption that they had been in touch. "A thousan' dollars is too much money for Purdy to pass up," muttered the Texan as his eyes swept the dead plain. "He knows he'd have to deliver her safe an' unharmed, an' the chances are he'd figure he could make Win shell out a good bit more'n the thousan'. Anyhow, if Long Bill ain't got back across the river yet, I've got two chances of locatin' her instead of one."

The Texan's attention riveted upon a spot less than a quarter of a mile away. Above the edge of a low cutbank, that formed the wall of a shallow coulee a thin curl of smoke rose and was immediately dispersed. So fleeting was the glimpse that he was not sure his eyes had not played him false. Long and intently he stared at the spot—yes, there it was again,—a gossamer wraith, so illusive as to be scarcely distinguishable from the blue haze of early dawn. Easing his horse from the ridge, he worked him toward the spot, being careful to keep within the shelter of a coulee that slanted diagonally into the one from which the smoke rose. A hundred yards from his objective he dismounted, removed his spurs, and crawled stealthily toward the rim of the cutbank. When within arm's reach of the edge he drew his gun, and removing his hat, wriggled forward until he could thrust his face into a tuft of bunch grass that projected over the edge.

Not ten feet below him Long Bill Kearney squatted beside a tiny fire and toasted a strip of bacon upon the point of a long knife. Long Bill was alone.

A short distance away a cayuse stood saddled and bridled. Noiselessly the Texan got to his feet and stood looking down at the man by the fire. The man did not move. Grease dripped from the bacon and little tongues of red flame curled upward, licking at the strip on the knife. The strip curled and shrivelled, and slipping from the point, dropped into the fire. Cursing and grumbling, the man fished it out with the knife, and removing the clinging ashes upon his sleeve, conveyed it to his mouth with his fingers. From a greasy paper beside him he drew another strip and affixed it on the point of the knife. As he thrust it toward the fire he paused, and glanced uneasily toward the cayuse which dozed with drooping head and one rear foot resting upon the toe. Apparently satisfied, he resumed his toasting, but a moment later restlessly raised his head, and scrutinized the lower reach of the coulee. Looking over his shoulder he submitted the upper reach to like scrutiny. Then he scanned the opposite rim while the bacon shrivelled and the little red flames licked at the knife blade. Finally as if drawn by some unseen force he deliberately raised his face upward—and found himself staring straight into the eyes of the Texan who had thrust the gun back into its holster. Seconds passed—long tense seconds during which the man's hands went limp, and the knife dropped unheeded into the fire, and the bacon burned to a charcoal in the little red flame. His lower jaw had sagged, exposing long yellow fangs, but his eyes held with terrible fascination upon the cold stare of the Texan.

"My Gawd!" he muttered, thickly when he could endure the silence no longer, "I—we—thought you was drownded."

"Oh, we did, did we? But we was afraid I wasn't so we went ahead an' spread those bills. Well, I'm here—do you want that reward?"

The question seemed to inspire Long Bill with a gleam of hope. He struggled to his feet: "Lord, no! Not me, Tex. I just tuck them papers 'long 'cause———"

"Where's the girl?"

"What girl—you mean the pilgrim's woman? I donno—s'elp me—I donno nawthin' 'bout it."

"Where's Purdy?"

"Who? Purdy? Him? I donno. I ain't seen him. I ain't seen him fer—it's goin' on a hell of a while. Last time I seen him———"

The sentence was never finished. Lightly as a cat the body of the Texan shot downward and hardly had his feet touched the ground than a gloved fist drove straight into Long Bill's face. The man crashed heavily backward and lay moaning and whimpering like a hurt puppy. Stepping to his side the Texan kicked him in the ribs: "Get up!" he commanded.

With a grunt of pain, the man struggled to a sitting posture. A thin trickle of blood oozed from the corner of his mouth. He raised a shaky hand to his face and inserting a long black nailed forefinger between his puffed lips, ran it along the inner edge of his gums and drew forth a yellow tooth. Leaning forward he spat out a mouthful of blood, and another tooth clicked audibly upon the rocks. With the other hand he felt gingerly of his side: "You've knocked out my teeth," he snivelled, "an' broke my rib."

"An' I ain't only just started. I'm goin' to knock out the rest of 'em, an' break the rest of your ribs—one at a time. You've got your guns on, why don't you shoot?"

"You'd kill me 'fore I c'd draw," whined the man.

"You've got me—exact. Stand on your feet—it's too far to reach when I want to hit you again." The man got to his feet and stood cowering before the Texan.

"Now you answer me—an' answer me straight. Every time you lie I'm goin' to knock you down—an' every time you drop, I'm goin' to kick you up again. Where's that girl?"

"Purdy's got her."

"Where?"

"Over—over to the hang-out."

"What hang-out?"

"Cass Grimshaw's—" Again the Texan's fist shot out, again Long Bill crumpled upon the floor of the coulee, and again the Texan kicked him to his feet, where he stood shrinking against the cutbank with his hands pressed to his face. He was blubbering openly, the sound issuing from between the crushed lips in a low-pitched, moaning tremolo—a disgusting sound, coming from a full-grown man—like the pule of a brainless thing.

The Texan shook him, roughly: "Shut up! Where's Purdy? I know Cass Grimshaw. Don't try to tell me he's into any such dirty work as this."

"Purdy's in Grimshaw's gang," yammered the man, "Grimshaw ain't in on it—only Purdy. If she ain't in the hang-out, I don't know where she's at. Purdy wouldn't tell me. He'd be afraid I'd double-cross him."

"What's he goin' to do with her?"

"Git the reward."

"An', you're in on it? You're the go-between?"

The man shrank still farther back against the wall: "Yes."

"When are you goin' to collect it?"

"Yeste'day a week——"

Once more the Texan's fist drew back, but the man grovelled against the dirt wall, holding his hands weakly before his battered face: "Not agin! Not agin! Fer Gawd's sakes! I kin prove it! Here's the paper! Kill me when you read it—but fer Gawd's sakes don't hit me no more!" Fumbling in his shirt pocket, he drew out the note Purdy had written and signed with the Texan's name. Carefully Tex read it and thrust it into his pocket.

"Where's Grimshaw's hang-out?" he asked, in a voice of deadly quiet.

"It's in a coulee—ten miles from here. A coulee with rock sides, an' a rock floor. A deep coulee. Ride straight fer Pinnacle Butte an' you'll come to it. It's up the coulee, in a cave."

The Texan nodded: "All right. You can go now. But, remember, if you've lied to me, I'll hunt you down. I ought to kill you anyway—for this." He tapped the pocket where he had placed the note.

"Purdy writ it—I can't write. I ain't lyin'. It's there—the cave—west side—crack in the rock wall." The man was so evidently sincere that the Texan grinned at him:

"An' you think when I go bustin' in on 'em, they'll just naturally fill me so full of holes my hide won't hold rainwater—is that it? You wait till I tell Cass Grimshaw you're sneakin' around tippin' folks off to his hang-out. Looks to me like Long Bill Kearney's got to kiss the bad lands good-bye, no matter which way the cat jumps."

A look of horror crept into the man's face at the words. He advanced a step, trembling visibly: "Fer Gawd's sakes, Tex, you wouldn't do that! I'm a friend of yourn. You wouldn't double-cross a friend. Cass, he'd kill me just as sure as he'd kill a rattlesnake if it bit him!"

"An' that's jest about what's happened." Both men started at the sound of the voice and glancing upward, saw a man standing at almost the exact spot where the Texan had stood upon the edge of the cutbank. He was a squat, bow-legged man, and a tuft of hair stuck grotesquely from a hole in the crown of his hat. With a shrill yaup of terror Long Bill jerked a gun from its holster and fired upward. The report was followed instantly by another and the tall form in the coulee whirled half around, sagged slowly at the knees, and crashed heavily forward upon its face.

"Glad he draw'd first," remarked Cass Grimshaw, as he shoved a fresh cartridge into his gun. "It give him a chanct to die like a man, even if he ain't never lived like one."

CHAPTER XXII

CASS GRIMSHAW—HORSE-THIEF

Lowering himself over the edge, Cass Grimshaw dropped to the floor of the coulee, where he squatted with his back to the cutbank, and rolled a cigarette. "Seen the smoke, an' come over to see who was campin' here," he imparted, "then I run onto McWhorter's roan, an' I knowed it was you—seen you ridin' him yesterday. So I slipped over an' tuk a front row seat—you sure worked him over thorough, Tex—an' if anyone needed it, he did. Set down an' tell me what's on yer mind. I heard you'd pulled yer freight after that there fake lynchin' last year."

The Texan squatted beside the horse-thief. "Be'n over on the other side—Y Bar," he imparted briefly. "Cass, I need your help."

The other nodded: "I mistrusted you would. Name it."

"In the first place, is Purdy one of your gang? Long Bill said so—but I didn't believe him."

"Why?"

"Well—he ain't the stripe I thought you'd pick."

The outlaw grinned: "Make a mistake sometimes, same as other folks—yup I picked him."

The Texan frowned: "I'm sorry, Cass. You an' I've be'n friends for a long while. But—Cass, I'm goin' to get Purdy. If I've got to go to your hang-out an' fight your whole gang—*I'm goin' to get him!*"

"Help yerself," Grimshaw grinned, "an' just to show you there's no hard feelin's, I'll let the tail go with the hide—there's three others you c'n have along with him."

"What do you mean?"

"I mean if you don't get him before supper, I'll have to. The four of 'em's got tired of the horse game. Banks an' railroad trains looks better to them. I'm too slow fer 'em. They're tired of me, an' tonight they aim to kill me an' Bill Harlow—which they're welcome to if they can git away with it."

An answering grin twisted the lips of the Texan: "Keep pretty well posted—don't you, Cass?"

"Where'd I be now, if I didn't? But about this woman business—I told Purdy to let the women alone—but you can't tell that bird nothin'. He knows it all—an' then some. Is she your woman, an' how come Purdy to have her?"

"No, she ain't mine—she's the wife of the pilgrim—the one we didn't lynch, that night———"

Grimshaw shook his head: "Bad business, Tex—mixin' up with other men's wives. Leads to trouble every time—there's enough single ones—an' even then———"

Tex interrupted him: "It ain't that kind of a mixup. This is on the level. She an' I was on Long Bill's ferry, an' the drift piled up against us so bad I had to cut the cable. We drifted ashore this side of Red Sand, an' while I was gone to get some horses, Purdy come along an' made off with her. I followed an' lost Purdy's trail here in the bad lands—I was half crazy yesterday, thinkin' of her bein' in Purdy's clutches—but, today, it ain't so bad. If I find her quick there's a chance she's safe." He paused and drew from his pocket the folded hand-bill. "The pilgrim offered a reward, an' Purdy aims to get it."

The other glanced at the bill: "I seen one," he said, gruffly. For a moment he puffed rapidly upon his cigarette, threw away the butt, and looked the Texan squarely in the eye: "There's a couple of things about that bill I've wanted to know. You've told me about the woman part. But the rest of it? What in hell you be'n doin' to have a reward up fer you? You spoke a mouthful when you said we'd be'n friends—we're friends yet. It's a friend that's talkin' to you now—an' one that knows what he's talkin' about. You're a damn fool! A young buck like you, which if you'd stay straight could be foreman of any outfit on the range—an' mebbe git one of his own started after while—goin' an' gittin' hisself outlawed! Fer God's sake, man—you don't know what you've gone up against—but—me—I know! How bad be you in?" The Texan started to speak, but the other interrupted. "If it ain't bad—if a matter of a thousan' or so will square it—you go an' fix it up. I've got the money—an' it ain't doin' me no good—nor no one else, cached out in an old iron kettle. You take it an' git straight—an' then you stay straight!"

The Texan laughed: "There ain't nothin' against me—that is nothin' that amounts to anything. I got a few drinks in me, an' cleaned out the Red Front saloon over in Timber City an' because I wouldn't let Hod Blake arrest me an' shove me in his damned little jail, he stuck up the reward. I'll just ride over when I get time, an' claim the reward myself—an' use the money to pay my fine with—that part's a joke."

As Grimshaw joined in the laugh, the Texan leaned over and laid his hand on the man's shoulder: "But, I won't forget—Cass."

The man brushed away the hand: "Aw, hell! That's all right. You'd of made a hell-winder of an outlaw, but the best of 'em an' the worst of 'em—there's nothin' ahead of us—but that." He jerked his thumb in the direction of the body of Long Bill that lay sprawled where it had fallen and changed the subject abruptly. "The woman's safe, all right—she's over to Cinnabar Joe's."

"Cinnabar Joe's!"

"Yes, Cinnabar an' that there Jennie that used to work in the Wolf River Hotel, they married up an' started 'em a little outfit over on Red Sand—couple hundred head of dogies. Purdy's got somethin' on Cinnabar, an'——"

"Somethin' on him!" exclaimed Tex, "Cinnabar's white clean through! What could Purdy have on him?"

Grimshaw rolled another cigarette: "Cinnabar's be'n in this country around six years. Him bein' more'n six year old, it stands to reason he done quite a bit of livin' 'fore he come here. Where'd he come from? Where'd you come from? Where'd I come from? Where'd anyone you know come from? You might of be'n ornery as hell in Texas, or New Mexico, or Colorado—an' I might of be'n a preacher in California, or Nevada. All we know is that 'long as we've know'd him Cinnabar's be'n on the level—an' that's all we're entitled to know—an' all we want to know. Whatever Cinnabar was somewhere's else, ain't nobody's business. Nobody's, that is, but Purdy's. He made his brag in the hang-out one night that when the time come, he'd tap Cinnabar fer his pile——"

"The damned dirty hound!"

"That's sayin' it ladylike," grinned the outlaw, "I told him Cinnabar was a friend of mine an' he was to keep off him, but Purdy, he's plumb disregardful of advice. Anyways, the woman's safe. Purdy's figurin' on leavin' her there while he dickers fer the reward."

The Texan rose to his feet: "Where did you say I'd find Purdy?" he asked. The other consulted his watch. "It's nine-thirty. At noon he'll be at the water hole, four mile north of the hang-out. Up till then they ain't no hurry. We'll plant *him* first, an' then I'll go along—me an' Bill Harlow——"

The Texan shook his head: "No Cass, this is my job. It's a long score I've got to settle with Purdy—startin' back a year. It leads off with a cut cinch. Then, there was the booze that Cinnabar Joe doped——"

"Cinnabar?"

"Yeh, when he was tendin' bar. I can see through it, now—since you told about Purdy havin' somethin' on him. Purdy got him to do it——"

"I don't believe Cinnabar'd of done that no matter what Purdy had on him."

"But he did, though. Then he switched the glasses, an' drunk it himself——"

"Some man!"

"I'll tell a hand! An' that same night Purdy took the pilgrim's girl out on the bench, an' dragged her off her horse——"

"I heard about it."

"An' then, yesterday, he found her unconscious there by the river." The Texan paused and when he continued his voice was low. "An' you know, an' I know what would have happened, if Long Bill hadn't showed up with those bills—an' then signin' my name to that letter to the pilgrim demandin' five thousan' dollars—an' last of all I owe him one for ridin' Cinnabar the way he's doin—I ain't forgot those switched drinks."

Cass Grimshaw nodded: "Quite a score to settle, take it first an' last," he paused, and the Texan noticed a peculiar twinkle in his eye.

"What's the joke?" he asked.

"There ain't no joke about it—only I was thinkin', mebbe you'd left out somethin'."

"Left out somethin'?"

"Yeh. What you think would of happened, an' what would of happened out here in the bad lands, if Long Bill hadn't come along is two different things. I was trailin' Purdy from the time he hit the bad lands with the girl. I wanted to find out what his game was an' when he run onto Long Bill I snuck up an' listened to their powwow. When I found out he aimed to take her to Cinnabar's, I figured, like you did, that she'd be safe, so I kind of loafed around to see if you wouldn't be along."

"You keep awful close cases on Purdy."

"Yeh—couple of pretty good reasons. I knew he was plottin' to bump me off, an' I kind of had some curiosity to find out when they figured on pullin' the job. But, mostly, it was on account of McWhorter's gal——"

"McWhorter's girl!" cried Tex, "what's McWhorter's girl got to do with it?"

"Nothin'—except that Purdy's be'n buzzin' around tryin' to get her—an' I don't mean marry her, neither—an' when he found out they wasn't nothin' doin'—that he didn't stand snake-high with her, he figured on gittin' her, anyway——"

"*God!*" The single spoken word ground between the Texan's tight-drawn lips, and as Grimshaw looked he noted that the gloved fists were clenched hard.

The outlaw nodded: "That's what I meant about leavin' out an' item—main item, too—I hope. You see, I seen you two ridin' together yesterday—when you sent her back home at the edge of the bad lands. An' that's what made me so damn mad when I thought you'd gone an' got outlawed, an' was mixin' it up with this here other woman. The man that gits McWhorter's gal don't want his trail tangled up with other men's wives. Marry her, Tex—an' take her out of this damn neck of the woods! Take her across to the other side."

The Texan met the man's eyes squarely: "I'm goin' to," he answered,—"if she'll have me."

"Have you, man! Make her have you!"

"I aim to," smiled the Texan, and Grimshaw noted that behind the smile was a ring of determination. "So you've be'n kind of—of lookin' out fer her, Cass?"

"Who the hell was they to do it, but me?" answered the man, roughly, "McWhorter's busy up to the lambin'-camp, miles away—an' she's there alone." The man paused, his face working strangely, "By God! If Purdy'd laid a finger on her I'd of—of *tore him to pieces*!" The Texan stared—surprised at the terrible savagery of the tone. The man continued, his voice dropped low: "It was that that outlawed me, years ago—killin' the damn reptile that ruined my little girl. I stood by the law, them days. He was arrested an' had his trial—an' they give him a year! *One year for that!* She died before he was out—her, an' the baby both. An' he died *the day he got out*—an' I was outlawed—an' I'm damn proud of it!"

The Texan reached out and gripped the man's hand: "I'm goin' after Purdy now," he said quietly. "But first, I'll help you with him."

It was but the work of a few moments to raise the body of Long Bill to the bench by means of a rope, carry it to a nearby mud crack, drop it in and cave a ton of mud onto it. As they raised him from the coulee Grimshaw had removed his guns: "Better take one of these along," he cautioned, "Purdy packs two—one inside his shirt—an' the dirty hound carries a squeezer in his pocket—don't play him fer dead till he's damn good an' dead, or he'll git you. Better let me an' Bill go along—there's four of 'em—we'll leave Purdy fer you—he's the only one that kin shoot right good—but the others might edge in on you, at that." The Texan shook his head as he examined the guns, carefully testing them as to action and balance. He selected one, and handed the other to Grimshaw.

"No, Cass, this is my job an' I'm goin' through with it."

The outlaw gave minute directions concerning the lay of the land, and a few words of excellent advice. "I've got a little scoutin' around to do first," he concluded, "but sometime along in the afternoon me an' Bill will drift around that way to see how you're gittin' along. If they should happen to git you don't worry—me an' Bill, we'll take care of what's left of 'em."

The Texan swung into the saddle: "So long, Cass."

"So long, boy. Good luck to you—an' remember to watch Purdy's other hand."

CHAPTER XXIII

CINNABAR JOE TELLS A STORY

Before Cinnabar Joe could fire again at the fleeing Purdy, his wife reached the door of the cabin and knocked his gun-barrel up so that the bullet sped harmlessly into the air. "Don't! Don't Joe!" she screamed, "he said—there was others, an' they'd——"

"I don't care a damn what he said! If the others don't spill it, he will. It ain't no use, an' I'd ruther git it over with."

Jennie noticed the dull hopelessness of the tone and her very soul seemed to die within her. "Oh, what is it, Joe?" she faltered, "what's Purdy got on you? What you gone an' done? Tell me, Joe!" The man laid the six-gun on the table and faced her with set lips. "Wait!" she cried before he could speak, "he said they was a woman—in the coulee. They'll be plenty of time to tell me, after you've got her here. Hurry! He said she'd rode a long ways. Chances is she ain't had nothin' to eat all day. An' while you're gone I'll git things fixed for her." Even as she talked, Jennie was busy at the stove, and without a word Cinnabar left the room, crossed the creek, and walked rapidly toward the mouth of the coulee.

"It ain't no use," he repeated bitterly, "but, I'll git Purdy first—or he'll git me!"

Back in the cabin Jennie completed her arrangements, and stepping to the door, stood with an arm against the jamb and allowed her eyes to travel slowly over the new horse corral and the unfinished stable. Joe's tools lay as he had left them when she had interrupted his work to give him the sandwich. Her fists clenched and she bit her lip to keep back the tears. The wind rustled the curtain in the window and she caught her breath in a great dry sob. "It *is* all a dream. It was too good to be true—oh—well." A horse splashed through the creek and she saw Cinnabar coming toward her leading a blaze-faced buckskin. A woman was lashed in the saddle, her feet secured by means of a rope that passed beneath the horse's belly, her hands lashed to the horn, and her body held in place by means of other strands of rope that passed from horn to cantle. Her hat was gone and she sagged limply forward, her disarranged hair falling over her face to mingle with the mane of the horse. She looked like a dead woman. Hastening to meet them, Jennie pushed aside the hair and peered up into the white face: "My Lord!" she cried, "it's—it's her!"

Cinnabar stared: "Do you know her?" he asked in surprise.

"Know her! Of course I know her! It's the pilgrim's girl—that he shot Purdy over. An' a pity he didn't kill him! That Tex Benton, he got 'em acrost the bad lands—an' I heard they got married over in Timber City."

"Who Tex?"

"No, the pilgrim, of course! Get to work now an' cut them ropes an' don't stand 'round askin' fool questions. Carry her in an' lay her on the bed, an' get the whisky, an' see if that water's boilin' an' pull off her boots, an' stick some more wood in the stove, an' then you clear out till I get her ondressed an' in bed!" And be it to the everlasting credit of Cinnabar Joe that he carried out these commands, each and several, in the order of their naming, and then he walked slowly toward the stable and sat down upon the newly hewn sill and rolled a cigarette. His tools lay ready to his hand but he stared at them without enthusiasm. When the cigarette was finished he rolled another.

In the cabin Alice Endicott slowly opened her eyes. They swept the room wildly and fixed upon Jennie's face with a look of horror. "There, deary, you're all right now," Jennie patted her cheek reassuringly: "You're all right," she repeated. "Don't you remember me—Jennie Dodds, that was? At the Wolf River Hotel?"

Alice's lips moved feebly: "It must have been a horrible dream—I thought I was tied up—and I broke loose and saw Long Bill and when I tried to get away there stood that horrible Purdy—and he said—" she closed her eyes and shuddered.

"I guess it wasn't no dream, at that. Purdy brung you here. But you're safe an' sound now, deary. Jest you wait till I feed you some of this soup. I'll guarantee you ain't et this noon—an' prob'ly all day." Jennie moved to the stove and returned a moment later with a cup of steaming soup. Supporting her in a sitting posture, she doled out the hot liquid by spoonfuls. Several times during the process Alice endeavoured to speak but each time Jennie soothed her to silence, and when the cup was finally emptied her eyes closed wearily and she sank back onto the pillow.

Presently her eyes opened: "Where—where is Tex?" she asked, in a scarcely audible tone. "Was he here, too?"

"Tex! You mean Tex Benton? Law! I don't know! He ain't be'n seen sence that night back in Wolf River."

"He didn't drown—and he's—somewhere—after Purdy—" the voice trailed off into silence and at the bedside Jennie waited until the regular breathing told her that the girl had sunk into the deep sleep of utter exhaustion. Then, with a heavy heart, she turned and stepped from the cabin, closing the door softly behind her.

Out of the tail of his eye Cinnabar Joe saw his wife step from the doorway. Rising, hastily from the sill he seized his hammer and began to pound industriously upon a nail that had been driven home two days before. And as he pounded, he whistled. He turned at the sound of his wife's voice. She stood close beside him.

"Now, Joe Banks, don't you stand there an' whistle like a fool! They ain't no more a whistle in your heart than they is in mine!" There was a catch in her voice, and she sank down upon the sill. The whistling ceased, and with rough tenderness Cinnabar laid a hand on her shoulder:

"It's tough on you, girl—after gittin' such a good start. When I told you awhile back that there couldn't nothin' happen, I overlooked one bet—Purdy."

"Oh, what is it, Joe? What's he got on you? Come, Joe, tell me all about it. I married you fer better or fer worse—I've took the better, an' I'd be a poor sport if I couldn't take the worse. Even if I didn't love you, Joe, I'd stick. But I do love you—no matter what you've got into. Tell me all about it, an' we'll work it out—you an' me. You ain't be'n rustlin' horses, have you? An' the bank stakin' us 'cause they trusted us to make good! Oh, Joe—you ain't! Have you Joe?"

The fingers tightened reassuringly upon the woman's shoulder and reassuring were the words with which he answered the appeal of the eyes that looked imploringly into his own:

"No, no, girl—not that. Not nothin' I've done sence—sence I growed up. I've played the game square sence then." The man seated himself beside her upon the sill: "It's a long story an' starts back, let's see, I was seventeen then, an' now I'm twenty-six—nine years ago, it was, I was workin' over near Goldfield in a mine. Everything was wide open them days an' I was jest a fool kid, spendin' my wages fast as I got 'em, same as all the rest of the miners.

"Out of the riff-raff that worked there in the mines was four men I throw'd in with. They'd drifted in from God knows where, an' they'd all be'n cowpunchers, an' their talk run mostly to the open range. They was counted hard in a camp that was made up of hard men, an' they kep' pretty much to theirselves. Somehow or other they kind of took a shine to me, an' it wasn't long till the five of us was thick as thieves. When we'd be lickered up, makin' the rounds of the saloons, men would edge along an' give us room at the bar. They didn't want none of our meat; although we never made no gun-play, they always figgered we would.

"Bein' a kid, that way, it made me feel mighty big an' important to be jammin' around with 'em. Lookin' back at it now, from my experience on the other side of the bar, I know that if that bunch had drifted into a place I was runnin' I'd spot how my guns laid under the bar so's I could reach 'em without lookin', you bet!

"There was Old Pete Bradley, one-eyed, he was, an' he didn't have no teeth but false ones that clicked when he talked an' rattled when he et. An' Mike Hinch, with a foretop of thick black hair that hung down over his eyes so it looked like he had to squinch down to see in under it. An' Scar Lamento, which he was a Dago or Spanish, an' had met up with an accident that tore his mouth down one corner so's he always looked like he was grinnin'. An' Wild Hoss Duffy. An' me. They wasn't none of 'em miners, an' they was always cussin' the mines an' wishin' they was back in the cow-country, so, come spring, we decided to beat it.

"Duffy, he know'd where there was a wild horse range up towards Idaho an' he wanted we should go up there an' hunt wild horses. Scar Lamento, he claimed there was more in it to go to Mexico an' start a revolution, an' Old Pete, an' Mike Hinch, they had each of 'em some other idee. But Duffy's horse range bein' nearest, we decided to tackle it first. We started out with a pack outfit—too little grub, an' too much whisky—an' hit up into the damnedest country of blazin' white flats an' dead mountains you ever heard tell of.

"To cut it short, we didn't get no wild horses. We was lucky to git out of there alive. We et the pack horses one by one, an' almost two months later we come out over in Idaho. We killed a beef an' spent a week eatin' an' restin' up an' drinkin' real water, an' then we hit north. We was busted an' one evenin' we come to the railroad. A passenger train went by all lit up an' folks settin' inside takin' it easy. We pulled into a patch of timber an' the four of 'em framed it up to hold up the next train. I was scairt out of a year's growth but I stuck, an' they left me in the timber to hold the horses. After a while a train come along an' they flagged her down an' there was a lot of shootin'—nobody hurt, the boys was just shootin' to scare the folks. I didn't know that, though, an' believe me, I was scairt. I was jest gettin' ready to beat it, figgerin' that they'd all be'n killed, when here they come, an' they'd made a good haul, too. We rode all night an' skirted through the mountains. Next mornin' we holed up. Old Pete, he said we'd divide the stuff up after we'd slep so we all turned in but Scar which we posted him fer a lookout.

"It was plumb dark when I woke up—dark an' still. I laid there a while thinkin' the others hadn't woke up yet. By an' by I got up an' hunted around. They'd gone—pulled out on me! They hadn't even left me a horse.

There I was, afoot, an' no tellin' how far from anywheres or what direction it laid. I learned, then, what it was to hate men. Fer a week I tromped through them mountains follerin' cricks an' crossin' divides. I et berries an' what little stuff I could kill with rocks an' clubs. I killed a deer with my six-shooter an' laid around three days eatin' on it. At last I come to a ranch an' worked there a month an' then worked around different places an' wound up in Cinnabar.

"I got a job drivin' dude wagons out of there an' Gardner, an' one evenin' I was comin' down the trail with my dudes, nine of 'em—an' out steps two men an' shoves six-guns in under my nose. I pulled up an' then I got a good look at 'em. It was Old Pete Bradley, an' Wild Hoss Duffy! Old Pete had me covered an' Wild Hoss was goin' through my dudes. Old Pete he recognized me about the same time I did him—an' he grinned. He never grinned again! It was a fool thing to do, but I was jest a kid—an' the dirt they'd done me was still fresh. I jerked out my gun an' begun shootin'. An' when I put it up Old Pete an' Wild Hoss was deader'n nits—an' I was so crazy mad that I'd jumped offen the seat an' was trompin' 'em into the trail. The dudes pulled me off, an' tuck up a collection an' give it to me, an' the company give me a reward, too. The railroad an' the express company had rewards out but I didn't dast try an' collect 'em, 'cause how was I supposed to know they was the ones pulled the hold-up?

"Well, I got kind of notorious fer savin' the dudes an' I had a good thing there until one day I seen a man hangin' around the depot. It was Mike Hinch—an' that night I blew. I worked around after that—cowpunchin', bartendin', minin' an' lots of other jobs, but I never would stay long in a place—till I hit Wolf River an' seen you. I figgered if I had to make a stand it might's well be there as anywheres so I stayed. I know'd Mike Hinch was on my trail. It wasn't that I was afraid of him—afraid he'd shoot me—'cause I'd took care to get so good with a six-gun, either handed, that he wouldn't stand no show. But, I'd learnt my lesson—that crooked work don't pay. I wanted to be on the level, an' I was afraid that Mike would somehow tip me off fer that hold-up, to git even for me killin' Old Pete an' Wild Hoss." Cinnabar paused and, his wife, who had been drinking in every word leaned toward him eagerly:

"But, Purdy? How did Purdy git in on it?"

"I was comin' to that. A year ago, Purdy had a little job of dirty work he wanted done an' he come to me to do it. I told him where to head in at an' then he sprung—what I've jest told you. I pulled my gun an' covered him, but—somehow I couldn't shoot him down in cold blood—not even fer that. He'd left his guns off a purpose. Then he lit in an' told how he was ridin' along Big Dry an' found a man layin' there with his back broke, which his horse had throw'd him off. Purdy seen he was all in an' while he stood lookin' at him the fellow got to mutterin' about a hold-up. Purdy fetched him some water an' the man—he was Mike Hinch—begged him to give him his gun which had fell out of his reach, so he could put hisself out of misery. Purdy thought if he was a hold-up, he'd have a *cache* somewheres, so he dickered with him, agreein' to pass him the gun if he'd tell where his *cache* was. Mike said he didn't have no *cache*. He was headin' to Wolf River to horn some money out of me to keep him from tippin' off the sheriff that I was in on that hold-up. So Purdy give him his gun—an' he shot hisself, but before he died he told Purdy that he was the only one left of the gang—I'd bumped off two, an' Scar Lamento had got killed down in Mexico." Cinnabar removed his hat and breathed deeply, "So now you've got it—straight. I'd ought to told you before—but, somehow—I kep' puttin' it off." He rose to his feet. "I'm goin' out an' git Purdy, now—I'd ought to done it long ago."

Jennie rose and laid a hand on his arm: "Jest one thing more, Joe? That little job of dirty work that Purdy wanted you to do—did you do it?"

Cinnabar grinned, "I did—an' I didn't. Ask Tex Benton—he knows."

"Tex Benton! That reminds me!" Jennie paused and pointed toward the cabin. "In there, she told me that Tex is huntin' Purdy. How it comes she's keepin' cases on Tex—an' her married—is more'n I know. But that's what she said."

Cinnabar stared at her: "Tex huntin' Purdy!" he cried, "well, if he is, it's good-night Purdy! An' I'm right now on my way to help him. It means I'll do time, but I'll back up Tex's play, an' between the two of us we'll git him."

Jennie shook her head: "No, Joe—not that way."

"What do you mean 'not that way'?"

"It's like—murder——"

"Murder!" exclaimed Cinnabar, "it ain't no murder to kill a skunk like him! He's got us right where he wants us. This is only the beginnin' of what he'll do to us. If I don't come acrost with whatever he says—up I go. An' if I do come acrost, up I go anyhow—he'll double-cross me jest to git me out of the way—an' where'll you be?"

"Listen, Joe," the woman had risen and stood facing him, "it ain't right to go huntin' him that way. I don't know if I c'n make you see it—like I do. You ain't a coward, Joe—you've always come through like a man. Everyone knows that. But if you go huntin' Purdy it would be because you was afraid of him——"

"Afraid of him! I'll show you how much I'm———"

"I don't mean that way, Joe! I know you ain't afraid to shoot it out with him. What I mean is, you're afraid to have him runnin' around loose—afraid that if he squeals, you'll do time. Now, it would be pretty clost to murder if you killed a man, no matter how ornery he is, jest to save your own hide———"

"But it ain't my own hide—it's you!"

"Now you're gittin' down to it. An' it ain't so much me right now, as it is that poor girl in there. There's two of us here that it's up to you to protect, an' the way to do it is to stay right here on the ranch till he comes for her———"

"But that'll be a week! In the meantime Purdy might tip me off."

"No chanct fer that. With Tex on his trail he ain't goin' to have no time for no tippin' off, an' he wouldn't anyway—not till he'd squeezed you dry. It's like you said, this is only the beginin'! When he's got everything he thinks he can git out of you, then he'll tip you off—an' not before. An' he's liable to show up here any minute—after her. When Tex begins to crowd him, he's goin' to try to make a git-away, with her. An' when he comes you make him wade through lead to git to the house! There's two guns in there, an' we'll keep one loaded while you're keepin' the other one hot!"

"What if he gits away? If Tex don't git him—an' he don't come back here?"

"He won't git away, but if he does, you're goin' to throw the saddle on your cayuse an' ride to Wolf River, an' you're goin' to the bank an' git your friends together an' tell 'em jest what you told me. Every man there is your friend an' they'll see you through. They've know'd you fer six years—an' they'll know the same as I know that there ain't no sense in throwin' you in jail fer what happened there on the edge of the desert. You done your time fer that when you was wanderin' through them mountains. You learnt your lesson then. An' it changed you from a fool kid that was headed straight to the devil into a square man. That's what the prisons are for—if they're any good—an' if the mountains done the job first, why there ain't nothin' left fer the prison to do, is there?"

"Tex Benton's a friend of mine, I'd ought to be out there backin' up his play."

"You're backin' up his play better by stayin' here an protectin' that woman. He's trailin' Purdy to save her."

"But, even if we do git Purdy, there's the others—his pals."

Jennie sniffed contemptuously: "I thought so, too, at first. But come to think it over you can't tell me he ever let anyone else in on this! That was a raw bluff to save his own hide. Why, his kind wouldn't trust one another nowheres with nothin'!"

Cinnabar removed his hat and ran his fingers through his hair. "Women ain't got no more education than what men has," he said, thoughtfully, "but sure as hell they can out-think 'em. I hope you're right all down the line—an' I guess you are. Anyhow, you better be, 'cause I'm goin' to do it like you say." His eyes rested for a moment on the new cabin. "But if you're wrong, an' back there in Wolf River they think the slate ain't wiped clean, an' send me up, an' the little outfit goes to the devil——"

His wife interrupted him: "Why, I'll get my old job back, an' wait for you to git out, an' we'll start all over again."

Cinnabar reached out and gathered the girl into his arms: "Yes," he answered, with his lips close to her ear, "an' either way, we'll know we done the best we know'd how—an' that's all anyone can do."

CHAPTER XXIV

"ALL FRIENDS TOGETHER"

Old Bat, with Endicott following closely, led the way through the darkness back along Timber City's main street. At the corner of the livery stable he paused: "W'ere you hoss?"

"Why, I—wait, I'll step across to the hotel and borrow one of Colston's." The half-breed nodded, and hurrying across the street Endicott entered the office of the hostelry. His appearance was the signal for a sudden awkward silence among the half-dozen men that sprawled in the chairs or leaned against the cigar case. Endicott's glance swept the faces of the men: "Where's Mr. Colston?" he asked.

The man with the long moustache, the one who had informed him that the ferry-boat still floated, opened a door that gave into the rambling interior: "Hey!" he called, loudly, "'s Y Bar went up?"

From the region beyond came an answer and the moustached one turned to Endicott: "Yup, he's went up. Don't know what room's his'n, but jest holler when you git to the top of the stairs, he ain't got to sleep yet."

At the head of the stairs Endicott paused, a light showed through the crack at the bottom of a door, and he knocked. The door opened and Colston, in undershirt and trousers, bade him enter.

Endicott shook his head, "No I want to borrow a horse."

"Goin' after 'em?" asked Colston. "Well, help yourself. The Y Bar horses are yours, now. But if I was you I'd wait right here in Timber City. A man that ain't used to the range will get lost at night before he's gone three miles. The chances are you'll never reach the river—and what are you going to do when you get there?"

"I'm going to cross—somehow. I'm going to find my wife. As for getting lost, Old Bat is going with me—or rather I'm going with him."

"Bat! What's he doing here?"

"Found out that the Texan had pulled out and came to get him. He knows Tex better than anyone knows him. He had guessed pretty accurately what was coming off here today, and he rode over to take the Texan back home."

Colston nodded: "Go ahead. If Old Bat starts on the trail you'll find your wife." He laid a hand on Endicott's shoulder, "and just bear in mind that when you do find her, you'll find her all right! I, too, know the Texan. He's been more like—like a son to me than an employee. The boy's got his faults—but he's a man! Barring the possibility of an accident on the river, you'll find 'em safe an' sound—an', when you do find 'em, mind you bring 'em both back. You're goin' to need Tex."

Endicott nodded: "I'll remember," he said, "and when we return, you have the papers ready, and we'll close the deal."

While the barn dogs saddled Endicott's horse, Old Bat led the way to the alley between the livery barn and the saloon, and throwing himself upon his belly, lighted matches and studied certain marks on the ground. Satisfied at length he regained his feet.

"What are you hunting for?" Endicott asked.

"Hoss tracks. Tex, she ain' got hee's own hoss. Me, A'm wan' know w'at kin' track A'm foller w'en we git 'cross de riv'."

"How are we going to cross?" asked Endicott as they swung along the trail at a brisk trot.

"We ain' 'cross yet. Firs', we swing down de riv'. We comin' to de ranch. Plent' ranch on dis side along de riv'. We git de boat."

"But, the horses? We can't take the horses in the boat."

"We com' w'ere we need de hoss we hont de ranch an' git mor' hoss."

At the river they halted for a few moments before heading down stream, and Endicott shuddered as he gazed out over the drift-choked surface of the flood. Old Bat devined what was passing in his mind.

"De riv', she look lak hell w'en you stan' an' see her go pas'. But she ain' so bad she look. W'en de boat git een de wattaire she ron so fas' lak de res', an' she 'bout de sam' lak she stan' still."

"Yes—but the boat—the heavy ferry—they couldn't handle her in the water."

"Dey ain' got for han'l. De riv' she han'l. W'en de boat com' on de plac', w'at you call, de ben'—w'ere de riv' she mak' de turn, de boat she gon git shov' on de bank. Mebbe-so dey don' gon on de bank, w'en de daylight com' some wan see um an' com' in de boat an' tak' um off."

Bat struck off down the river with Endicott following. After an hour's ride through the darkness they came to a ranch. Bat opened and closed the wire gate and led the way along the winding wagon road to the house, a log affair, nestled in a deep coulee. A dog rushed from the darkness and set up a furious barking, dodging in and out among the legs of the horses in a frenzy of excitement. A light appeared in the window and as the two riders drew up before the door it opened, a man thrust his head out and swore at the dog. When the animal subsided he peered at the horsemen: "Whut's up?" he growled surlily.

"Have you a boat?" Endicott asked.

"A boat! What the hell am I runnin', a cow outfit or a summer resort? A boat! Er mebbe you think I fish fer a livin'? Mebbe I'm runnin' a ferry? Mebbe I want the hull damn country raisin' hell around here all night! No, I hain't got no boat! An' I never had none, an' don't want none!" The man's senseless anger seemed to increase as though the imputation that he might have owned a boat were in some way an insult. "What the hell would I want of a boat?" his voice rose almost to a scream, and he shook his fist almost in Bat's face.

The old half-breed leaned slightly forward in the saddle: "W'at de hell! W'at de hell! W'at de hell you wan' wit de ponch on de nose—but you git wan jes' de sam'!" As he spoke, his fist shot out and landed squarely in the man's face, and as he staggered back into the cabin, the half-breed put spurs to his horse and the two rode swiftly into the dark. "Dat do um good—mebbe-so nex' tam som' wan com' 'long he ain' stan' an' holler 'W'at de hell! W'at de hell!' so mooch."

A boat was procured at the fourth ranch, and turning the horses into the corral, the two pushed out into the river. Daylight was beginning to break and, keeping close in, they scanned the shore eagerly for sign of Long Bill's ferry. Hour after hour they drifted, Endicott overruling Bat's suggestion that they stop for food. It was sometime after noon that the half-breed stood up and pointed toward the other side. "A'm t'ink mebbe-so de boat on de odder side. 'Long tam A'm watch de drift. De heavy stuff—de tree an' de beeg log, dey mos' all on odder side. A'm t'ink dat better we cross. A'm t'ink dat boat lan' befor' dis—we com' pas' it."

"But how are we ever going to buck this current? If we've past it we'll have to go up stream to find it."

"We hont de ranch an' git de hoss an' ride 'long de edge."

"But, suppose they haven't landed? Suppose they've drifted on down?"

The half-breed shrugged: "S'pose dey gon' on down—we can't ketch um. Dey got de beeg start. De riv' she car' de ferry joost so fas' lak she car' de leetle boat. S'pose dey gon' too far for ride back, dey com' back on train. But, me—A'm t'ink dey lan' befor' dis. We com' bout feefty mile. You fol' Ol' Bat—we fin' um."

The half-breed, who more than once that day had proven himself more willing than proficient with the oars, surrendered them to Endicott and for more than an hour the Easterner battled with the yellow, turgid flood before he finally succeeded in driving the boat ashore in the mouth of a coulee. Abandoning the boat, they struck out on foot up river where, a mile or more above they had passed fences. When they finally located the ranch house Endicott was near to exhaustion.

It was mid-afternoon and he had eaten nothing since the night before, every muscle in his body ached from his labor at the oars, and the skin of his feet was rubbed raw by the grind of the high-heeled boots. The people at the ranch knew nothing of the wrecked ferry, the men holding with Bat, that the chances were it had grounded far above. Declining their invitation to remain over till morning, Endicott procured horses and an ample supply of food and, with the hearty approval of Old Bat, the two struck out up the river.

"He said it was nearly seventy miles to Long Bill Kearney's ferry crossing and only three ranches between," said Endicott as the horses laboured out of a deep coulee, "and if anything's happened to their horses and they haven't struck one of those ranches, they're going to be in a bad way."

"Dem all right. Dat Tex, she got de gun, she shoot de jack-rabbit, de leetle owl, mebbe-so de deer—dey ain' gon' hungry w'ile he got de gun."

It was slow work exploring the margin of the flood. The late darkness overtook them with scarcely twenty miles of the distance covered, and they camped on the top of a high bluff where they built up a huge fire visible for many miles up and down the river. Daylight found them once more in the saddle, exploring the mouths of coulees and scouring every foot of the scrub-bordered bank. It was nearly noon when, from the edge of a high cliff that overlooked the river, they caught sight of the abandoned ferry-boat. The crest of the rise of water had passed in the night and the boat lay with one corner fast aground. Putting spurs to the horses they raced back from the river until they reached a point that gave access to the coulee. The keen eyes of the half-breed picked up the tracks at the bottom of the ravine even before the horses had completed the decent, and it was with difficulty that he restrained the impatient Endicott from plunging down the ravine at the imminent risk of destroying the sign. Picketing the horses beside the trail the two proceeded on foot, Old Bat in the lead, bent slightly forward with his eyes darting this way and that, studying each minutest detail of the disturbed ground. Following closely, Endicott hung on each word and grunt and fragmentary observation of the old Indian. In vain he plied Bat with eager questions but he might as well have sought information from the sphinx. The old man paid him not the slightest attention but proceeded on down the coulee pausing and staring at the sign for a full minute at a time, again almost running with his eyes fixed on the ground until brought up again, frowning and muttering by some new baffling combination of tracks. After what seemed an interminable length of time they reached the mouth of the coulee where Endicott sank wearily onto the end of the water-logged boat and watched the half-breed work back and forth, back and forth, over the little strip of beach. Endicott had long ceased to ask questions and when at last, Bat straightened up, removed his hat, and wiped the sweat from his forehead upon the sleeve of his faded shirt, the information he conveyed was voluntary: "I ain' quite mak' it out. Firs' t'ing dey lan' here Tex, she ain' got on de boots. De 'oman she sleep—mebbe-so w'at you call, knock out. Tex car' her an' lay her on de grass w'ere she leetle bit flat," he paused and pointed to a spot that looked no whit different from any other spot of grass to Endicott's untrained eyes. "Only wan hoss lan'—dat Powder Face, an' ron lak hell up de coulee. Tex, she gon' up de coulee an' by'm'by he put on de boots an' climb oop on de bench. After w'ile com's a man on a hoss off de bench. He ketch oop Powder Face an' com' down here an' git de 'oman an' ride off—he lif her oop an' tie her on de saddle an' ride off leadin' Powder Face. By'm'by Tex com' long on beeg hoss an' nodder man on leetle hoss. Tex git off an' look roun' an' fin' de 'oman gon'—he joomp on de hoss an ride lak hell after de man an' de 'oman."

Endicott was staring, white-lipped into the half-breed's face. He leaped up and seized the man's arm roughly. "Did he catch them?" he cried.

Bat shook his head: "*Non*—not yet. We fol' 'long on de trail—we fin' dat out. Com' we git de hoss."

"But, maybe it was Tex who got here first and rode away with her," cried Endicott as they hastened toward the picketed horses. "Surely you can't tell from those tracks———"

The other interrupted him: "*Oui!* De track don't lie. Ol' Bat, she know 'bout dat. Me—A'm know Tex track an' when she tromp 'roun' she shov' de mud on de odder man track—eef de odder track ain' dere firs' how in hell Tex kin shov' de mud on it?"

"And this happened yesterday! Oh, Alice! Alice!" The man's voice broke on the name, and glancing into his face, Bat saw that it glistened wet with the sweat of torture.

As they mounted he offered a word of advice and encouragement: "Dat better you ain' los' de, w'at you call, de guts. Mebbe-so you 'oman all right. We fin' um safe on som' ranch house."

The trail of the four horses was so plain that even Endicott found no difficulty in following it across the bench. Bat struck into a steady trot which was maintained till he pulled up sharply at a point where the trail dimmed to nothing upon the hard lava rock of the bad lands. The half-breed studied the ground: "De leetle hoss turn back," he announced, "Tex, she gon' on in. He los' de trail, now—he ain' kin pick it oop in here—he ain' Injun. He', w'at you call, goin' it blin'."

Unhesitatingly the old half-breed followed along a ridge and dropped off into a coulee. He rode slowly, now, with his eyes on the hard rocky ground. Several times he dismounted and Endicott's heart sank as he watched him search, sometimes upon hands and knees. But always the old man straightened up with a grunt of satisfaction and mounting proceeded confidently upon his course, although try as he would, Endicott could discern no slightest mark or scratch that would indicate that anyone had passed that way. "Are you really following a trail?" he asked, at length, as the Indian headed up a coulee whose wind-swept floor was almost solid rock.

The old man smiled: "*Oui*, A'm fol' de trail, all right. Two hoss, shod, mak' good trail for Injun. Eef dey swim een de wattaire lak de feesh, eef dey fly een de air lak de bird, Ol' Bat he no kin pick oop de trail—but, by Goss! Eef dey walk, or ron, or stan' still dey got to mak' de sign on de groun' an' me—A'm fin' dat out—" The words died in his throat as he jerked his horse to a stand. From behind a projecting shoulder of rock a man stepped directly into their path.

"Stick 'em up!" The command rang with a metallic hardness in the rock-walled coulee, and Bat's hands flew upward. From the rear Endicott saw that the man who barred the way was squat, bow-legged, and bearded, and that he held a gun in either hand. For one sickening instant he thought of Alice in the power of this man, and reckless of consequences, he forced his horse to the fore. "Damn you!" he cried leaning forward in the saddle, "where's my wife?"

Old Bat cried out a warning, and then stared in surprise at the man on the ground who was returning his guns to their holsters, and grinning as he did it.

"Damn me, where's your wife?" repeated the man, "ain't that a kind of a rough way, pardner, to ask a question of a stranger? Or mebbe you're jest na'chelly rough, an' can't help it." The metallic hardness was gone from the voice. Endicott noticed that a tuft of hair stuck through a hole in the crown of the man's hat, and that upon close inspection the bearded face had lost its look of villainy.

"But—my wife!" he persisted, "you brought her here! She———"

"Not me," interrupted the man, "I didn't bring her nowheres. An' besides she ain't here."

"Where is she? And who did bring her! Speak up, man!"

"She's safe enough. You don't need to worry about her. She's over to Cinnabar Joe's ranch on Red Sand. Purdy took her there yesterday."

"Purdy!" shouted Endicott, "do you mean the Purdy that———"

"Yup," interrupted the other, "the Purdy that you took a shot at a year ago an' creased. Why in hell couldn't you of shot a half an inch lower that night?"

"How do you know she's safe?" cried Endicott. "How do you know he ever took her there? I wouldn't trust Purdy out of my sight!"

"You an' me both," grinned the man, "an', I didn't. I trailed along from the time they hit the bad lands till he delivered her at the ranch. He's after the reward an' he had to keep her safe."

"But the people at the ranch—this Cinnabar Joe?"

"Ace high all around—the breed, there, he knows 'em."

"How did Purdy know about the reward?"

"Long Bill Kearney, he brung the bills along."

"Long Bill! He's another fine specimen! She's not safe as long as those two scoundrels are at large. Where are they now? And where's Tex?"

"Well, Long Bill, he's quite a piece away from the bad lands by now. I 'spect he wishes he was back—but he won't come back. An' Purdy, he's prob'ly wishin', by now, that he'd listened to me. God knows, I tried to make a horse-thief out of him, but it wasn't no use—he's crooked. An' Tex, he's busy an' don't want to be disturbed."

"Busy?"

"Yup. Busy killin' some folks—Purdy an' some others. I wanted he should let me an' Bill Harlow go 'long an' help—but he wouldn't. Said he wanted to settle with Purdy hisself."

"Who are you?"

"Me? I'm Cass Grimshaw."

"Ha!" cried Bat, climbing from the saddle, "A'm lak A'm shake you han'. A'm know 'bout you. You de bes' hoss-t'ief in Montana, *sacre*! Me—A'm Batiste Xavier Jean Jacques de Beaumont Lajune———"

"Is that one word—or several?" grinned Grimshaw. "An' as long as we started in passin' poseys back an' forth, I've heard tell of both of you birds. You're Tex's side kick an' your regular name's Bat, ain't it? An' this here's the pilgrim that nicked Purdy over in Wolf River an' then cussed out the lynchin' party to their face, thereby displayin' a set of red guts that was entirely onlooked for in a pilgrim. So, bein' as we're all friends together, let's hit it out an' see how Tex is makin' it." He turned to Endicott, "Onless you'd ruther hit fer Cinnabar Joe's?"

Endicott shook his head: "No! If my wife is safe, my place is right here beside Tex. This is my fight as much as it is his—more so, for it's on her account he's after Purdy."

"That's what I call a man!" exclaimed Grimshaw extending a hand which Endicott shook heartily. "Here's a gun—but let me slip you the word to lay off Purdy. Nick away at the others, there's three more of 'em—or was—but Tex he wants Purdy. Of course if anything should happen to Tex—that lets us in. We'll pick up Bill Harlow on the way. Come on, let's ride!"

And as they rode, Endicott smiled grimly to himself. A horse-thief, a half-breed, and he, Winthrop Adams Endicott, "all friends together." And in this friendship he suddenly realized he felt nothing but pride. The feel of his galloping horse was good. He raised his eyes to the purpled peaks of the distant Bear Paws, and as he filled his lungs to their depths with the keen, clean air his knees tightened upon his saddle, his fingers involuntarily closed about the butt of the gun that protruded from the waistband of his corduroy trousers. "All friends together," he muttered, and again he smiled—grimly.

CHAPTER XXV

JANET PAYS A CALL

Janet McWhorter rose early upon the morning following her talk with the Texan. Dressing hurriedly, she blew out her candle and hastened to the door. Toward the east the coulee rim showed dimly against the first faint blush of dawn. She wondered if the Texan still slept and whether she ought not to waken him and ask him to breakfast. As she stood in the doorway, man and horse emerged from the stable. She withdrew into the blackness of the room and in the dim light of the unborn day watched him mount. She saw the big roan try to sink his head. Noted the ease with which the man foiled the attempt. Heard the sound of his voice as he spoke to the unruly horse as one would speak to a mischievous child. Then, horse and rider disappeared in the darkness of the valley. The girl stood there in the darkness until the sound of hoof-beats died away. There was a certain rugged grimness in the scene. It was like the moving finger of fate—this silent horseman riding away into the dawn. Her lips moved: "I wish you—luck!" she breathed, "even if—even if—" She stepped from the cabin and glanced up at the paling stars. "Oh, I know!" she exclaimed, bitterly, "I saw it in his eye when I mentioned the reward. It isn't the reward he wants—it's *her*!" Hastening to the woodpile, she gathered kindlings and returned to the house and prepared her father's breakfast.

Neither by word or look did McWhorter refer to the conversation of the evening before. The meal concluded he betook himself to the lambing-camp. Left alone, Janet washed and put away the dishes, tidied up the cabin, fed her orphan lambs, and looked after the little "hospital band" of sheep. Then she pitched a forkful of hay into the corral for the bay mare and returned to the cabin. Picking up a magazine, she threw herself into a chair and vainly endeavoured to interest herself in its contents. Ten minutes later she flung the magazine onto the table and, hastening into her own room, dressed for a ride. Stepping to the wall she removed a six-gun and a belt of cartridges from a peg and buckled the belt about her waist. Drawing the gun from its holster, she examined it critically. Her thoughts were of Purdy, now, and she shuddered: "I must never be without this—after yesterday." She stepped to the door of the cabin and glanced about her. "He said the next time it will be his turn—well, we'll see." An empty tomato can lay on its side, its red label flapping in the breeze. Levelling the gun the girl fired and the tomato can went spinning over the short-cropped buffalo grass. And without stopping it kept on spinning as she continued to shoot, until with the last shot it came to rest, a ripped and battered thing a hundred feet away. "Maybe it will be his turn—and maybe not," she muttered grimly. "He's the one person in the world I could kill." She cleaned the gun, reloaded it, and walking to the corral, saddled the bay mare.

Cinnabar Joe sat in the doorway of his unfinished stable and squinted down the barrel of a high-power rifle. A six-shooter lay beside him on the sill, cleaned and oiled and loaded. "Shines like a lookin' glass," he observed, and throwing the gun to his shoulder, sighted at a rounded rock that protruded from a cutbank a quarter of a mile away. "If that had of be'n Purdy's head, an' I'd of pulled the trigger—there wouldn't of be'n no more Purdy," he grinned. "He better not stick his nose in this here valley," he muttered, "but, at that, I'd rather be out there huntin' him."

From beyond the stable came the sound of galloping hoofs. Dropping the rifle, Cinnabar reached for his six-gun and whirled to meet the laughing gaze of Janet McWhorter. "Why, what's the matter? You look as though you wanted to kill me!"

The man summoned a grin: "Nerves, I guess. Don't mind me. Be'n smokin' too much, maybe."

"What's all the artillery for? You look as though you were going to start a war."

"Maybe I am. But speakin' of artillery, you're pretty well heeled yourself. Coyotes be'n killin' lambs?"

"Yes, the worst coyote on the range killed one of them yesterday and then offered to pay for it. I mean your friend Purdy."

"*My* friend Purdy!"

"Yes—your friend, and Dad's friend, too. If you men wouldn't tolerate such characters around—if you'd try to clean them out of the country instead of doing everything in your power to make it easy for them, they would soon be wiped out."

"But, we'd git wiped out first—an' besides they ain't all like Purdy."

"They're all criminals. They all ought to be in prison."

Cinnabar shook his head: "No, there's plenty of criminals that hadn't ought to be in prison: an' there's plenty of folks that ain't criminals that had ought to be in prison. Trouble is—the gauge ain't right that they measure 'em with."

"All men talk alike," sniffed Janet, "where's Jennie?"

"In the house, feedin' a woman the first square meal she's et in the Lord knows when."

"Woman! What woman?"

"I never seen her before. Jennie says she's the pilgrim's wife—fellow name of Henderson, or Kottmeyer, or some such a name. About a year back, in Wolf River he took a shot at Purdy, an' come near gittin' him, 'cause Purdy had toled her out fer a ride an' then drug her off her horse—they wasn't married then."

"Is she—all right?"

"All right? Yes, I guess she's all right, now. She slep' most of yesterday afternoon, an' all night."

"What are you going to do with her?"

Cinnabar's lips tightened: "When she's able to travel, we're goin' to git her back to her folks."

"And claim the reward?"

"Reward?"

"Yes, didn't you know that there is a reward of a thousand dollars for information concerning her?"

Cinnabar shook his head: "No. I didn't know that. No. We won't be claimin' no reward. So, that's his game, is it?"

Janet swung from the saddle: "That isn't his game," she said, "I thought it was, at first. But, do you know, I believe he really loves her."

Cinnabar stared open mouthed: "Loves her!" he roared, when he could find his voice. "That damn snake couldn't love no one!"

The girl's face went a shade paler: "You know him?" she asked.

"Know him! You bet I know him! I know he's the orneriest livin' white man! They ain't nothin' he wouldn't do—onless it was somethin' decent!"

"And yet—I can hardly believe it. There's something about him so—wholesome—so clean—and he has really fine eyes."

Cinnabar Joe placed his hands on his hips and stared at the girl in astonishment. "You ain't be'n into old Mac's bottle, have you?" he asked, at length. "Wholesome! Clean! Fine eyes! Why, he's the slimiest, dirtiest, evil-eyedest lookin' scoundrel that ever draw'd breath!"

Janet winced at the words: "When did he bring her here?" she asked after a moment of silence.

"Yesterday afternoon."

"Yesterday afternoon! Why, he—told me last night that he hadn't found her!"

"You ain't none surprised that he'd lie, be you?"

Janet nodded thoughtfully: "Yes, I am," she answered. "He didn't look like he was lying. Oh, there must be some mistake! Did you know him before he worked on the Y Bar?"

"Y Bar!" Cinnabar laughed, "that bird never seen the Y Bar onless he's be'n tryin' to run off some Y Bar horses."

"Run off horses! Is he a horse-thief, too?"

Cinnabar waved his arms in despair: "Oh, no," he asserted, emphasizing the ponderous sarcasm of his words with a dolorous shaking of the head, "he ain't no horse-thief. He's—judge of the supreme court. An' the reason he lives in the bad lands is because all the judges of the supreme court lives in the bad lands."

The girl interrupted him: "Don't try to be facetious. You do it badly. But the fact is, he don't live in the bad lands, he don't look like a horse-thief, he don't act like a horse-thief—and I don't believe he is a horse-thief—so there! When he struck out this morning on Purdy's trail——"

"On Purdy's trail!" Cinnabar fairly shouted the words. "Who's on who's trail? What's all this mixup about? Purdy ain't no horse-thief! He's a wet nurse in a orphan asylum! He's clean lookin' an' wholesome. He wouldn't lie!"

"Purdy!" exclaimed Janet, "have you been talking about Purdy all this time?"

A sudden gleam of comprehension shot from Cinnabar's eyes: "Who did you think I was talkin' about," he grinned, "the Gazookus of Timbucktoo?"

The girl broke into a peal of silvery laughter. A weight seemed suddenly to have been lifted from her heart—a weight that had borne heavier and heavier with the words of Cinnabar Joe. There was a chance that her Texan would prove to be the man she wanted him to be—the man she had pictured him during the long hours of the previous afternoon when alone in the cabin her thoughts had reverted again and again to the parting at the edge of the bad lands—the touch of his hand on her arm, the strong, firm grip of his fingers, and the strange rapturous something that had leaped from his eyes straight into her heart. But, all that was before she had known of—the other woman. The laughter died from her lips, and her eyes narrowed slightly. Cinnabar Joe was speaking:

"An' I suppose you've be'n talkin' about Tex Benton. She told Jennie he was on Purdy's trail."

"How did she know?"

"Search me. Jest naturally know'd that if he wasn't dead, that's what he'd be doin', I guess. How'd Purdy git holt of her, anyway?"

"This woman and Tex were washed ashore when the ferry broke its cable, and while Tex was trying to get some horses, Purdy came along and found her."

"Where's the pilgrim?"

Janet shrugged: "Oh, he don't count. He's merely the wronged husband."

Cinnabar looked straight into her eyes: "Know Tex?" he asked, drily.

"I've seen him. He borrowed Blue, and he spent last night at the ranch."

"Well, then, believe me, you've seen some man! An' don't you go makin' no more mistakes like you jest made. If them two was together they had a right to be. An' they'll come clean with a good reason. They's some things a *man* won't do—an' runnin' off with another man's wife is one of 'em."

"Do you know him?" There was more than a trace of eagerness in the girl's voice.

"I'll say I know him! An' I'm tellin' it to you, sister, if he's on Purdy's trail, I'd rather be in hell with my back broke than be in Purdy's shoes right now."

The girl turned abruptly and walked toward the house, and as Cinnabar followed her with his eyes, he smiled: "If them two could only hit it out—she'd make a fine woman fer him. By Gosh! With a woman like that to kind of steady him down, Tex could be a big man in these parts—he's got the guts, an' he's got the aggucation, an' so's she. I misdoubt he'd marry into no sheep outfit though, at that."

CHAPTER XXVI

THE OTHER WOMAN

At the door of the cabin Jennie greeted her caller effusively. Alice Endicott, who had insisted upon dressing, had finished her breakfast and was sitting propped up among the pillows on the bed.

"This is Janet McWhorter, our neighbour," introduced Jennie, taking the girl by the hand and leading her to the side of the bed, "an' this is Mrs.—Mrs.—why, do you know I can't call your married name to save me. I never seen yer husban'—an' he's always spoke of in these parts as 'the pilgrim.'"

"Endicott," smiled Alice, as her glance noted with swift approval the girl's riding boots, her corduroy skirt, her grey flannel shirt, the scarf of burnt orange, and the roll-brim Stetson—noted, too, the six-gun and the belt of yellow cartridges. Each well-appointed detail bespoke the girl of the open range. But the Eastern woman perceived instantly that the gliding grace of her walk was never acquired in the saddle, nor were the well modulated tones of the full, throaty voice with which she acknowledged the introduction, a product of the cattle range.

"I am very glad to meet you—Mrs. Endicott." Their hands met, and as Alice looked into the girl's eyes, she wondered at the peculiar glance that flashed from their blue-black depths. It was not exactly a glance of hate, but rather of veiled antagonism, of distrust—almost of contempt. Alice's own eyes had been frankly friendly, but as they encountered the look, they fell before the blue-black eyes, and she turned appealingly toward Jennie. But the woman did not notice. She chattered on:

"Ontil yesterday, I ain't seen Mrs. Endicott sence that night, it's a year back, when Tex Benton brung you to the hotel in Wolf River an' wanted the room—" Janet McWhorter sat down abruptly in a chair beside the table and became suddenly interested in fingering the rims of the cartridges in her belt. Jennie continued: "An' I jest give him a good blessin', 'cause I don't trust no cowpuncher—or didn't then—ontil he explained how it was. An' then he went away, an' Old Bat come an' tuck you off, an' we heard afterwards how you an' Bat, an' the pilgrim an' Tex hit down through the bad lands an' crossed the river, an' you an' the pilgrim was married in Timber City——"

Alice gave a little cry: "Oh, and he's there now! Worrying his heart out! He don't know where I am nor what's become of me! Oh, I've got to go to him! I've got to get word to him, somehow!"

Janet McWhorter looked up quickly, the blue-black eyes resting in frank surprise on the woman's face. Her husband! Why should she be so concerned about her husband? Must get back to him! Was she tired of the Texan already? Had her experience with Purdy taken the romance out of the adventure? Or, was the concern assumed for the benefit of her hearers? No. The girl decided the concern was not assumed—it was a very real concern—and there were real tears in the woman's eyes.

Jennie sought to soothe her: "There you go again, deary. We'll git you back to him as soon as ever we can. But there ain't no way with the river where it's at. But, tell us how come Purdy to have you tied up, an' what's Tex Benton got to do with it—an' your man in Timber City? I be'n most bustin' to hear about it."

"Oh, it all happened so suddenly—I hardly know myself. It seems like some horrid dream—some fantastic nightmare. We came to Timber City, Win and I, to be there on our anniversary. Win is going to buy a ranch, and while he was talking business I rode out on the trail a little way, and when I returned it was dark, and there was a crowd of men in front of the saloon and they were shooting. And one of them told me there was a man inside—a Texan. Somehow, I just knew it was Tex—our Tex—the one we came to know so well and to love a year ago. So I told them to stop shooting and I would go in and try to straighten things out. Tex had been drinking a little and he was obstinate. He had defied the marshal to arrest him and he absolutely refused to submit to arrest. I don't blame him much. The marshal is a fool and he thought, or pretended to think, that Tex was some terrible desperado, and he intended to hold him in jail indefinitely until he could look up his record.

"Tex managed to get out of the building and he jumped onto a horse and dashed right through the crowd, sending them sprawling in all directions. As he started down the trail they began to shoot at him, and men began to mount horses to ride after him. I knew they would kill him—and what had he done? Nothing! Except shoot a few bottles and things and break some windows—and they would have killed him for that!

"I knew they wouldn't dare shoot me, so before they could get onto their horses, I swung into the trail behind him so they would have to stop shooting. On and on I dashed through the darkness. At first I could hear the sounds of pursuit, yells and curses and shots, but my horse was faster than theirs and the sounds died away. He had almost reached the river when I overtook him. His horse had gone lame and we barely made the ferry-boat ahead of the mob. He tried to send me back as he led his horse onto the ferry—but I knew that the moment he shoved off from shore those fiends would kill him—he wouldn't have had a chance. So before he could prevent me, I followed him onto the boat and cut the rope that held it and we drifted out into the river—but the men on the bank didn't dare to shoot. He would have put back then if he could, but the current was too strong and it carried us farther and farther from shore.

"Then a great tree drifted down against us, and to save the boat from being swamped, Tex seized the ax and hacked the cable in two. The tree hit his head and knocked him senseless for a time. I bandaged it the best I could by the light of the lightning flashes, and we drifted on, fighting the flood and the trees. The boat sprang a leak and we bailed and bailed, and the next thing I knew he was shaking me, and day was just breaking, and we were close to shore. And he tied the rope to the saddle of my horse and made him jump overboard and we followed. That's the last I remember—jumping into the water—until I awoke, it must have been hours later, to find myself tied—and I got loose, and saw Long Bill Kearney beside the river, and I flew back to the horses, and just as I was about to escape, there stood that unspeakable Purdy, grinning at me." Alice paused and pressed her hands to her eyes as if to keep out the sight, "And, oh, the things he told me—the awful things—the threats—the promises—that were worse than the threats. I must have lost consciousness again—for the next thing I remember—I was here in this room, and you were bending over me."

The two listeners had sat spellbound by the narrative and at its conclusion, Janet McWhorter leaned forward and took one of Alice's hands in both of hers. And when Alice looked again into the girl's eyes lifted to her own, she read something akin to adoration in their depths.

The girl's lips moved: "And you did that—risked your life—everything—to save his life—to keep him from being shot!"

"It wasn't anything," protested Alice. "It was the least I could do. He risked his life for ours—Win's and mine—last year—and—why, I love that boy—like a sister. I never had a brother and—I need one."

"And maybe he needs—a sister," murmured Janet softly. And at the words Alice Endicott glanced swiftly into the girl's face, and her eyes glowed suddenly with the light of great understanding. Her own troubles were forgotten, and into her heart welled a mighty gladness. She pressed the hands that held her own.

"Do you know him?" she whispered.

The girl nodded: "Yes—a little. He borrowed one of our horses—and I rode with him when he went back to get you and bring you to the ranch. And I rode to the edge of the bad lands with him when he took Purdy's trail. And then he sent me back."

"Then, he *is* safe! Oh, I'm glad—glad! Purdy told me he had drowned, but I didn't believe him. I knew he would come to my rescue." She paused and her face clouded, "but, now, I am safe and he is in danger. Purdy may kill him——"

"Don't you go frettin' about that, deary," broke in Jennie. "If they's any killin' to be done between them two, Tex'll do it. Purdy's a gunman all right, but he'll never git Tex. Tex is the best man—an' Purdy knows it—an' his kind ain't never no good when they're buffaloed."

"But, he might shoot him from ambush!"

"He better do it all to one shot, then. 'Cause, believe me, Tex, he'll hit the ground a-shootin'! An' now you two make yerselves to home while I run out an' tell Joe—I'm just a-bustin' to tell him an' he'll want to know."

As the woman hurried toward the stable, Alice patted the girl's hands. "He's splendid," she whispered, "splendid!" Janet's eyes did not meet hers, and she continued, softly: "He's just a boy—impulsive, lovable. And yet, at times he's so very much a man. And there doesn't seem to be anything he can't do. Always, no matter what the emergency, he does the right thing at the right time. And he has another side—once when I ventured to say that Corot would have loved to paint a certain sunset we were watching, he quietly informed me that Corot could not have painted it—could not have got into the feel of it—and I knew that he was right."

"He gets drunk," said the girl, without raising her eyes, "I could hate a man that gets drunk."

"I didn't say he is a saint. But I happen to know that when he makes up his mind not to drink, no power on earth can make him take even a single drink."

"He wouldn't drink at the ranch—I offered him a drink because I thought he needed one—and he did—but he refused it."

"Do you know why?"

The girl shook her head.

"Because he promised me he wouldn't take a drink until after he had talked with my husband. Win wants to see him on business. Wants to persuade him to keep the place he's held for a year, as foreman of the Y Bar. Win is going to buy the Y Bar."

"The Y Bar!"

"Yes, do you know the Y Bar?"

The girl nodded slowly: "I was born there, and lived there the most of my life. Dad moved over here onto Red Sand while I was away at school. The Y Bar is—is like home to me."

"Mr. Colston says he's the best foreman he ever had. You should hear him speak of him—of his taming a great wild stallion they call the Red King——"

"The Red King!" cried Janet, her eyes wide with excitement, "I know the Red King—I've seen him often on the range. He's the most wonderful horse in the world. They said nobody could ride him. Once or twice men tried it—and the Red King killed them. And, did Tex ride him?"

Alice nodded: "Yes, he rode him—tamed him so the great wild horse would come when he whistled. But he wouldn't brand him. And then, one night, he leaped onto his back without saddle or bridle and rode him straight out onto the open range—and turned him loose!"

The girl's eyes were shining: "Oh, I'm glad—glad! Wait till you see the Red King, and you will be glad, too. He's the embodiment of everything that's wild, and free, and strong. I should hate to think of him—branded—labouring under the saddle like a common cow-horse."

"That's just what the Texan thought—so he turned him out onto the range again. It was a great big thing to do—and it was done in a great big way—by a man with a great big poetic soul." There was a long silence during which the little clock ticked incessantly, Alice spoke again, more to herself than to the girl: "What Tex needs is some strong incentive, something worth while, something to work for, to direct his marvellous energy toward—he needs someone to love, and who will love him. What he needs is not a sister—it's a wife."

"Why didn't you marry him, then?" flashed the girl.

Alice smiled: "He never asked me," she answered, "and I couldn't have married him, if he had. Because, really, I've always loved Win—for years and years."

"Maybe he won't ask—anyone else, either. If he asks me, I won't marry him. I won't marry anybody!" She concluded with a defiant toss of the head.

"I certainly shouldn't either, if I felt that way. And if he should ask you, you stick to it, or you will spoil my plans——"

"Your—plans?" questioned the girl.

"Yes, I've got the grandest scheme. I haven't told a soul. When we get settled on the Y Bar I'm going to send for a friend of mine—she's a perfectly beautiful girl, and she's just as adorable as she is beautiful. And I'm going to make her come and pay us a long visit. I'm a great believer in propinquity, and especially out here———"

Janet sniffed audibly: "She'd probably get lost the first thing———"

"That's it, exactly!" cried Alice enthusiastically. "That's just what I'm counting on—and who would find her? Why Tex, of course! There you have it—all the ingredients of a first-class romance. Beautiful maiden lost on the range—forlorn, homesick, wretched, scared. Enter hero—rescues maiden—if I could only work in a villain of some kind—but maybe one will turn up. Anyway, even without a villain it's almost sure to work—don't you think?"

Alice repressed a desire to smile as she noted the girl's flushed face, "I—I think it's perfectly horrid! It's a—what do they call it? A regular frame-up! Suppose he don't love the girl? Suppose he don't want to marry her?"

Alice laughed: "Well, then you may rest assured he won't marry her! He won't marry anyone he don't want to, and as the Irish say, 'by the same token,' when he finds the girl he wants to marry, he'll marry her. If I were a girl and he wanted to marry me, and I didn't want to marry him, I'd jump onto a horse and I'd ride and ride and ride till I got clear out of the cattle country."

Janet stood up and drew on her gloves. "Well, I must be going. It's nearly noon. Good-bye. Glad to have met you, I'm sure."

"Good-bye," called Alice, as the girl stepped from the door, "and when we get settled at the Y Bar, do come over and see us—make us a nice long visit. Please!"

"Thank you, so much! I certainly shall—come to see you at the Y Bar."

Alice Endicott smiled as she watched the girl stamp away toward the corral.

Declining the pressing invitation of both Jennie and Cinnabar Joe to stay for dinner, Janet mounted and rode across the creek.

"Well, I never!" exclaimed Jennie, as she watched her out of sight, "she acted like she's mad! An' here I thought them two would hit it off fine. Ain't that jest like women? I'm one myself, but—Gee, they're funny!"

Out on the bench Janet spurred the bay mare into a run and headed straight for the bad lands. A jack-rabbit jumped from his bed almost under her horse's hoofs, and a half-dozen antelope raised their heads and gazed at her for a moment before scampering off, their white tails looking for all the world like great bunches of down bobbing over the prairie—but Janet saw none of these. In her mind's eye was the picture of a slenderly built cowboy who sat his horse close beside hers, whose gloved hand slipped from her sleeve and gripped her fingers in a strong firm clasp. His hat rested upon the edge of a bandage that was bound tightly about his head—a bandage bordered with tatting. His lips moved and he was speaking to her, "For God's sake, don't hinder—help!" His fine eyes, drawn with worry and pain, looked straight into hers—and in their depths she read—"Oh, I'm coming—Tex!" she cried aloud, "I must find him—I must! If he knows she's safe—maybe he will—will stop hunting for Purdy! Oh, if anything should—happen to him—now!"

"Little fool of an Eastern girl!" she exploded, a few miles farther on. "If she did come out here and get lost and if he did find her, and if—she'd never make him happy, even if he did marry her! But that Mrs. Endicott—I like her." She pulled up abruptly upon the very edge of the bad lands and gazed out over the pink and black and purple waste. Her brow drew into a puzzled frown. "I wonder," she whispered, "I wonder if she *did* know I was just crazy about her Texan?" And, with the question unanswered, she touched the bay mare with her spurs and headed her down a long black ridge that extended far into the bad lands.

CHAPTER XXVII

SOME SHOOTING

When the Texan left Cass Grimshaw he headed due north. He rode leisurely—light-heartedly. The knowledge that Alice was safe at Cinnabar Joe's left his mind free to follow its own bent, and its bent carried it back to the little cabin on Red Sand, and the girl with the blue-black eyes. Most men would have concentrated upon the grim work in hand—but not so the Texan. He was going to kill Purdy because Purdy needed killing. By his repeated acts Purdy had forfeited his right to live among men. He was a menace—a power for harm whose liberty endangered the lives and happiness of others. His course in hunting down and killing this enemy of society needed no elaboration nor justification. It was a thing to be done in the course of the day's work. The fact that Purdy knew the ground, and he did not, and that the numerical odds were four to one against him, bothered him not at all. If others of the same ilk had seen fit to throw in with Purdy they must abide the consequences.

So his thoughts were of the girl, and his lips broke into a smile—not the twisted smile that had become almost habitual with him, but a boyish smile that caused a fanlike arrangement of little wrinkles to radiate from the corners of his eyes, and the eyes themselves to twinkle with mirth. As men of the open are prone to do, he voiced his thoughts as they came: "She sure give me to onderstand last night that runnin' off with other men's wives is an amusement that wouldn't never meet her popular approval. It's, what do the French call it—a *faux pas* that's not only frowned on, but actually scowled at, an' made the excuse for numerous an' sundry barbed shafts of sarcasm an' caustic observations of a more or less personal application, all of which is supposed to make a man feel like he'd not only et the canary, but a whole damn buzzard—an' wish he hadn't lived to survive doin' it." The man glanced up at the sun. "Time I was gettin' outside of this lunch she packed up for me—chances are I won't want to stop an' eat it after awhile." Dismounting, he seated himself with his back against a rock and unrolled the sandwiches. "She made 'em," he observed to Blue, "regular light bread, an' good thick ham between." He devoured the sandwich slowly, and reached for another. "Cass said to *make* her have me," he smiled; "hell of a lot he knows about women, but—the dope's right, at that. Boy, those eyes! An' that hair, an'—an', oh, the whole *woman* of her! If a man had a girl like that to go home to—an' she loved him—an' he knew she was thinkin' about him—an' pullin' for him to—to make good! There wouldn't be nothin' to it—he'd just naturally have to make good. Janet

McWhorter—Janet Benton—Mrs. Tex Benton—Mrs. Horatio Benton—hell! I hope she don't go in for the Horatio part. It's almost as bad as Winthrop Adams Endicott! Tex is better—if she ever thinks to inquire about my other name I'll tell her it's Mike, or else I'll go plumb to the other extreme an' call it Percy or Reginald. I ain't got her yet—but believe me! She's goin' to have a war on her hands till I do get her!

"I'll just admit that she'll marry me—what then? It's time I was kind of takin' inventory. Here's what she gets: One cow-hand an' outfit—includin' one extra saddle horse, a bed-roll, an' a war-bag full of odds an' ends of raiment; some dirty, an' some clean; some tore, an' some in a fair state of preservation. Eight hundred an' forty dollars in cash—minus what it'll take to square me in Timber City. An'—an'—that's all! She ain't goin' to derive no hell of a material advantage from the union, that's sure. But, if I've still got my job it ain't so bad to start off with. Other assets, what we used to call incorporeal hereditaments back in law school—fair workin' knowledge of the cattle an' horse business. Health—good. Disposition—um-m-m, kind, to murderous. Habits—bad, to worse. Let's see: smokin'—that's all right: chewin'—prob'ly be allowable if indulged in out doors only. Swearin'—prob'ly won't be an issue till the kids get old enough to listen. Gamblin'—prob'ly be limited to poker—friendly games an' pifflin' limit. Drinkin'—let's see, the only year since I can remember I don't drink nothin' I quit better than eight hundred dollars to the good—first time I ever had eight hundred dollars all at once in my life. What happens? Get to drinkin' for a half a day, an' Bing! Off comes a hundred, maybe two hundred to pay up for the hell I raised! Does it pay? Not for a married man! Not for me! An' besides, what was it she said when I turned down the drink she offered me? She said, 'I'm glad—I hate the stuff.'" He paused, smiling reminiscently, "drinkin's lots of fun—but, a man's got to pay for his fun—more ways than one, he's got to pay. If it'll make her happy to not drink, an' onhappy to drink—the way I look at it, it's a damned mean man that would pay for his own belly-wash with his wife's happiness! That about concludes the takin' stock, then: Drinkin'—once! Drinkin'—twice! Drinkin'—three times—an' *out*! I'm a non-drinker, a teetotaller, a pop-lapper, an' a grape-juice swizzler! At that, if I'd known that last drink I had back there in Timber City was goin' to be the very last doggone drink I was ever goin' to get, I'd kind of strung it along a little—sort of sipped it slow an' solemn as become an obsequy. Instead of which, I tossed it off light-hearted, casual, even what you might call flippant—an' it's the last drink I was ever goin' to have!"

He rose, brushed a stray crumb or two from his shirt, and mounted: "Come on, Blue, let's get this stuff over with, an' wash our hands, an' hit for Red

Sand. Cass says Cinnabar Joe's place ain't only about four miles above McWhorter's."

Thirty minutes later the Texan slowed his horse to a walk. Rock-fragments appeared, dotting the surface of ridges and coulees. Small at first, these fragments increased in size and number as the man pushed northward. He knew from Cass Grimshaw's description that he was approaching the rendezvous of Purdy and his gang. Far ahead he could see the upstanding walls of rock that marked the entrance to the gorge or crater which marked the spot where some titanic explosion of nature had shattered a mountain—shattered it, and scattered its fragments over the surrounding plain. But the Texan was not thinking of the shattered mountain, nor of the girl on Red Sand. He hitched his belt, glanced at the revolver in its holster, and slipping his hand beneath his shirt, made sure that Long Bill's six-gun lay ready to his hand. He proceeded slowly, pausing at frequent intervals to scan the rock-dotted plain. The mouth of the gorge showed distinctly, now. He pulled up his horse and studied the ground. He decided to dismount and proceed on foot—to work his way from rock-fragment to rock-fragment. A slight sound caused him to glance swiftly to the left. Not fifty feet away the malevolent face of Purdy stared at him above the barrels of two six-guns. Directly before him he saw another man, and to the right two more. And every man had him covered. His eyes returned to Purdy, and his lips twisted into their cynical grin. "Well—why in hell don't you shoot?"

"Want to git it over with in a hurry, do you?" sneered the outlaw. "Well I don't! I'm goin' to git you all right, but I'm goin' to take my time to it. When you skipped out a year back fer fear of what I'd do to you, you'd ought to stayed away."

The Texan laughed: "Just as big a damned fool as ever, Purdy. Just as big a four-flusher, too. You better shoot while you've got the chance. 'Cause if you don't I'll kill you, sure as hell."

Purdy sneered: "Gittin' in yer bluff right up to the last, eh? Thought you could sneak up an' git me when I wasn't lookin', eh? Thought—" The sentence was never finished. The Texan's expression suddenly changed. His eyes fixed wildly upon a point directly behind Purdy and he cried out in sudden alarm:

"Don't kill him, Cass! He's mine!"

Like a flash, Purdy whirled, and like a flash the Texan was out of his saddle and behind a rock. And as Jennie had predicted, he hit the ground a-shootin'. His own horse had shielded him from the others whose attention had been momentarily diverted to their leader. Instantly Purdy discovered the ruse—but too late. As he whirled again to face the Texan, the latter's gun roared, and one of Purdy's guns crashed against a rock-fragment, as its owner, his wrist shattered, dived behind his rock with a scream of mingled rage and pain. Three times more the Texan shot, beneath the belly of his horse, and the two outlaws to the right pitched forward in crumpled heaps and lay motionless. Frenzied by the noise, the big blue roan plunged blindly forward. The man in front made a frantic effort to get out of his way, failed, and the next moment, crashed backward against a rock-fragment from which he ricocheted from sight while the great blue roan galloped on, reins flying, and stirrups wildly lashing his sides.

"That leaves just the two of us, Purdy," drawled the Texan from the shelter of his rock, as he reloaded his gun.

A vicious snarl from the hiding place of the outlaw was the only answer.

"I told you you was a fool not to shoot while you had the chance. I'm goin' to get you, now. But, seein' that you wasn't in no hurry about it, I won't be neither. There's quite a few things I want you to hear—things you ought to know for the good of your soul."

"You don't dast to git me!" came exultingly, from behind Purdy's rock, "if you do, what'll become of *her*—the pilgrim's woman? She's right now layin' tied an' gagged in a mud crack where you nor no one else won't never find her. What'll become of her, if you git me?"

The Texan grinned to himself, and after a moment of silence, called hesitatingly: "Say, Purdy, you wouldn't do that! Wouldn't let a woman die like that without tellin' where she is."

"The hell I won't!"

"Come on, Purdy, tell me where she is? You might as well. If I get you, what's the use of leavin' her there to die? An', if you get me, why you'll have her anyway."

A sneering laugh answered him: "You don't dast to git me—an' leave her where she's at!"

The Texan's voice hardened: "Oh, yes I do, Purdy. 'Cause I know, an' you know, that she's safe an' sound at Cinnabar Joe's—an' she'll stay there till Cinnabar can get word to her husband."

A volley of oaths greeted the statement: "Cinnabar don't dast to open his yap! He'll go up fer the rest of his life if he does. I'll fix him!"

"You won't fix no one, Purdy. You're goin' to hell from here. An' whatever you've got on Cinnabar you'll take with you. When I told you to tell me where the girl was I was just givin' you a chance to do one decent thing before you cashed in—but you couldn't do it, Purdy. There ain't a decent thing in you to do. Why, even Long Bill Kearney was a man fer about a second before he died."

"What do you mean—Long Bill—died?"

"Ask him," answered the Texan grimly, "you an' him will be close neighbours—wherever you're goin'." Inadvertently the Texan leaned a little to one side, as he shifted his position. There was a quick report, and a bullet tore through a loose fold of his shirt sleeve. "Pretty fair shootin', Purdy," he drawled, "little bit wide—you'd have nicked me if you'd held in against the rock."

So intently did each man watch the other that neither noted the four men who approached stealthily from rock to rock and finally crouched behind an irregular buttress of rock only a short pistol shot away. Their vantage point did not permit any view of the man who had been knocked down by the galloping horse nor of the contestants themselves, but the exchange of shots could be followed with ease and accuracy.

Cass Grimshaw nudged Endicott and pointed to the bodies of the outlaws: "He got two," he whispered, with grim approval. "An' he got 'em right out in the open. They must have seen him comin' an' laid for him before he got to their hang-out."

"Hey, Tex," called Purdy after a long interval, "we ain't goin' to git one another peckin' away like this behind these rocks."

"No—*we* ain't goin' to git *one another*—but *I'm* goin' to get *you*—like that!" He fired as he spoke and his bullet chipped the rock and tore through Purdy's hat brim. "Missed, By Grab! But, that pays up for puttin' a hole in my shirt. You was a fool for fallin' for that old gag I put over on you!"

"An' I wouldn't of fell fer it neither, if it hadn't of be'n fer luck—you outlucked me—if you'd of said anyone else except Cass, I wouldn't of fell fer it."

"That wasn't luck, Purdy—that was brains. If I figured on murderin' a man tonight—an' he knew it—do you suppose I wouldn't jump quick if I thought he was sneakin' up behind me with a gun? You bet I would!"

"Murderin'!" Purdy's voice sounded shrill with a quavering note of fear. "What—what do you mean—murderin'?"

"Why, I run across Cass awhile back. I told him I was huntin' you an' he said I'd find you an' three more over here. Said you an' them had planned to bump him an' Bill Harlow off tonight, an' you was busy arrangin' the details. He wanted to come along—him an' Bill—but I told him they wasn't no use—if they was only you an' three more like you, I could handle you myself. Him an' Bill are goin' to ride over after awhile an' see if I need any help—but I don't do I, Purdy?"

The Texan's words were drowned in a perfect tirade of curses. Purdy's voice was shrill with fear. "I've be'n double-crossed! It's a lie! Everyone's agin me! I ain't never had no show!" The voice trailed off in a whine. A few moments of silence followed, and then above the edge of Purdy's rock appeared a white handkerchief tied to the end of a gun-barrel. Taking careful aim, the Texan fired. The white flag disappeared and the gun struck the rocks with a ring of steel.

"You shot at a white flag!" screamed Purdy.

"You're damn right I did! An' I'll shoot at the low-lived pup that tried to hide behind it too. My God, Purdy! No head—no guts! The only things about you that's a man is your pants, an' shirt, an' hat—an' I spoilt the hat!"

"Listen, Tex, listen!" the man's voice was frantic with appeal. "Let's make medicine. You c'n have the pilgrim's woman—I don't want her—I only wanted the reward. I was only kiddin' about bumpin' you off! Honest I was! Listen! Let me go, Tex! Let me git away! Cass has got me framed-up! I aimed to quit him an' turn straight! Listen—they's a girl, Tex. Over on Red Sand—I give her my word I'd quit the horse game an' start an outfit. Listen—I——"

"Who is she?" the voice of the Texan cut in like chilled steel.

"McWhorter's girl——"

"You're a damned liar!"

"D'you know her?" the words came haltingly.

"Some," answered the Texan, drily, "she an' I are goin' to be married tomorrow." The words had been uttered with the deliberate intent of taunting Purdy, but even the Texan was not prepared for the manifestation of insane rage that followed.

"You lie! Damn you! Damn you! You've always beat me! Yer beatin' me now! You son of a—, take that!" With the words he leaped from behind his rock and emptied his gun, the bullets thudding harmlessly against the Texan's barrier, and instantly he was behind his rock again.

Cass Grimshaw grinned at the others. "He's baitin' him—prob'ly be'n baitin' him fer an hour till Purdy's gone plumb mad."

"De Injun she would stake um out an' build de leetle fire on hees belly. But A'm t'ink dat hurt worse lak Tex do it."

Endicott gazed in white-lipped fascination upon the scene. "Let's make him surrender and turn him over to the authorities," he whispered.

Grimshaw shook his head: "No—not him. If you knew him like I do, you wouldn't say that. By God, I turned one man over to the authorities—an' they give him a year! An' when he got out I give him what he had comin'. Think, man what he'd of done to your wife———"

The sentence was cut short by the sound of galloping hoofs. All four craned their necks for sight of the rider. Grimshaw and Bill Harlow drew their guns, expecting to see the fourth man of Purdy's gang come rushing to the aid of his leader. But not until the rider was within a hundred feet of the two combatants did they catch sight of her. At the same instant they saw the Texan, hat in hand, frantically wave her back. Janet McWhorter saw him, too, and pulled the bay mare to her haunches at the same instant a shot rang out and Purdy's bullet ripped the Texan's hat from his hand. Almost before her horse came to a stop, the girl's gun was in her hand and she sat—tense—expectant.

With glittering eyes fixed upon the girl, Purdy laughed a wild shrill laugh, that echoed among the rocks like a sound from hell. The words of the Texan burned like words of living fire. "*Goin' to be married tomorrow!*" Deliberately he raised his gun and fired—just at the instant the bay mare threw up her head with a nervous jerk to rid her mouth of the feel of the cruel spade bit. The next second she reared high and crashed to the ground carrying her rider with her. With a loud cry the Texan sprang to his feet and started for the girl, and at the same moment the horse-thief that the big blue roan had knocked senseless among the rocks rose to his feet and levelling his gun at the running man, fired. At the sound of the report the Texan staggered, turned half-way round and fell sprawling among the rocks. Purdy leaped to his feet and, gun in hand, started for the prostrate Texan. The rock-ribbed valley became a roar of noise. Janet, one leg pinned in the stirrup, fired across the body of her horse. Fired swiftly and accurately. The running Purdy staggered this way and that, drew himself stiffly erect, threw his hands high above his head and spun around like a top, and as the sound of the girl's last shot died, pitched forward and lay very still.

From the rock buttress to the left, Janet saw men running toward her. She could not tell whether they were friends or foes—it mattered not—her gun was empty. At thought of her gun, she gave vent to a pitiful little cry and covered her face with her hands. Then the men were at her side pulling at the body of her horse. Her leg was freed and someone stood her upon her feet. She lowered her hands and stared into the bearded face of Cass Grimshaw!

"Good shootin', sis!" he patted her shoulder gently, "why, what's the matter? D'ye think you missed him—look!" he pointed to the body of Purdy.

"Oh—oh!" moaned the girl and covered her eyes again. "I've—I've *killed* a man!"

Grimshaw looked puzzled: "No, sis—you ain't killed no *man*! Not by no stretch of imagination he ain't no man!"

"But—he's a human being—and—I killed him!"

As the horse-thief stood looking down upon her heaving shoulders the puzzled look in his eyes gave place to a decided twinkle, which an instant later changed to a look of mild reproach: "Say, sis, who do you think you be? Claimin' *you* killed Purdy! Why, there ain't no more chance you killed him, than there is that I didn't." He extended his hand in which an automatic pistol of large calibre lay flat in the palm. "This here gun shoots jest twict as swift as yours. Agin your eight hundred feet of muzzle v'losity, I've got almost two thousan'—an' I'd got in two shots before you begun! Then, too, if you'll take a look around, you'll see that some other folks has got pretty fair claim on him. Take Bill here, his 30-40 rifle shoots half-agin as swift as my automatic—an' he begun shootin' when I did. An' look at the breed, yonder, stickin' fresh shells in his gun. I bet that bird never missed— an' he shot jest a hair before I did. An' the pilgrim he shot, too—but I wouldn't bet on him—he might of missed—but the rest of us didn't. An' I ain't sayin' you *missed*, mind you. 'Cause I think you got him every crack out of the box. But he was dead 'fore you started shootin'. Yup—what you done was to pump about a quart of lead into a dead man, 'fore he could hit the ground—an', believe me—that's *shootin'*! But the killin' part—that goes to the fastest guns."

The girl's eyes lighted: "Oh, I—I'm glad I haven't got that on my conscience. I'd hate to think that I had killed—even him." The next instant she was gone, and they watched her as she bent low over the Texan, who had struggled to his elbow.

"Janet—darling," he whispered, "do you know—about—*her*?"

The girl blushed furiously at the words, and the blue-black eyes shone like twin stars. "Yes," she breathed, "I know. She's at Cinnabar Joe's—and she told me all about it. And, Tex, I think she's fine!"

The Texan nodded: "She is, an'," he indicated Endicott with a nod of his head, "there's her husband over there shaking hands with Cass, an' he's just as fine as she is—they're real folks, girl—but, never mind them. What I want to know is—will you marry me tomorrow, dear?"

"Tomorrow!"

"Might's well be tomorrow as next week—or next month! Come on—please! You can't get away from me, so you might as well. An' besides here I am, shot in the leg an' if you don't give me my own way I'm likely to run a fever, an' have to get it cut off—so it's up to you, sweetheart—a one-legged man a month from now, or a two-legged one tomorrow. Which?"

The girl bent very close: "I—I think I'd rather have a two-legged one—darling." And the next instant the man's arms were about her and her lips were crushed to his.

"Say, Cass," whispered Bill Harlow, with an eye on the girl who was bending over the wounded man. "I never shot at Purdy—I got that damned skunk down there in the rocks that shot Tex."

"Me, too," chimed in Old Bat.

"I shot at him, too," said Endicott.

"Hell!" answered Grimshaw, with a wink, "so did I—but, don't never let her know."

There was a moment of silence which was broken by Endicott, who stepped forward and grasped the speaker's hand. "I am proud to be admitted to the friendship of Cass Grimshaw, horse-thief, and—gentleman," he said, and turned away to see the Texan looking at him with a twinkle in his eye.

CHAPTER XXVIII

BACK ON RED SAND

While Cass Grimshaw and Bill Harlow rounded up the horses, and transferred the girl's saddle from the dead mare to one of the animals belonging to the outlaws, Endicott and Bat assisted Janet to bind up the Texan's wound.

When at last they were ready for the trail, Grimshaw called Endicott aside: "You an' the breed come along with me," he whispered, "you must be middlin' anxious to see yer wife, an' I'll take you to Cinnabar Joe's. The girl, there, she knows the way, an' they can follow along slower," he paused and winked, "he won't be wantin' to ride no ways fast—on account of that leg."

Endicott's eyes lighted with sudden understanding as he glanced at the two figures who stood side by side near the horses: "By George!" he exclaimed, "I wonder——"

"Wonder—hell! Give 'em a chance! Come on, we'll pull out. Bill, he'll h'ist him onto his horse, an' then he'll stay an' drop them corpses down some mud crack."

As Endicott leaped from his horse in front of Cinnabar Joe's cabin, his wife rushed from the door and threw herself into his arms.

"Oh, Win—Win—dear!" she sobbed, "oh—can you ever forgive me? But—it was the only way—they'd have killed him!"

Endicott soothed her: "Forgive you! I have nothing to forgive, dearest. I know it's all right! At first I was a little—worried, but Old Bat came along—and after that, I knew it was all right—but come on, let's go inside and you can tell me all about it!"

Cinnabar Joe greeted Grimshaw and Bat at the horse corral: "Seen Tex?" he asked anxiously. Grimshaw nodded: "Yeh—we seen him."

"Did he—git Purdy?"

Grimshaw shook his head: "No—he didn't git him. He almost, but he didn't quite."

Without a word, Cinnabar turned, entered the corral, and stepped out a few moments later leading a saddled horse.

"Where you goin'?" asked Grimshaw.

"To Wolf River."

"Wolf River! What's goin' on in Wolf River that you're so hell bent to take in?"

Cinnabar hesitated just an instant, then he spoke: "You might as well know it as the rest of 'em. I'm goin' to give myself up, an' I want to beat Purdy to it. He's got somethin' on me—a hold-up that I was partly mixed up in, way back when I was a kid. I never got none of the money, an' I've be'n on the level since. I figgered I'd payed fer that long ago. But, if Purdy got away, he'll tip me off. It's goin' to be hard as hell on her." He nodded toward his wife, who stood at some distance talking earnestly with Old Bat.

Grimshaw leaned over and laid a hand on the man's shoulder: "Put up yer horse, boy," he said; "you've got a nice little outfit started here—you an' her. Stay right with it—an' stay on the level. Forgit anything that might of happened a long time ago. It's the things you do now, an' what yer goin' to do that counts. Tex didn't git Purdy—but they was five more of us there to back up his play. We was all of us more or less handy with our guns. An' between the whole of us—we managed to git him. Purdy's dead, Cinnabar—dead as Julius Cæsar, an' all his pals is dead—an' whatever he had on you died with him."

"There comes Tex, now!" cried Cinnabar, pointing to two riders who appeared outlined for a moment against the opposite valley rim, before beginning the descent of the slope. "He's ridin' McWhorter's blue roan. But who's that with him? Why—it's McWhorter's girl! But, what horse has she got? She busted out of here two or three hours ago ridin' her bay mare!"

As the two riders approached across the narrow valley, Grimshaw fingered his stubby beard: "There's a pair to draw to," he muttered.

"Do you mean———?"

"Yes—that's just what I mean! But, they rode a damn sight faster than what I would, at that."

"Hey, Bat! You old reprobate!" called the Texan, as his horse ascended the bank from the creek, "take Cinnabar's cayuse an' beat it for Wolf River! An' you make him scratch gravel! Now's the chance to do me a good turn on account of them four-bits I give you—way back in Las Vegas—remember?"

The old half-breed grinned broadly: "*Oui*, A'm 'member dat fo'-bit." Reaching into his shirt he withdrew a half-dollar suspended from his neck by a greasy thong of rawhide. "See, A'm ain' fergit. Dat fo'-bit she giv' me chanc' to pay heem back 'bout seex-seven hondre tam'. W'at you wan' in Wo'f Reevaire? Nodder pilgrim to hang, eh, *bien*?"

Joining in the laugh that followed the old half-breed's sally, the Texan rode to his side and handed him some yellow bills. "You hit the trail now—an' hit it hard. An' you show up here tomorrow morning with a preacher an' a round yellow ring—savvy?"

"*Oui!* De pries' an' de ring! *Voila!*" The old man looked straight into the eyes of the girl who sat her horse close beside the Texan. "You gon' mar' heem tomor'?"

Janet, blushing furiously, laughed an affirmative.

Bat nodded: "Dat good. You git de bes' dam' man on de worl'! Dat Tex mebbe-so she git to be de gov'—de w'at you call, de *president*! But, som'tam' he lak de bad boy an' you got to knock hell out of heem to mak' heem good. Ol' Bat—he know. For er long tam' A'm know heem. You lov' heem lak hell. Een de eye A'm see it—an' een de eye A'm see you gon' to mak heem stay good———"

"Hey, you old leather image!" laughed the Texan, "what are you tryin' to do—scare me out?"

"Ba Goss! A'm lak A'm see you scare wan tam'! You bet A'm ride wan hondre mile to laff on you. You git de dam' fine 'oman. Now you got to mak' her, w'at you call, de happiness. Bye-m-bye, Ol' Bat, she git to ol' to ride de range—to cook. Den A'm joos' stay 'roun' an' look aftaire *les enfants*. A'm show um how to ride, an' shoot, an' t'row de rope—joos' so good lak de *pere* kin do, *ah voila!*"

Janet fled precipitously for the cabin, and as Bat mounted Cinnabar's horse and headed out onto the trail, the Texan turned to Grimshaw: "Slip over to McWhorter's tomorrow, Cass," he invited—"I'd like to have you there."

Grimshaw hesitated just a moment: "You're sure you want me? You ain't askin' me just so I won't feel—left out? An' how about the others? How about yer—wife? She never has had no time for us horse-thieves."

The Texan smiled: "She's learnt a lot in the last couple of hours, Cass. If you ain't at the weddin' she'll be the most disappointed one of all."

"All right, boy—I'll come. I got to be goin' now." He ran his fingers over his stubby beard, "Sure is goin' to be hell to shave."

As the Texan swung from his horse, a feminine shriek of joy directed his attention toward the cabin, where in the doorway Alice and Janet stood locked in each other's embrace—laughing, crying, talking all at once, while Endicott smilingly beckoned to Tex.

"Oh, you darling!" Alice was saying, "I'm so glad! I picked you for him the moment I laid eyes on you—and then I nearly spoiled it all by my eulogy."

"But—" stammered Janet, "what about the other girl—the one from the East—that you were going to invite out? You said she was beautiful—and—and adorable and—you were just going to *make* her marry him!"

"From the East!" Alice exclaimed, "I'm sure I didn't say anything about the East. I said there was a girl friend of mine—and I did say she was beautiful and adorable—and she is—and I said I was going to invite her to come and make me a long visit—and I *did* invite her—before she left the room in a huff—and went tearing off into the bad lands to find her lover——"

Janet smothered the rest of the sentence in kisses: "Well, anyway—you didn't make her marry him," she said, "because she intended to marry him anyway—if she could get him to ask her!"

A couple of hours later while the three women were in the cabin preparing supper, Tex, and Endicott, and Cinnabar sat outside and talked and listened to the sounds of laughter that floated through the door.

"Look at old Whiskers comin'," said Tex, indicating a horseman who appeared around the corner of the barn.

Cinnabar chuckled: "Whiskers! Why man, that's yer new dad! That's old Colin McWhorter—an' if you don't make a hit with him, believe me—he'll cut your head off!"

The huge Scotchman dismounted, nodded and addressed Cinnabar Joe: "Ha' ye seen my daughter?" Before Cinnabar could answer the girl herself rushed from the door and threw herself into the big man's arms: "Theer, theer, wee lass, ha' they hurt ye? Ye're face is red like the fire-weed! I'll——"

"No! No! Dad! I'm—so happy! I'm—I'm going to be married tomorrow! I want you to meet my—Mr. Benton—Tex! And, oh Dad—you'll just love him! I knew it was all a mistake—about that horrid hand-bill—here are Mr. and Mrs. Endicott—they know him well—and Cinnabar and his wife have known him for years."

McWhorter stood glaring at Tex who returned him look for look. "Was it for thot I looked after her a' her life—educated her—thot she sh'ud marry a common cowpuncher!"

The Texan stepped directly before him and reaching up a finger tapped the irate man's breast: "Look here, old timer. I'm a common cowpuncher, just as you say—but, at that, I don't take off my hat to any sheep-man! You an' I are goin' to be big friends, once we get strung out. I like you already. I've got you sized up for one of the biggest hearted old specimens on the range. But, at that, you like to get your growl in—an' get it in first. Well—you've growled—an' you haven't fooled no one—nor scairt no one. If you want a little further dope on me here goes. I'm from Texas—come from good enough folks down there so they haven't been able to beat the Old Man for Congress in twenty years. I've be'n somethin' of a black sheep—but the black's wearin' off in spots. I've got as good an education, I reckon, as anyone here—an' a damn sight better one than I need in my business. I walk on my hind legs an' eat with a fork. I've got a job—eighty bucks a month, an' found—foreman of the Y Bar outfit, over across the river. Some day I expect to own an outfit of my own!" He ceased suddenly, and reaching out, drew the girl from her father's arms and held her to his side, "An' last of all—an' as far as I can see, the only thing that really matters—I love this little girl——"

"Losh! Lad!" cried the old Scot, his eyes a-twinkle. "Ye fair talk me off my feet! 'Tis na wonder she took ye—ye ne'er gi' her a chance to say no!"

"Supper's ready!" called Jennie, from the interior of the cabin, and it was a merry company indeed, that filed in and took their places at the table—extended for the occasion by means of planks carried in from Cinnabar's unfinished stable.

"I've just bought an outfit, over on the other side," said Endicott, when the last vestige of Jennie's pies had disappeared from the plates, and the thick cups had been filled with black coffee. "And Cinnabar, do you know where I could find a foreman?"

"On the other side!" exclaimed the Texan. "You! Didn't know there was an outfit for sale over there! What is it, Win—sheep, or cattle?"

"Cattle."

Cinnabar shook his head.

Endicott continued, "He must be capable, sober, understand the cattle business, and—married."

"Don't know no one that would quite fill the bill," grinned Cinnabar Joe.

"Hey, Win," cut in Tex, "how would I do? I'm capable of some things—sometimes. I've got Cinnabar, here, for a witness that upon certain occasions I've be'n sober. I understand the cow business or old Dad Colston wouldn't of made me foreman—an' tomorrow, everyone here's goin' to be witnesses that I'm married! How about it—don't that fill the bill?"

Endicott laughed: "I guess that fills the bill, Tex," he said. "You're hired!"

"But—what outfit did you buy, Win?"

"The Y Bar," answered Endicott, "and Colston told me that if I couldn't find you for foreman, I'd sure be out of luck."

"The Y Bar!" Tex reached over and grasped Endicott's hand. "Boss—you've got the best outfit in Montana!"

"Not—boss—Tex. What you meant was 'Partner.' You see I forgot to mention that the man who accepted the position would have to accept a half-interest in the outfit—his time and his experience—against my money." A dead silence followed the words—a silence broken a moment later by the sound of Janet, sobbing softly against her father's shoulder—and by the big Scotchman's rumbling words: "Theer, theer, wee lassie—theer, theer."

AN EPILOGUE

The ceremony that took place the following afternoon in the McWhorter cabin was impressive in its extreme simplicity.

At the conclusion of the wedding feast, McWhorter arose, passed into his own room, and returned a moment later with a bottle of wine, which he held to the sunlight: "'Tis auld," he said, reverently, "an' of famous vintage. Its mate was drunk years ago at my ain' weddin' in Sco'lan'. I ha' saved this—for *hers*." Very carefully he broke the seal, and withdrew the cork, and poured a little of the precious liquid into each thick glass: "We will drink," he said, solemnly, "to the health an' prosperity of—my children!" They drank, and the old Scotchman divided the remaining wine as before. "An' now, Meester Endicott can ye not propose us a toast?"

Endicott rose and allowed his eyes to travel slowly over the upturned faces about him. He began to speak: "Here we are—we and our women—a cattleman, and a sheep-man; a minister of the gospel, and a horse-thief; an ex-bartender, a half-breed, and a Harvard man who until a year ago was of the strictest and most hide-hound sect of the New Englanders—and as Cass Grimshaw so aptly phrased it yesterday—'We are all friends together.' Let us drink—to the wonderful free-masonry of the cow-country!"